I0617591

THE HARD-BOILED DETECTIVE

1

BY **BEN SOLOMON**

PRINTED BY THE HARD-BOILED DETECTIVE, CHICAGO

These stories first appeared as part of *The Hard-Boiled Detective*
subscription series from January 2013–May 2013

Copyright 2013 The Hard-Boiled Detective
Cover copyright 2014 The Hard-Boiled Detective
All rights reserved.
This book or any portion thereof may not be reproduced or used in any
manner whatsoever without the express written permission of the
publisher except for the use of brief quotations in a book review.

This is a work of fiction. Names, characters, corporations, institutions,
organizations, events or locales are either the product of the author's
imagination or, if real, used fictitiously. The resemblance of any character
to actual persons (living or dead) is entirely coincidental.

First Printing, 2014

ISBN-13: 978-0692269947 (The Hard-Boiled Detective)
ISBN-10: 0692269940
The Hard-Boiled Detective
www.thehardboileddetective.com
info@thehardboileddetective.com

Editorial Consultant: John Budz
Back cover photograph by James Iska

CONTENTS

Prologue

PROLOGUE

I won't tell you his name. One Tom, Dick or Harry's as good as another.

Or the city that serves as his beat. You'll figure it out, all right.

His time? Vanished. Call it 1926. 1933. 1959. Any time you like.

The point, see, is that his actions speak for him.

Not some lousy stencil on some lousy frosted panel.

His world is that never-changing urban jungle

where asphalt runs like quicksand,

where back alleys swirl into whirlpools.

Where shadows outnumber street lamps and victims outnumber winners.

His stories? An endless parade of statements to the cops.

Yarns as timeless as a code of honor,

as timeless as a thirst for justice,

as timeless as man's corruption and sin.

It's the stuff that makes him the hard-boiled guy he is.

Statement No. 1:
Pierre-Louis Leblanc

I wonder if you found a trace of anything in the basement. Nobody will tell me. No one's saying a thing about it. I'm betting it's clean. Real clean. Like an infant's rap sheet. Like nothing happened. But I'm sticking to my account.

I'll go through it all again. Sure I will. I must look a sight, bruised face, torn up coat and all. My head and jaw ache like hell, but we'll skip that for now. You'll get your story, all right. For my own reasons. Sure. But you'll get it from me just one more time, get me?

I don't much care for your procedures or your methods—can't say I much care for your manners, either, as far as that goes. So get me—*this is the last time.* Is there someone else out in the squad room that needs to hear it? Get him in here pronto. After this, we're through. You can do what you like after, for all I care.

Maybe I'm the only one who can cobble it together. Start to finish. Sure. From the trumped up beginning to the big bang finish. That's what you're after, right? The shooting? You boys are all hopped up on that. Up and down the line, everybody cuts straight to that—the incident. But I've got my own interests to look out for. Remember that I came to you, get me? Nobody had to send for me.

Just one more thing, as long as I'm at it. You play patient with me and we'll all get along. And I'll tell it swell. My own way. Start turning up the heat, any one of you, and I might go dumb on you. Everyone got that? OK? Just so long as we're all clear. OK.

It started with Lucilla. It ended with Lucilla. Doesn't every case need a dame? She introduced herself as Lucilla Leblanc. Sure, I didn't buy it, either. Turned out to be the right name, all right. Just the wrong broad. Matter of fact, there was a whole line of Lucillas going back on the mother's side. Any of you ever learn her maiden name? Landusky. Lucilla Landusky. Anything's an improvement over that.

Mrs. Lucilla Leblanc swung into my office on the morning of the fifth. *Swung's* an accurate way to put it. A fine looker, all right. That surprises you? You'll catch on. She knew damn well how men looked at her. If I wasn't such a cynic I might have fallen for her routine, and right now you'd be grilling someone else. I put her at thirty-five. Light brown, shoulder-length hair. She wore it pulled back that first time. She came in on the slim side. A striking five-nine, but that's in heels. Her clothes smart, new, topped off by a dark blue pillbox with a half-veil that masked the color of her eyes. So there she was—attractive, well fixed, with something to hide. You could say she interested me immediately. Sure.

After the intros, we got down to particulars. She ran hot and cold as she spoke. One moment stern and jittery, the next cool and tempting. At the time I figured her for the high-strung type, or maybe testing the waters. Maybe both. What she wanted, she said, was a tail job, which was fine by me. I was supposed to tail her husband, she said.

"You want the old man shadowed," I nodded. "What for, Mrs. Leblanc?"

As coyly as she could manage it, she said, "I want you to catch him with *her.*"

"That is delicate," I said. "You don't strike me as the demure type, Mrs. Leblanc."

With abrupt confidence she replied, "You strike me as the impertinent type."

"Sometimes my line of work calls for it."

"Does it?"

"I've been working it into a big ad campaign I'm planning: 'Private & Personal Investigations. Discreet & Impertinent.' Catchy, don't you think?"

"It appears I'm wasting your time."

"It's just that matrimonial cases aren't my usual line, Mrs. Leblanc."

"Hmm. I would have thought that was bread and butter for a trade like yours."

I said nothing.

"In that case," she began to purr—she looked like she purred a lot—"What if we say this? Let us say my husband's life has been threatened and I need you to follow him. Just by some off chance? As a precaution, let us say. To play it safe."

"Just to play it safe."

"I am prepared to pay handsomely, with an attractive bonus for results."

"Just like that."

"Just like that." She had a wicked smile. I liked it.

She worked a crisp fifty dollar bill out of her clutch and placed it on the desk. She nudged it across the blotter. I kept my eyes on those eyes behind the veil.

"No," she was purring again. She made purring seem like the most natural thing. "We'll make that one hundred dollars to start." Another Grant emerged from the bag. "I'll pay an additional one hundred dollars if I get what I want."

"You usually get what you want, Mrs. Leblanc?"

"Usually." She wore that wicked smile like melted chocolate.

"I see."

"What does that mean?"

"How do you know I can get you what you want?"

She surveyed the room. "You are a private detective, aren't you?"

"The stencil on the door says so."

"And you have followed people on occasion?"

"I've published monographs on it."

"Then we shouldn't have any trouble, should we?"

"Are you looking for trouble?"

"You're becoming impertinent, again."

"That one's on the house, Mrs. Leblanc. So, all together, that's two hundred bucks."

"That's the offer," purring through curled lips. "I like a man who can handle big math problems."

"So does my accountant. But you wouldn't like him. He's not nearly as impertinent as I am."

We kept up the clever banter while she carefully produced a small photograph of Mr. Leblanc.

"Is this recent?" I asked. "Somebody else has been torn out of it."

"Yes, fairly recent. Taken in the last six months or so."

"But the tear?"

"Will the picture do or not?"

"Sure, sure. It'll do," and I grinned as I considered the photo.

"Are you laughing at me?"

"You amuse me, Mrs. Leblanc, you really do, and no, I'm not being impertinent. I find it amusing that a lady such as yourself comes into my modest office. It amuses me that you're willing to pay me liberally just to pretend that you're not pretending why you're here. It amuses me to think that you must be so used to getting whatever you want. Do I amuse you at all, Mrs. Leblanc?"

"Not in the least. And you are being impertinent again." Her voice ran cold but her tongue traced that wicked smile.

I glanced at the man in black and white. Thinning, white hair. Pockets of shadows beneath the eyes. Hollows in the cheeks. He must've had a good twenty-five years on her. More like a *bad* twenty-five. It didn't add up that he should be the one stepping out. Complete confidence in a client is the exception in this racket. Everybody's hiding something—I wouldn't be in business, otherwise. But a certain level of belief is critical. The veil and the money were obvious. I could live with that. But the photo? That photo presented doubts.

"It's a funny species," I said.

"How's that?"

"This'll do. What makes you think he's running around?"

"A woman knows these things."

"Uh-huh."

"Perhaps my generous proposal will overcome any second thoughts as well as your aversion to this kind of work."

Second thoughts—she hit that one on the head. "OK, sister, you got me. I'll shadow your Romeo and see what gives."

"I know he'll be going out again tonight. He never leaves before seven. You can start tonight, can't you?"

"I may have to shift around a few things, but I'll pencil it in, Mrs. Leblanc."

"I'm writing down our address. Also my telephone number. My private line. I'll expect a full report in the morning. Will there be anything else?"

There's always something else. There had to be something else. Loads of something else. I shook my head.

Lucilla Leblanc snapped shut the little clutch, rose slowly, smoothed her skirt. She sauntered to the door, and lingered before it, laying her fingers on the doorknob. She pivoted towards me, gradual. She met me with a hard stare, a hint of that wicked smile arching her mouth. She breathed the word "impertinent" so faintly I barely got it. She threw the door wide and swung out.

I pushed back from the desk, crossed the office, and shoved the door shut. The echo of sharp high heels faded in the corridor. It's a quiet building.

Sure, I didn't buy her name, and her story played like a dodge. The one hundred bucks—that made me a believer. I picked up the two Grants, held them between my thumb and fingers, and slid them against one another. "Sure," I thought to myself. "Impertinence pays. Sure it does."

I spent part of my afternoon at the library. *Who's Who* and the like led me to *The Bankers' Annual.* I found Leblanc, all right, Mr. Peter-Louis Leblanc. Private banking, investment banking, etcetera. The house of Mercer, Leblanc and Furst. Big money. Serious money. The kind of dough a flatfoot or P.I. dreams about when he sees an RKO movie. Everything jived with Lucilla's info, right down to the exclusive address on North Lake Shore Drive.

As for the lady herself, I found something entirely different—zip. No listings, no society page blurbs, no nothing. For whatever reason, Mrs. Leblanc was under wraps. Way under.

After knocking off my homework, I blew in a call to the answering service. No messages. For better or worse, that made Lucilla the only game in town. I grabbed a quick bite in the Loop before heading to Leblanc's.

At 6:45 p.m. I parked the coupe on the inner drive. My spot furnished a clear view of the Leblancs' building, one of those gray stone monoliths opposite the lakefront. They lined them up that way, like a string of concrete forts, our last defense in case of Canadian attack. I lit a cigarette and waited.

At 6:55 a shining, black Packard pulled up. A hulking bus of a crate. Mr. Leblanc exited the lobby at seven on the dot, overdressed for the warm, fall evening. I recognized him easy, even bundled up. He displayed the enthusiasm of a hamper full of wet towels. He moved sluggishly, shuffling his way around the front of the Packard. I turned over the engine of my coupe and let her idle. The porter hopped out of the car and held the door. Leblanc, stiffly bent, worked himself in behind the steering wheel. He did not need, or did not want, a chauffeur. The porter let fly a goodbye salute. Leblanc did not.

You couldn't ask for a better tail-job. A subject made to order. Dull, easy. The Packard circled the block, headed north, and hung a left on Fullerton. The old boy held his route due west for quite a ways, well beyond hitting the sticks. He took a right at River Road, heading north. I checked my fuel gauge.

Two miles up River Road, Leblanc swung into the drive of a sprawling, Colonial number. The Palmer Mansion had nothing on this baby. Tall, iron gates fronted the edge of the property for a good block or more. The expansive lawn served as a parking lot. I took a quick tally, counted better than one hundred cars, and let loose a silent whistle.

Leblanc circled the rows of vehicles twice before parking his machine. He eased his way out the driver's side, stiffly. He brushed his coat, and paraded down to the oversized double-doors of the mansion. A duo of solemn doormen gave him the nod. The entry doors swung wide.

I settled for a spot on the side of the lawn opposite Leblanc's. I took my time approaching the house, unsure if the doormen would hang out the welcome sign. Despite lollygagging, I overtook a pair of old dames strolling arm and arm. I meant to skirt them when one made a slight misstep—her upper body heaved forward, the arms snapped upward, and her evening bag sailed off for a good ten-foot trip.

"Oh heavens!"

"Allow me, mademoiselle," I called.

Bounding beyond the couple, I snatched up the purse and wiped it on the sleeve of my coat with exaggerated delicacy. I returned to offer up the bag with a slight bow. I straightened up with a start, as if seeing double. Turned out I *was* seeing double. Turned out I was in the presence of Doreen and Laureen Messmer, identical twins. Kind of sweet and cute types, modeled in that overweight, spinsterish manner. They giggled as Doreen accepted her bag. Or maybe it was Laureen. I never did get the names straight—the only name that interested me was *Leblanc*.

I expressed mock outrage that these two damsels arrived unescorted. I worked my way between them and offered each my arm. They tittered in their fashion and smiled at each other and tittered some more. I sauntered through the double doors, a Messmer on each arm. The solemn doormen made extra room for us as we barely squeezed by.

The telltale sounds struck home as soon as you passed through those oversized, double doors. The mechanical whirring and chunking of slots, the flapping burps of cards shuffling, the sharp rattling of dice being shaken. Just inside I spied a cloakroom to the left, a wide staircase to the far right. An enormous bar began beneath the stairs that extended the length of the room. The rest of the first floor gave over to the crowded gaming tables.

"Do you partake?" one of the twins turned to me. "I'm sure my sister could use one, and I don't know why I should feel so parched myself."

"That's because you're just an old lush, my dear," the other said with a smile.

I replied it was oak with me.

On the way to the bar we passed the roulette table. I got myself a gander at a painfully serious Leblanc. Impressive stacks of chips towered in front of him. His coat remained buttoned. Either the old boy had thin blood or he didn't expect to stay long.

I made sure we found just the right barstools, close enough to the action. I could keep an eye on Leblanc in the bar mirrors with a strategic turn of my seat. I witnessed the old man's folly—nothing but straight number bets. To be precise, he played one number and only one number. Bet after bet, turn after turn of the wheel. Even the simple Messmer twins could've predicted Leblanc's fate.

Leblanc lost an entire stack of chips by the time we knocked off our first drink. His stakes shrank by half as we finished our second round. When Doreen, or maybe Laureen, raised her third nip, she spilled it in her sister's lap. I glanced over at the roulette table. Leblanc had gone bust.

The Messmer sisters excused themselves to the powder room. Leblanc stood to leave. He tossed a large, glittering coin to the croupier and plodded in the direction of the door. I casually approached the roulette table and leaned in with, "The old boy had it bad tonight."

"Sometimes you wins, mister," the croupier said. "Sometimes you lose."

I spied Leblanc at the exit. "He must have lost a small fortune."

"We don't keep no score, mister."

It felt good to step outside, away from the stale casino atmosphere. The air had that crisp autumn snap to it, the type that wakes up your spirits. The soft moonlight renewed things. It could fool you into thinking the world's at peace, we're all good, we're all innocent.

I reached for a cigarette, eyeballing Leblanc's silhouette shambling down the line of silent automobiles. As I struck a match, the sulphur flared up and died down, and the silhouette dropped out of sight like a shot.

I zigzagged down the lot, hunting for Leblanc. I found the old bird doubled over on elbows and knees. He strained to breathe, slow and shallow, in a rasp that outdid the crickets. He didn't look injured any. I bent down and braced his shoulders with my hands.

"What is it?"

He shook his head.

"You want a doctor?"

He shook his head. "A moment," he gasped. That's all he said.

I glanced up. No one to the left, the right, or behind us. We were alone. "You want to sit up?"

"A moment." That's all.

We held our wrestlers' posture for five minutes before he felt steady. I helped him onto the running board of the car next to us. His breaths grew longer and deeper. He managed, "Thank you, sir."

"I still think I should get you a doc."

"No, no, I don't think that will be required. Merely a moment's rest."

"Perhaps you'd like to duck back inside."

"I will not spend one minute more in that *place* than I have to."

So we sat. We cooled our heels on that strange running board in the middle of nowhere way the hell up River Road. I couldn't puzzle out what we were doing there, or whether it had anything to do with Lucilla Leblanc.

"I just realized, sir," he found his breath, "I must be keeping you from something."

"Don't give it a thought. You well enough to get on?"

"Certainly, sir. Yes. A little strain is all. Business concerns, you know."

"Sure. Maybe you need some time off."

"Ah. Yes, I shouldn't be surprised. But then there are obligations, aren't there?"

"I don't know. Are there?"

"Partners, wives, employees."

"I always considered myself a pretty good first obligation."

"Ah. What you've got there is a young man's game." As he spoke he raised his shoulders and crossed his arms. Thin fingers kneaded the upper arms.

"You getting a chill?"

"I worry most for my wife," Leblanc said. "The poor, lost thing. Lost for some time. Perhaps I've lost my way, too, from time to time. There are those who say, those who advise me, I shouldn't trouble about her. But confound it if that doesn't go against the grain. I don't believe that should be so difficult to understand."

"I get you."

"Do you, sir?"

"Sure, sure. You're OK. A little balled up, maybe, but you'll make out."

"Balled up!" he laughed, and he smiled to himself. He turned the smile on me, and I have to say it was a good smile. It tempted me to come clean, but I resisted.

"Think you can tool home all right?"

"Tut! I know I can, sir. I thank you, but I don't require looking after."

That's the first time a tail job told me the tail wasn't necessary. Of course, I followed him all the way back to North Lake Shore Drive. Leblanc arrived in one piece, without incident.

From that moment, I took his side. I was all for Leblanc, all right. I didn't know the score, but that made no difference. You're always taking sides, and I knew it like you know right from wrong—I'd stand against anyone who wasn't for Leblanc.

I rang up Lucilla the following morning at nine o'clock sharp. She picked up on the second ring. She played it cool, her tone dismissive, her words abrupt. Kitten had lost her purr.

"I've been waiting for your call. You always sleep in so late?"

"I wanted to make sure I didn't disturb you, Mrs. Leblanc."

"Never mind that. Did you catch them together?"

"No."

"No?"

"No."

"So where did he go?"

"He drove out to a club in the boondocks. Up north on River Road."

"Not that awful gambling house."

"I've seen worse, Mrs. Leblanc."

"How'd he make out?"

"He dropped a pile."

"He can afford it."

"Then he collapsed in the parking lot."

"Collapsed?"

"Your husband may not be a well man, Mrs. Leblanc."

"I see. Where did he go after that?"

"Did you get what I said about his health?"

"We already have a family physician. I asked where he went after that."

"Straight home, Mrs. Leblanc."

"I see." The line went quiet for a moment. "You better try again tonight."

"Yes, Mrs. Leblanc."

"He'll see her again. I know he's going to see her soon. I want you there, and I want you to call me as soon as you catch them together."

"Yes, Mrs. Leblanc."

Somehow, with Kitten's purr lost in the shuffle, I began to care even less for my client. As for Mr. Leblanc, I'd figured on tailing him again no matter what—wild Lucillas couldn't keep me away. I couldn't put my finger on the trouble, but it was there, all right. I'd decided to stick a while longer.

Leblanc followed his casino routine for the next three nights. Those solemn doormen at the club on River Road let me come and go without any static. I played my part, sitting in for a few hands of blackjack, throwing craps, just for show. As far as concerns Leblanc, I always made sure to blend in, just another faceless sucker among the crowd.

Leblanc opened each night with a pile of chips that could buy and sell anyone of us several times over. And each night he threw it away at the roulette table. Betting always on thirty-three. Always going belly up. The ritual went like clockwork save for one detail: it struck me that his table stakes grew smaller, one night to the next. I chewed it over plenty, and the more I chewed on it, the less I came up with.

I fell into the habit easy. I knew what to expect and faithfully phoned in my non-reports to Kitten every morning. She offered nothing much in the way of response. I had to confess to her that I didn't see what I was getting paid for. Kitten insisted I keep at it, so we left it at that. Not that I was looking for her permission, but I didn't tell her that.

That leads up to that final night. I had a good view of Leblanc from a nearby craps table. He came across more tense than usual. The way he curved over the table, the hunch of his shoulders, that grim pan. The final straw could've been anything, but when it came, he snapped. His hands balled into fists and softly pounded the table. Contempt washed over his face. He jerked to his feet, cashed in his chips without a word, moving abruptly, awkwardly. I remained in the background, casually hanging back—I saw no reason to sweat it.

Leblanc strode to the parking lot with a briskness I hadn't expected. I didn't think the old guy had it in him. His car sat a lot farther down than mine. I approached my coupe, keeping watch, and waited. Leblanc crossed the lawn, reached the Packard, and maneuvered himself in behind the steering wheel. I dug into my shirt pocket for a smoke. A soft, male voice from behind caught me off guard.

"Beg pardon, can I trouble you for a match?"

It happened just as I turned. It happened fast. It felt like a sack of cement crashing into my jaw. I caught a blurred, split-second glimpse of the johnny who jumped me before crumpling into the grass. Then everything dissolved to smoke. I never saw Leblanc again.

I came to, slow, with a grinding headache. The sunshine didn't help any. It took a few moments to register my surroundings as the passenger seat of the coupe. A sharp, throbbing pain kicked in along my jaw. Between the throbs, my memory flashed back to me in spurts. Sitting up made the pain worse. I found my billfold next to me on the seat. The Grants were gone. So was Leblanc's snapshot. Everything else in order. A gaze through the windshield placed me just off the intersection of 22nd and Cicero. I identified the Hawthorne Works looming ahead on the right. I fingered my jaw, painful to the touch, but my teeth felt intact.

I needed coffee before anything else. I had enough pocket change for that. I exited the car and assessed the damage in the side mirror. The bruising bloomed like a Technicolor experiment. I spotted an owl wagon about half a block up so I tested the waters, and my legs, and set off on foot.

Funny how being roughed up can turn any lousy cup of coffee into the best you ever had. The stiff manning the counter kept sneaking peeks at my face. The register girl was kind enough to offer some aspirin. The gravel in my head gave way to something softer during the third cup. The raging headache subsided to a dull grinding and I could actually think. A lot of good that did me.

I still came up empty regarding Leblanc's nightly sojourn. The man was no mean gambler, that's for sure. Not betting on one number. Not night after night. Beats me what got to him. And then somebody got to me, all right. I made as much sense out of it as trying to read a tote sheet in Chinese.

The big daddy question of them all threw me for a loop. I don't know why I didn't catch it sooner, laying there right in front of me. But when it struck me, it struck as hard as any blackjack to the jaw.

The headline in *The American* read, "Banker Commits Suicide." Above the fold, a photograph of Peter-Louis Leblanc. He hadn't smiled for the camera. The snapshot must've been taken years before the one the missus had forked over.

Suicide is never pretty. They all pull off their own level of ugly. The more you know the poor sap, the worse it plays out. A single witness stumbled on Leblanc's Packard, the lone auto in a Hyde Park lot, half a city away from his home and office. A spent, old man, flung back in the driver's seat. Like an abandoned marionette. Done in by a large caliber rod, probably a forty-four. The slug blew a huge crater through the top of his skull. Chips of bone, fragments of brains and bits of flesh sprayed across the Packard's interior. Late at night. No letter. No note. Discovered by a stock boy on his way home from an all-night drugstore. The stock boy said, "I've never seen anything like it." Sure.

The American ran a second picture, a portrait of Leblanc with his wife. That shot displayed her light hair, a wide face, and she appeared about the same age as her husband. That baby posed another question. Now we had two Mrs. Leblancs on the loose, one as phony as an alderman's promise. As if my head didn't ache enough.

My anger kicked in faster than the aspirin. I raced up north to the Leblancs' apartment building—I never gave the speedometer a thought. I handed my card to the concierge, told him I knew the late Mr. Leblanc, said I'm sure his wife would want to see me. He hesitated, a questioning look screwing up his face. He caught sight of the bruising, the soiled jacket, my whole, rough-and-tumble demeanor—he dropped the questioning look and buzzed upstairs at once.

The elevator opened directly onto a foyer and connecting hallway. The Leblancs must've let the entire floor. My whole walk-up could've fit in the foyer with room to spare. A subdued butler showed me to a large sitting room. Mrs. Leblanc sat dead center, surrounded by a warehouse worth of furniture. There were straight-back chairs and lounge chairs, loveseats, small sofas, end tables, coffee tables, console tables, table lamps, floor lamps, floor rugs, throw rugs. She appeared stiff and uneasy in her cane chair. As animated as asphalt. I took a seat in a wingback, right across the Oriental rug from her.

Mrs. Leblanc looked just like her picture in the newspaper, all right, with a few years thrown in. The regal widow, sure. Encircled by that hodgepodge of luxury. I could've expected the old dame to be plenty sad or upset. Heartbroken, even. Maybe the whole affair would leave her numb. Maybe everything would come crashing down on her later. I gave her a careful once-over—Mrs. Leblanc was terrified. You could see it on her face. As plain as anything. Alone and terrified.

I declined the offer of something to drink. I wasn't in the mood to have anything spilled in my lap—the old dame looked that shaky. I didn't feel in top form myself. A light-headedness tried gumming up the works I call a brain, but I ignored it. Mrs. Leblanc asked after my health, but making small talk didn't interest me. Neither did paying my respects. I cut to the chase.

"Mrs. Leblanc, what are you afraid of?"

A soft gasp escaped her lips.

I continued. "You don't believe he killed himself, do you? I can't think he did. He didn't strike me as the type. But I barely knew your husband, Mrs. Leblanc. It'd mean a lot more coming from you."

She parted her lips, and then hesitated. She looked about to speak, but kept mum. An air came over her that put a distance between us, as though she saw through me and into the next room.

"Mrs. Leblanc."

She squinted in my direction, like I was difficult to make out all that way across the Oriental.

"What did you tell the police?"

She mouthed the word "nothing" without making a peep.

"But you could tell them something, isn't that right, dear?"

She closed her eyes, nodded, and drew in her upper lip.

"What do you know about it, Mrs. Leblanc?"

She started rocking in the cane chair.

I spat at her. "What do you know?"

"I," she paused. She glanced upward. "He couldn't. He just—" She paused again and took a breath. "I cannot accept it. Pierre-Louis would not do such a thing. Such a harsh thing. Such a vile thing."

"I'm with you as far as that goes, Mrs. Leblanc."

"Pierre-Louis was a very gentle man, in his own way. Serious. Perhaps too serious, but also gentle."

I had to keep pressing. "What else?"

"He liked snow. Did you know that?"

"What do you know about his trouble, Mrs. Leblanc? Tell me about that."

She squeezed her eyelids shut, placed an index finger to her lips and bobbed her head. I waited. She drew heavy breaths in a stop and start fashion. I leaned forward. The thin creaking of the cane chair squeaked as she rocked in place. Then, like a piercing alarm, like a fire alarm, the telephone rang with shocking loudness. Mrs. Leblanc let fly, "I blackmailed my husband!"

The old girl had come through. Her eyes opened and scrutinized me, again with that unsure squint. They held terror, all right. I sat still. The phone continued to ring. A third ring. A fourth.

"Maybe it's important," I said. She put her index finger to her lips and waited. "The butler?"

"I've left instructions."

After ten rings the telephone went silent. Mrs. Leblanc was ready to talk.

"I'll confess everything. I can't tolerate the shame. I must talk to someone. Can I trust you? You look like someone I can trust."

"There's no reason in the world you should trust me, Mrs. Leblanc. Just because I was all for your husband doesn't mean I'm for you as well."

"I see, yes." She spoke faintly, almost to herself, as softly as rainfall. "But I feel as though I can trust you. Did my husband trust you?"

"In a small way, I think he did."

"Is it all right if I tell you everything?"

You could see the old gal had reached the final station. Any strength, any resilience she'd once had was shot. Nothing left inside. Nothing left to lose. "I'm not going to stop you, Mrs. Leblanc."

"You see, I knew. I knew Pierre-Louis was seeing someone. He didn't love me anymore, or maybe he knew I hadn't loved him for years. Or maybe he just gave up. Perhaps that's why he found someone else. I don't know, really. After all that time, why should that have hurt me?"

"So you wanted to hurt him. To get back at him."

"To a point, I suppose so. What I wanted most of all was to run away from everything. Imagine that. At my age. But I would have had nothing, you see. Pierre-Louis made me sign all these documents before we married. We were happy and I didn't mind. Perhaps I was being young and foolish. That was so very long ago. One can hardly start over at this age. Now even so, when Mr. Jupiter first suggested we blackmail Pierre-Louis—how could I entertain such a notion? That's all it was to me at first. Just a silly notion, or his way of poking fun at me."

"Mr. Jupiter, the gambler."

"Yes, some call him that. I first met him at his club—I'd gone there on a lark. I'd begun going out nights when Pierre-Louis said he was working late. Soon after, Mr. Jupiter and I met again, quite by accident, in a restaurant near here."

"Fancy that."

"Yes. He began calling me and calling me. Finally, I just gave in. He was the most charming gentleman, really, and made the most pleasing companion. For a time. Until we began discussing my husband. I don't know what I was thinking. He was so young. I acted so foolishly."

"A younger fella. I see. What'd he work out for your husband?"

"At first he wanted to know if Pierre-Louis had any weaknesses. That's a funny sort of thing to be asked. And now, now Pierre-Louis is gone." She glanced upward.

"Don't drift out on me, Mrs. Leblanc. You said Jupiter wanted to know about your husband's weaknesses."

"Yes, yes, that's what he asked. I told him what came to mind, though not exactly what you'd call a weakness, was Pierre-Louis' obsession with his privacy and reputation. Any type of notoriety simply outraged Pierre-Louis. He refused to pose for the camera. Avoided every kind of publicity. He never even advertised in the journals, you know. Some businessmen are more discreet than others. Pierre-Louie was, well, practically invisible."

"But did OK for himself. And for you."

"I must say so. I really must."

"Jupiter must've smelled opportunity."

"I saw a change come over Mr. Jupiter. He became excited and distracted. 'This one is going to be easy, my dear, so easy.' I remember that's what he said, and his voice was cold and frightened me. 'So easy.' When I offered a slight protest, he grabbed me painfully hard. By my wrist. 'Isn't this what you want?' he asked. He pushed me away, said we were all alike, and marched off. I never saw Mr. Jupiter after that." She added in a whisper, "Just the thought frightened me."

"He was all fixed."

"Yes, he was. And I'm to blame for it. And now I'm to blame for Pierre-Louis."

"You think Jupiter's involved?"

"Pierre-Louis would never do anything like that, you see? He was a proud man. And something—"

"Do you think Jupiter could've been involved in your husband's death, Mrs. Leblanc?"

"Jupiter?"

"Do you think Jupiter killed your husband, Mrs. Leblanc?"

"I don't know," she whispered. "I don't know." The words ran fast and breathless. "I know I am afraid of him." She went all petrified again.

"I think I'd like to meet this Mr. Jupiter." That gave her a terrific scare. Maybe I shouldn't have said it.

I left Mrs. Leblanc like I found her. There was nothing I could do for her. That didn't interest me, anyway. Still, I couldn't ignore that sense of sorrow that washed over that home. Maybe I just felt sorry for all of us. Take it as you like. I caught a maid on the way out and suggested she look in on Mrs. Leblanc. Maybe sit with her for a bit. "I'd die before I show that old crow any consideration." That was the maid's flat response. The staff had taken sides, and Mrs. Leblanc lost out.

I stopped home for a shower and a change, but an unscheduled collapse delayed me. That wrap on the jaw must've been harder than I figured.

The twilight ride to River Road went by in no time. My thoughts distracted me. Mostly I pictured Mr. Leblanc, discarded like last year's suit. No longer in style. Out of step. Then I reflected on Mr. Jupiter—finding him and taking care of him one way or another.

I reached Jupiter's club after sunset. The hatcheck girl referred me to a floor manager who looked more like a bouncer. He referred me to a set of double doors at the far end of the game room. A little sign in gold above the doorway read, "Private Office." A couple of torpedoes flanked each side of the entry.

"Jupiter's private office?" I asked.

Bruiser number one had a comeback ready: "Whatever you say, brother."

"I'd like to see him."

Bruiser number two chirped, "So would his wife and her attorney."

"Nix that," spat the first bruiser. "He ain't here, brother."

"He'll want to see me."

"As much as you want to see him?" That from number two.

"More," I said.

"Don't matter," shrugged number one, "cause he ain't in."

"You boys ever try this routine on the radio?"

"Radio?"

"Why, you want to manage us?"

"I'll tell you boys what. You tell Mr. Jupiter that the P.I who was tailing Leblanc is waiting for him at the bar."

"I will if I see him, brother."

"That's *Leblanc*," I emphasized.

"Say, I think I uncorked a nice Leblanc eighty-eight, once."

"Just tell him." I headed for the bar.

The second one called after me, "Maybe you should send him a cable, maybe."

I pulled up to the bar, wondering if I'd made my point. An empty stool was all the company I wanted and I found it. I ordered a highball. The first sip went down rough, which was fine with me. Jupiter's establishment didn't impress me, or his reputation, and it pleased me that his liquor followed suit. I enjoyed my displeasure for less than ten minutes. The interruption arrived in the form of a thin wheeze.

"So you have ferreted me out." The voice sounded soft and grainy and short on air, like a pump organ without enough juice.

I spun around to view the celebrated Mr. Jupiter. Put him around sixty. And a round man, all together. Dull, blonde hair circled his round head so closely you couldn't make out for sure if he was going bald. The eyes, tiny slits close to his nose, held two, tiny balls that glistened like black pearls. His monkey suit brought out the roundness of his shoulders, chest and gut. His short, round fingers displayed too many rings with too many stones. The capper, which was just right because it fit so wrong, was a short cigarette holder wedged between his tiny, round teeth. No doubt this egg couldn't belong to the real Mrs. Leblanc.

"Far from Rome," I mused.

"Pardon?" Jupiter wheezed.

"Nothing," I replied.

One of the gargoyles from the office hovered a little too close. "No need to crowd, Geoffrey," Jupiter said. "Our friend here might think we're expecting trouble." He bent towards me. "Should we be expecting trouble?"

I was all set to crack wise, but Jupiter kept wheezing and speaking.

"We dismiss all troubles here. My guests leave all their troubles outside when they enter my house. Look at them. Complacent. Content."

"Going bankrupt."

"I rather think hopeful. They find hope in my house. One more spin, one more roll. A turn of the right card could change everything."

"You're just a goddamn romantic."

"Why do you mean to bring trouble into my house?" The color in his round face went up one, rosy notch.

"Nothing you haven't brought on yourself."

"You're referring to this man? This Leblanc?"

"That's right."

"Well. I never heard of this Mr. Leblanc." He smiled to me. He turned and smiled at Geoffrey.

"He was an important man to know," I said. "A powerful man. In private banking."

Jupiter let out a thin sigh. "Well, as to that." He worked a gold cigarette lighter from his waistcoat pocket. "What need do I have for a private banker?"

"You're greedy."

"Even greed has its limits."

"No it doesn't." I felt like pushing just for the sake of pushing. "Not in your case."

Jupiter worked his thumb on the lighter. "Well, in any case, I have never met your Mr. Leblanc. I can't even say I've seen the fellow."

"And one of your best customers, too. Supported you plenty, night after night. That is, after you set him up. I'm sure it was easy for you to find some pretty, and pretty cheap, young thing to take him in."

"I don't associate with cheap!"

"Everything about you is cheap, Jupiter. I've looked around. Cheap and rotten and corrupt."

"You cannot speak to me like that in my own house!" He meant to be threatening, but the buzzing rasp came off like a whining child.

"It must have proved a cinch to pull the badger game on a man like Leblanc. Then a simple matter of blackmail. On the installment plan. That built-in method of laundering the cash—very smooth. I'll hand you that."

"You have no idea what you're saying." Jupiter ran a shaky hand across his short crop of hair.

"Leblanc became one of your best customers. Until he'd had enough. That's when he became troubled, and that turned him *into* trouble. You can't ignore a man with Mr. Leblanc's influence and connections. So I suppose he had to be removed. Ditched in Hyde Park with a hole blown through the back of his head."

"I repeat—you have no idea," Jupiter's shark eyes glared, "no idea what you are saying. Doesn't sound like anything we'd be involved in. No, wouldn't do for us at all." Jupiter controlled his words through clenched teeth. The red in his round face and neck boiled up another level.

"I find that hard to believe, Mr. Jupiter. Especially when I look around a cheap joint like this."

"Joint? You refer to my house as *a joint?*"

"I wouldn't be surprised if every dealer is packing. You telling me those aren't heaters in Geoffrey's pockets? No one's hands are that big."

"I must," he said with an extended wheeze, "afford myself some protection. It is *de rigueur*, after all, in a house like this. It is required and expected."

"Shall I tell you what I think, Mr. Jupiter?"

"You've told me enough!" He meant to go on but couldn't find enough air.

Geoffrey pitched in, "Tell me to take a poke at him."

Jupiter's round head made an abbreviated shake. "Later."

"I'm counting the hours," I smiled at Geoffrey.

"Enough," Jupiter wheezed.

"You're down to two syllables."

"Why—"

"Why what? Why am I here? Why did I want to talk to you? I'm beginning to wonder why my talking should make you look like a Pekingese with a case of the jitters. I could bring up honor and justice and that whole routine, but let's boil it down to this. I'm looking to do right by an old egg who deserved better. And I wanted to say it to your face, accuse you straight up. You and your confidence game killed Leblanc just as sure as if you pulled the trigger—of course you haven't the stomach for that yourself."

"Enough!" His wheezing bellow became a spasm of coughing.

"I've had my say, Jupiter. I'm done for now."

"Mmm, most apropos." Jupiter gulped some air, smiled, and bit hard on the cigarette holder.

Maybe that's not the shrewdest of moves, blowing your top like that when you're in another guy's territory. Especially when the other guy's got more torpedoes than I've got socks. Maybe I was being just hardheaded, but sometimes my line of work calls for it. So, sure, I received an escort, compliments of Mr. Jupiter.

It took three of them to walk me to my car, but only one to lay me out. It could've been worse, but it was bad enough. Two hard jabs to the jaw, the same jaw that was already as purple as a Crown Royal Whiskey bag, followed up by a knee to the stomach and a kick to the ribs. I remember throwing one wild punch that missed by a mile.

As I gasped for air, just before I descended into a black cloud inside my head, I heard a faraway voice: "What's that sickly, breathing sound?" The second bruiser laughed, "Oh, now I know. He sounds like Mr. Jupiter!"

There's not a whole lot of difference between almost blacking out and blacking out all together. Either way it was a while before my brains unscrambled and I could make out someone murmuring to me.

"Mister. Psst! Mister! Are you with me?"

The cloud began to lift and the ache kicked in.

"I say, can you hear me?"

I opened my eyes just enough to see a face nose to nose with mine.

I winced. "I don't know if I can hear so good, but I can smell your breath all right."

"If you're coming round then, I mean to speak to you."

"Yeah, I'm coming round. But I don't get it."

"Right. I'll be off, but you give me fifteen minutes. Meet me in the supply cellar. You know where that is?"

"You tell me."

"Down the right side of the building. Towards the rear. Got that? On the right, towards the back you go, you'll find steps going down to a door. It'll be unlocked, but don't let anyone see you. Just give me fifteen and I'll be waiting for you."

He scrambled to his feet, first crouching and peeking over the fender of my car. He straightened up, glancing left and right.

"Hold on," I said, "Hold on."

He inched backwards while speaking in a loud whisper. "We can't talk now. Shh!"

"I know you," I called.

He hissed as loud as he could while creeping backwards. "You—don't—really!"

"You work the roulette wheel. Leblanc always sat at your table."

"It's—more interesting—than that!"

"So why should I want to talk to you?"

I could barely hear him as he reached the end of the row of cars. "I'm Mrs. Leblanc's friend!"

"Who?"

"Mr. Jupiter!"

With that he was gone. Sure, my head felt like a crazy game of pinball was going on inside. My jaw felt like an overinflated tire ready to blow. The whole thing screamed set up, but I figured I was close to the end. Real close. And his last line really was a grabber, wasn't it? I wasn't ready to leave. Not just yet. Not by a long shot.

I lay crumpled in the grass next to the coupe. I swung an arm up and over and caught hold of the passenger door handle. It took a few tries, but I released the catch and opened the door. The tough part was pulling myself up into the car and onto the seat. I thought I'd give the pain down my ribcage a chance to subside—it didn't take it. I popped the glove compartment and pocketed my thirty-eight. It wasn't just the pain I had going for me. I could feel the pain surging into a rich anger.

No one paid any attention as I staggered along the south side of the building to the cellar entrance. Ten jarring steps took me down to a second door. I worked it with my left while my right held fast to the revolver in my jacket pocket. The knob turned easy and the door swung easy. I inched forward onto a landing. Adjusting to the dim light from below, I could make out another set of stairs twelve feet ahead. I closed the door behind me, carefully. I stopped, listened, then walked to the end of the landing. The cool, damp air from the basement hit me as I began my descent. I felt my head start to clear. The low ceiling blocked the view except for the stairs beyond my feet. A faint voice rose from below.

"You can't be serious. I mean, you don't mean to do this. He'll be here any mo. Why me? Why? Why me?"

That was the croupier, the fake Mr. Jupiter. Sure. I held still, waiting to hear his playmate. The reply came like a cool, emotionless purr.

"You bore me, Freddie. You really do. How long did you expect I'd put up with the likes of you?"

I stole down the steps, one at a time. I reached the room at the bottom jammed with crates and cartons and shelves and barrels. I let the voices guide me.

"You look so surprised, Freddie. Really."

The cold laugh led me around to a small clearing. That's where I found the fake Mr. Jupiter, on a folding chair, rigid as a mannequin, the muzzle of a large automatic pressed hard against his temple. Gripping the butt end of the automatic, the first, or rather, the fake Mrs. Leblanc.

Kitten threw me that wicked smile. "You look like crap."

It wasn't much of a reunion, but Kitten felt chatty, and I got to straighten out a few things. I'd figured it mostly right.

Leblanc was merely the latest in a series of marks. Kitten claimed it was almost too easy for Freddie—she called him Freddie Bath—to cultivate Mrs. Leblanc as Jupiter. Mrs. Leblanc, she pointed out, got her husband's affair all wrong. Kitten, of course, was the dame he was seeing, but not until *after* Mrs. Leblanc and Freddie got together. The strait-laced husband never laid a finger on Kitten, never came close, never even tried. That's something she never understood.

Everyone took the bait on cue, including the mister's *acquiescing* to the blackmail. Kitten loved throwing in those big, Dale Carnegie words. According to her telling, the real Mr. Jupiter's involvement was limited to the payoff-laundering scheme, a service that cost her twenty percent off the top. What she hadn't figured on was Leblanc growing righteous. And she hadn't figured on Freddie getting cold feet when physical action was called for. That's when she put me on Leblanc's tail, about the time he started cutting back on his payments. Eventually she decided to end their arrangement, in a one-sided sort of way, but she didn't have time to pull me off. It was Kitten, not Freddie, who sapped me down in the parking lot.

Running Leblanc off the road proved easy as pie. That goes for hijacking him to the South Side. Thrusting a forty-four down an old man's throat and squeezing the trigger? Splashing his brains across the car roof? A cakewalk for her kind of woman. That left taking care of a stooge who couldn't pull his weight.

"You've probably known lots of Freddies," I said.

"There's always another Freddie creeping around the next dark corner," she shrugged.

"You're not going to let her do me in, are you? You can't let her!"

"This is her show, Freddie."

"But you can't!"

"I sure can, Freddie. There's nothing in this whole, sweet world anyone can do to save you."

I waited to make my play. She pressed the gun hard into Freddie's temple. Did she suspect I was holding? Maybe she did, maybe she didn't. I waited.

"Say something," she purred to me. "Say something impertinent."

Freddie lost it. His pale lips vibrated. He made this gurgling noise and babbled a rapid-fire string of nonsense. I didn't know what the hell he was trying to say. Kitten increased the pressure on the barrel until Freddie's head pressed against his shoulder.

"I wasn't talking to you, Freddie." She stared at me, that wicked smile showing her teeth. "Go on," she said.

I kept quiet.

"Go on!"

"Maybe later," I replied.

"It's later than you think."

With smooth ease she wheeled the automatic in my direction. Freddie nearly collapsed. I waited. As the gun drew about, Kitten squinted her left eye. The forty-four came to rest, pointed at my heart. She smiled again, nearly laughing. I was ready.

"Go on. Say something—"

I made my play and Kitten didn't flinch. I leaned to the side fast, jerked up my pocket, squeezed off two shots. Bang—the first cut her chest open and her whole body recoiled, taking her back one step. Bang—the second blew through her gut as she went down. She collapsed fast and hard. Dead before you could count ten. The wicked smile faded even quicker.

The act of shooting, the deafening echo of the volleys, the sharp smell of spent bullets and burned cloth—it left me stunned, my nerves raw. My hand remained locked on the thirty-eight sticking out the hole in my pocket, trained on a target that was no longer there. Then Freddie caught my eye, cowering with his gaze fixed on something behind me.

The something wheezed: "Why do you bring trouble into my house?"

I meant to turn around but never got the chance. The heavy, padded weight crashed down hard and fast and I went out cold.

Sure, I woke up on Cicero Avenue. Again. Beats me why Cicero. I found the first cup of hot coffee I could, couldn't keep it down, but managed the second cup all right. That's when I came straight round to see you boys.

So, here I am. Plenty worse for wear, but trying to do what's right. See, this is about justice and honor and all the other stuff that fair play's about. That's why I came in. Sure.

I came in because I want to do just one last thing. I want to report a stolen thirty-eight.

Statement No. 2:
Vincent Grigio

I t's bad business to plug your client. It's bad business, bad for P.I.'s everywhere, just plain bad all around. Sometimes my line of work calls for it.

Vincent Grigio? He had no idea what he was paying for when he hired me, the poor sap. You ever come across a born victim? You know the type. The bird who gets soup dumped in his lap. That mug waiting for a bus in the rain and gets doused by a passing motorist. The gink whose best pal in the world runs off with his ever-loving wife. That was Vincent Grigio in a nutshell. But what do I know? I only saw him twice. And hardly to his best advantage.

Grigio fashioned one sad figure. That's the truth. And now I get to spin you his sad ending. Gentlemen, it's a tale of blackmail, passion, and justice. Justice turned on its head, all right, but justice nonetheless. I know you boys have your own version of justice to dole out. The D.A.'s only a telephone call away, isn't that right? You'll get your chance, all right. And the city's lawyer will get his. Sure.

I can't begin to dream up the story concoctions that the little one and his partner have fed you. There might even be the hint of truth to them. What I lay down will be straight up. You can take that to the bank. I'll give you the whole yarn, the full treatment. Sure I will. Then you can clap me in bracelets and heap on whatever charges you like—if you think you can make them stick.

Did I mention blackmail? As far as charges are concerned? Whatever variety, blackmailers are as low-life as they come. None of us are complete innocents. I guess we're all that way—it's a flawed species. Even cops. Sure. Blackmailers seize upon those flaws, expose and exploit our weaknesses, kick us when we're down. Then kick us again. They take the ugliest kind of advantage of the corruptible, and no one, not one of us, is immune to that. Maybe you think I get carried away. Maybe you think they're not the lowest life form out there. I guess even leeches need something to aspire to. But just in case I haven't made myself clear on this—I hate blackmailers.

That's what Vincent Grigio said he was up against when he telephoned. That was Tuesday the thirteenth. Over the wire, his voice came across young, nervous, and weak. Call him shaky. I kept asking him to speak up. He kept clearing his throat. A regular clay pigeon made to order.

Grigio agreed to my fee, and asked to see me as far away from his digs as possible. And he didn't want to be caught anywhere near my office. He agreed to meet me that afternoon at a watering hole in Old Town, an old, reliable dive.

The joint felt nice and somber when I walked in, about as lively as stucco. A smitten couple cooed at a table off to the side. A party of four college types gabbed in the middle of the floor. I took three joes settled in at the bar for regulars. Those regulars sat silent and still as parking meters, like they'd been screwed into their barstools.

This lone johnny had a table to himself in the farthest corner. He perched forward on his chair, both hands wrapped around the martini glass. The rim of the glass pressed against his pencil mustache. His gaze had an unregistered look about it, focused on who knows what—his body may have been in the room, but his thoughts sure weren't.

He struck me as an everyday, plain sort. Black hair slicked back and down, a la Valentino. Small, dark eyes. Conservative, business dress. I tagged him for taller than average with a slight, wiry build. Maybe thirty years old, at the outside. Maybe closer to twenty-five.

He never saw me coming. I stood by the table and gave him a moment. He bobbled the glass when I finally spoke up. A splash of liquor leapt for his tie.

"You spook easy, Grigio."

"Sorry," Grigio said. The narrow lips formed a pained grin. He cleared his throat and dabbed his tie with a napkin. "Please sit down. What will you have to drink?"

I took a chair, ordered a black coffee, and offered Grigio a cigarette. He apologized and declined. I lit up and Grigio sucked on his glass. We waited for my joe, and I watched Grigio. He had nothing to say, and he didn't look me in the eye while he didn't say it.

"One coffee. Black." The waitress's years of experience showed in her surly tone.

I exhaled, "You waiting for something?"

She got wise and took a powder.

I prodded Grigio, but he kept dancing. First he had to apologize for the out-of-the-way meeting place. Then he thanked me for meeting him under such *unusual* circumstances. I saw nothing so unusual, and told him so. That surprised him. He thanked me anyway.

"There's nothing to thank me for, yet," I said. "What's your kick?"

"Sorry?" Grigio said. He cleared his throat.

"You're sure one for the apologies."

"Yes. I suppose I am."

"What's your racket, Grigio?"

"I beg your pardon?"

"What's your lay, your gig? What line are you in?"

"Oh, yes." He cleared his throat. "I practice law."

"So you're a mouthpiece, are you?"

"Yes, I am a lawyer."

"You don't have to appear in court, do you?"

"No, no. Nothing at all like that. The firm I've recently joined deals exclusively in corporate law."

"Mesmerizing."

"You're probably joshing, but I actually find it quite exciting, at times. It's a fascinating discipline."

"Sure, sure. That's swell. And would you say we've sufficiently broken the ice?"

"I don't understand."

"Let's have the story, Grigio. What kind of trouble are you in?"

Grigio apologized again. I half-wondered when he'd get around to apologizing for apologizing. I had to coax it out, every step of the way, but here's the yarn he told me. A little tale about little leaguers and their little league badger game.

Grigio met the twist after a Pump Room dinner party. A business get-together, he said, celebrating a client's successful merger negotiations. The blowout broke up not too late, but not too early—Grigio's blabber was full of ambiguities like that. And him a lawyer.

So back to the twist. They met up, after a fashion, when Grigio hoofed it back to his car. That's when he spotted this figure across the street. Leaning against a parked car. Facing him, all smiles. It made Grigio go self-conscious. He searched for his keys and tried real hard to look like he wasn't looking, if you know what I mean.

At the same time, someone else waited, too, someone in the shadows. This someone waited for the right distraction, for the right moment. Grigio popped the door lock, and paused. He glanced over his shoulder at the figure across the street. That's when the blackjack cracked the back of Grigio's skull, and with plenty of gas behind it. That was lights out for Mr. Vincent Grigio.

When he came around, Grigio found himself in this run-down hotel room. Peeling paint, chipped plaster, etcetera. Long on etcetera. The throw rug at his feet showed more wear than the batter's box at Wrigley Field.

Grigio's head felt like Cream of Wheat, and all the strength had been sucked out of his body. His mouth and tongue as dry as a sandbox. He'd been flopped in an old armchair, his hat and coat gone. Someone had popped the collar button of his shirt and loosened his tie.

Curious enough so far, but here's where it starts to get saucy. On display in front of the unmade bed, less than five feet away, the skirt was back, posing like. Doing a real Alice White or Jean Harlow number. Pure cheesecake. Grigio wanted to stand but couldn't muster the legs for it. He couldn't get his mouth to operate, either. Ain't that a charming panorama? It gets better.

During this point in his telling it, Grigio showed signs of the DTs. Sweat broke out on his tall forehead. A shaky right hand twisted the band on his left ring finger. I rallied him on.

Grigio described his companion as "pretty young." He wouldn't say how young. Short and slim with short, bobbed hair. A blonde. Wearing a button down blouse and dark gray slacks. He gawked as the thin fingers worked open the first button of the blouse. Then the second. All very oh, so slowly.

Grigio moved his tongue and moistened his lips and swallowed hard. The words came out hoarse, but they came out, all right. "Where am I? How did I get here? Why am I here?"

His questions fell flat as the blouse slid off and billowed down to the floor. The gray slacks peeled off next. Then Grigio watched as the panties shimmied down around skinny ankles.

Grigio braced himself, squeezing the arms of the chair. He pushed hard as he could, struggling to stand, but his playmate straddled him with such force that he collapsed back helpless. He closed his eyes as the warm body lowered onto his, the hips grinding into him. Warm breath tickled his ear, and he heard the words, "I know what you want. You know you want it."

Then a quick, hard bite on the neck opened his eyes. He lunged, grabbing at arms, hips, anything he could to free himself. That's when it really broke loose.

"I've got enough." That statement came from a third party in the room. The words froze Grigio halfway out of the chair. His playmate giggled and snorted and shook with laughter. The third party jeered, "I've got enough, Babe. I've got more than enough."

The low, smooth voice belonged to a tall man, narrow and dark, stepping out of a closet door on the other side of the bed. Grigio failed to catch sight of the camera, at first. His eyes fixed on the pistol tucked in the man's belt.

"Who are you?" Grigio croaked. "What do you want?"

"I could ask you the same," the man smiled. "I did wonder, though, if you got any hobbies?" The man aimed the camera at Grigio. "I just got me this. Been trying my hand at it. Got some great shots of you and Babe, here."

"Babe?"

"Quite the little ham, this one." The man shrugged.

Babe whispered, "Ride 'em, cowboy," hopped off Grigio, and flopped onto the bed.

"I'm just thinking, maybe," the dark man quipped, "maybe you might like a copy or two for your family album." He kept the words light enough, but delivered them with the severity of a mortician.

A wave of dizziness flooded Grigio's head. He felt nauseous. He forced down a painful swallow and felt a line of ice slip down his spine. He blinked with dull eyes at the cameraman.

"Let's just make it a package deal." The cameraman's pan went all grim. "Every print and negative. The works. You're probably thinking all this can really add up, but I'm sure you'll find my prices real reasonable. After all, I ask you, how can you put a price on cherished memories? How can you?"

Grigio cleared his throat. "How much?"

"We'll be in touch."

"Tell me how much. Please."

"We'll be in touch. It's time for you to leave. Babe, get your rags back on, already."

"Tell me," I interrupted Grigio, "did you consider trying him?"

"Trying him what?"

"Did you consider making a move and taking the camera away from him?"

"I told you. He had a firearm. And there were two of them."

"But his hands were full."

"I'm not used to coming to blows. I am not a violent person."

"Uh-huh. And maybe you weren't exactly feeling up to snuff."

"That's right."

So Grigio couldn't, or wouldn't, stand up for himself. Sure. He hauled himself up and out of the chair. Locating his crumpled hat and coat on a dresser, he scooped them into his arms like a bundle of laundry. He staggered towards the door.

"Don't forget this." The dark man tossed a billfold at Grigio's feet.

Grigio nearly passed out stooping over, but he retrieved the wallet, clutching his hat and coat close to his chest. He leaned his face against the door. "I'm sorry," he muttered.

The man yapped. "What was that?"

Grigio half-yelled and half-blubbered, "I'm sorry."

"We'll see how sorry." The dark man spoke low and steady. "You think about exactly how sorry. Now get out."

Grigio cracked the door just enough to squeeze through. A stale smell hung in the hallway. It just about overcame him. He stumbled his way down the corridor, a boisterous laughter tailing him muted by the thin walls. When Grigio hit the stairway, he lost his lunch. Like I said, a born victim.

"Is that it?" I asked.

"Yes. That's all there is to tell. That's my entire story."

"When was this?"

"Three days ago."

"That was Saturday."

"That's correct."

"And they called today?"

"Yes."

"They made you sweat for three days. Very big of them. How is it your wife didn't go to the dinner?"

"How did you—"

I spun a make-believe ring on my finger, nodded at his left hand.

"She had to babysit her niece. I believe the firm preferred me to attend stag, anyway."

I asked Grigio if anyone at work could be mixed up in this. Any of his clients, maybe.

"Oh, my gosh," he said. "No, of course not. That would make no sense. I've only just joined the firm. I've been with them seven months."

"And you haven't told your wife anything about it."

"How do you know that?"

"Lucky guess. How long have you been married?"

"Less than one year."

"A newlywed. That's swell."

"Do you need the precise date?"

"Never mind that. So, they've contacted you. By telephone?"

"Yes, they certainly have."

"What'd they say? Give me everything you remember."

"They said they weren't messing around—that's how he spoke. And they meant business."

"Sounds like a real tough crowd."

"And they want five hundred dollars!" He repeated in an exaggerated whisper, "Five hundred dollars."

"That's a lot of scratch."

"It is indeed."

"Have you got it?"

"No, I haven't any savings to speak of."

"They've done they're homework, all right. Can you get it?"

"I'll need some time for that."

"What can you come up with now?"

"Possibly two hundred? Possibly?"

"Don't ask me, Grigio. I'm just doping this out."

"At least one hundred right away. Is that good? I can't let the wife find out. She can't know anything about it. How much will do?"

"It all depends."

"Tell me what it depends on."

"It all depends on what you want to do about it."

"I just don't know. That's why I telephoned you, for Pete's sake."

"Sure. Is there anything else you didn't tell me? Something you forgot to mention? Or maybe left out by accident on purpose?"

"Isn't that enough?"

"Okay. Let me give it to you as straight as I can, Grigio. You can play it one of three ways."

"Very well, I've got three choices."

"That's right. All of them stink, but that's the fix you're in. Get me?"

"I know, I know. I'm sorry."

"Sure. The first choice is to call the cops."

"I can't, I can't do that." Sweat began beading up again on his high forehead. He patted the mustache with the back of his hand.

"You know what they're pulling is against the law. Big time. This is a major crime being committed here, Grigio. Nothing penny-ante about it. You have every right to bring these creeps to justice. Wouldn't you like to see them behind bars? You're a lawyer, for chrissake."

"No," shaking his head. "Can't do that. No."

"All right. You have to be sure."

"Can't. Not that, please. No police."

"All right. The second choice: pay up."

"Pay up?

"Sure. Pay up and be done with it—as long as you realize you might never be done with it. See, if you're good for the five hundred, they may figure you're good for another five. Then maybe a thousand. Maybe two. Get me? They could figure it like that."

"Oh my God!" Grigio got loud again and glanced around. He cleared his throat and found his whisper. "I'm ruined."

"It ain't necessarily so. Sometimes they do take the money and run. They're walking a fine line, themselves. Remember this, Grigio: they don't want you calling cop, either."

"I understand."

"From the sounds of things, we're dealing with small-timers. They might be perfectly happy to take the five Cs and blow town."

"I see."

"Good. You've got a lousy decision to make, so the better you understand the score, the better all round."

"What's my third choice?"

"You fight them."

"You don't mean with fisticuffs?"

"I mean anyway you can. Blackmailers are just about the worst of the worst. They deserve every lousy break we can give them. It might be that we can arrange to take them, for good."

"Those are my choices?"

"Unless you're considering a move to Pago Pago."

"Pago Pago?"

"Sure. Pago Pago. Zanzibar, if you prefer."

"Yes, yes. I understand. God." Grigio forced down a tiny sip. "Tell me. What would you do?"

"It's not my call, Grigio."

"I see. Choices. Choices? I know what I don't want to do, but I know what I can't do."

Grigio gave me this pitiable look right out of a tearjerker. I knew what I wanted him to do, all right. But I was a good boy and played it straight down the line. I didn't even blink. I let him hash it out for himself.

"That's it," he declared. "That's all there is to it. I may be doomed, but I have to fight, God forgive me."

Now he was apologizing to the almighty. He threw a good slug down his throat, and the belt gave him a jolt. His eyes opened wide in more ways than one.

"Okay," I leaned in. "Forget about the amount of dough involved. I'm telling you these guys are strictly bush league. You can tell by the way they set it up, the way they played you, and the payoff they're after. Could be they've never done anything like this before. This could be their maiden voyage. Sure."

"You mean they're a couple of amateurs?"

"That's in our favor, Grigio. How'd they'd leave it with you?"

"The man said he'd call back tomorrow. We'd make arrangements when we talked again."

"That's fine, Grigio, just fine. I need you to do a couple of things in the meantime. Can you do a couple of things?"

Another full belt hoarsened his voice. "Anything you say. I'm listening.

"Agree to the money. You can tell him you don't know how you're going to get it, but you'll get it. Next, when you set up the meeting—sure, you make it a bar. It's got to be a bar, Grigio, get me? You'll only meet them in a public place, and a bar's as good as any. It has to be. The last thing—get two, fifty dollar bills and ten ones. Stack them with the fifties on the outside, the ones in between, and tuck it in an envelope. You bring that envelope to the meeting. Got that?"

"I thought I was going to fight."

"The money's strictly for show. Just in case. You're going to hold it all the time. Probably never even leave your sight."

"Is that all?"

"Just call me when it's set up."

"Will it work? I mean, can you make it work?"

Maybe I struck Grigio as the clairvoyant type. I had no idea whether or not I could pull this off. It sounded like we were dealing with a couple of lightweights, all right. That afforded a certain amount of optimism. So why not put up a good front? Maybe because neither one of us really knew what to expect. The smaller the operator, the more likely you'll draw a wildcard. You can depend on seasoned pros, but you can never tell what a rookie might pull. Especially one with a roscoe snug in his belt. But I didn't see any reason to make Grigio feel lousier than he already did. So I lied without missing a beat. Sometimes my line of work calls for it.

"You're going to make *them* pay, Grigio. They'll never know what hit them."

Grigio rose from his seat, and for the first time I realized his full, gawky splendor. He stood an easy six-plus, skinny like a rail, with an awkward posture. He extended a thinly tapered hand.

"I sure can't thank you enough."

"That's why you pay me."

"Well, yes. The sum we agreed to on the phone. There'll be no trouble on that account. I assure you."

Grigio picked up his bowler from the chair next to him, placed it on his noggin at an awkward tilt, and tipped the brim. I watched him as he cut out. His silhouette achieved something of the cliche cowpoke in its slight, bowlegged bounce.

The next morning I made some stops on the way into the office. I blew in around ten thirty. That's Wednesday the fourteenth. I checked with my service—no calls. I made it a point to stick around until something broke.

The call came in a little after four. Grigio reported that the exchange was full steam ahead. His caller referred to himself as Mr. Grey. This Grey instructed Grigio to be at the Columbia Tavern at Clark and Belmont at seven that evening. That was seven o'clock sharp, of course. Alone, of course. And, of course, with the dough.

Grigio got us a bar, all right. You couldn't ask for more of a dive than the Columbia, a hole that suited me just fine. I asked Grigio if he had pulled together the envelope like I wanted. Sure, he said, he'd prepped it just like I instructed. I told Grigio he was doing swell. I'd take care of the rest and see him at the Columbia. I rang off before he could apologize for anything.

The idea was simple, the idea was basic—you turn the tables. You play your mark for the sucker and set him up on some other rap. You just never know how much finesse is going to be called for, or if your mark will play one of those damn wildcards. That thought kept me spinning. I grabbed an early dinner at the Belden before heading over.

The crowd at the Columbia was impressive, being the middle of the week and all. I held up the bar with one shoe on the foot rail, lingering over a draft, seeing if I could finger our Mr. Grey. I might of overlooked him if not for this beautiful pair of legs a couple stools down. Every joe within drooling distance kept cheating a look at those gams, every joe but one—that made him stand out like Elmer Fudd at a boardwalk beauty pageant.

This bird occupied a little table on the other side of the room. No companion, no drink. Set back stiff in his chair. Arms folded. A gaunt figure, dark skin like a rusty tan. Hard to judge at that distance, but I guessed around thirty-five. A burning cigarette dangled from his lips. He stared through the blue-white smoke from deep-set pockets beneath bushy eyebrows, zeroed in on the front door. He sat and gazed without hardly moving a muscle.

Was that the gink? Could of been—he struck me as small time, all right. He should of bought a drink, but must've been too cheap or too hard up. I observed him chain-smoke two cigarettes, and he wiped his nose on his jacket sleeve three times. He wore an oversized cap, uncommon for guys his age except cabbies and newsies. Then there was that scar. It ran from just above the left corner of his mouth to his ear. I don't know how Grigio missed that one. This mug had been taught a lesson before. I'd have to teach him another. Sure.

Adolph caught my eye from a ways down the bar. He jerked his head twice towards the mug I was giving the once-over. I shrugged, my hands palms up. He strolled down the counter to me, glass and towel in hand.

"Can I get you a fresh one?"

"No thanks."

"You're not sure? About the fish?"

"I'm pretty sure. Doesn't matter. It'll pan out soon enough, one way or another. Never seen him in here before?"

"Nope."

"Has he had anything to drink?"

"Nope."

"We'll have to do something about that. You still remember the Lone Star gag?"

Adolph made an exaggerated nod and wink. He strolled away whistling.

Grigio entered the bar five minutes ahead of schedule. Mud caked his shoes and trouser cuffs—it hadn't been raining, but that's a born loser for you. Right off he spotted the same guy I spotted. Grigio was spotted. He removed his bowler and carried it with both hands as he maneuvered around the tables with that gawky, awkward gait. He tripped once and almost upset a party of four.

Grigio reached Grey's table. At first they exchanged nothing except a silent stare. A waitress came up to Grigio's side. Mr. Grey spoke to Grigio. Grigio sat down. The waitress spoke to Grigio. He shook his head and she left. Grey watched her leave and spoke again. He put out his cigarette, then turned to keep watching the waitress, all the time yapping. He turned back to Grigio with a pointing finger, then stopped talking. Grigio dropped his head and lowered the bowler to his lap. Grey offered a few more words, hunching his shoulders and gesturing with one hand. Grigio, for whatever reason, had clammed up but good.

I abandoned my beer, strode over towards Grey and Grigio, yanked a chair from the next table over, and joined the party. Grey's eyes flashed my way. He spat low and reserved. A smooth and strong tone it was. Made me think of a viola, of all things.

Grey said, "We've got a private conversation going, mister."

"I'm with him, pal," I said. "Sorry I'm late, Mr. Grigio."

Grey gave Grigio the bug eyes. Grigio's thin mustache squirmed as his lips formed the slightest of guilty smiles.

"Say, what gives, Grigio?"

"Mr. Grigio was rolled once," I said. "He didn't care for it. I'm here to make sure he isn't rolled again."

"Grigio, we agreed to meet alone."

"Skip it, Grey. Mr. Grigio isn't about to be steamrolled. And he's not interested in gamesmanship. He's here to settle up with a blackmailer."

"Say, I don't have to stand for none of this. Grigio, we already have a deal."

"I didn't hear Mr. Grigio agree to anything. If you insist on screwing around, we can end this right now and you can take a hike."

Grey stood up. Unsure of himself, he went for tough. "Take a hike, you say?"

"Sure," I smiled. "Maybe we'll bring in some law."

"The law?"

"How's by you, Mr. Grigio? You prefer the nineteenth or twentieth district?"

"You guys don't want no trouble, do you? Don't you just want the merchandise?"

"Of course we want it, Grey. That's why Mr. Grigio's here. That's why you're here. Sit down and let's see if we can come to terms."

"Aw, come on, you guys," Grey beseeched both of us. One doesn't get beseeched a whole lot in this burg. "I don't mean to play tough guy. I just don't like for some stranger to yank me around."

"Sit down if you want to make a deal, Grey."

Grey sat down. "Mr. Grigio knows my deal. Five bills for the photos and negatives. I didn't catch your name?"

"I didn't pitch it. We're all men of the world here, aren't we, Grey? Let's be realistic about this thing. You think a simple lawyer like Mr. Grigio can cough up five bills? Just like that? He hasn't even made partner, for chrissake. Two-fifty. That's more in the ballpark."

"I don't get it." Grey's pan displayed dumb astonishment. Grigio pulled up the bowler just below his eyes. "This isn't how it's supposed to go. I had this all worked out. What I've got should be worth plenty to Grigio, or to his wife, even."

"Threats, Grey? Don't turn ugly on me. We were conducting a real nice business transaction and then you have to go and say a thing like that."

"But I should get at least four hundred out of this. I mean, I went to an awful lot of trouble. And I got this partner—"

"Mr. Grigio appreciates your position. He'll be willing to go up to three hundred. That's three hundred dollars, Grey. Think on that. You ask yourself how much you made last month. In the last year. You ask yourself. Mr. Grigio will give you three hundred dollars for all the prints, all the negatives. A one-time swap. You can take it or leave it."

Grey lit another cigarette, the scar pinching inward with every suck on the butt. Grey tried to think. You had to admire the effort. I trained my focus on Grey but hard. I said, "You bring the envelope, Mr. Grigio?"

Grigio cleared his throat. He placed the bowler on his lap and gingerly groped inside his breast pocket. He came out with the envelope, offering it like a rotten fish.

"Drop it on the table, if you'd be so kind," I said.

The number ten fell to the center of the table with a slap. Grey's greedy fingers darted for the envelope. I struck the back of his hand with a stinging whack, then slowly picked up the package. I coaxed out the wad, just enough to expose the fifty dollar bill on top.

"That's the color of Mr. Grigio's money. Where's your product?" I placed the packet back in the center of the table.

Grey leaned forward in order to dig out a bandana concealed under the back of his jacket.

"Put it on the table," I said.

Grey laid down the bandana, ever so careful. He went pale as a golf ball. "That's all of it. You don't have to look through them."

"Inspect it," I said to Grigio. I kept my stare fixed on Grey. By this time, Grey couldn't take his eyes off mine.

"Is it all there, Grigio?"

Grigio's face scrunched up as he unfolded the kerchief and fingered through its contents. He winced and kept closing his eyes, reviewing the prints with sideways glances.

"Is this everything, Grey?"

Grey showed worried eyes. "That's the whole lot."

"The whole ball of wax?"

"Everything I got."

"It better be."

"It is, I'm telling you."

"Good. Now, listen up. There's one last thing."

Grey used the end of his butt to start off another. His eyes darted between the operation and my stare. "What's that, mister?"

"It's a bit delicate, I'm afraid."

"S'okay."

"I'm sure you can imagine that this whole affair has been quite uncomfortable for Mr. Grigio."

"So what?"

"So, to put it bluntly, he has a problem taking your word for it. That there will be no more pictures or demands. You understand Mr. Grigio's position."

"I guess so. What's it to me?" Grey cheated a quick glance at Grigio. Then at the envelope of money.

"Mr. Grigio would like us to toast the deal. That gesture would afford him some confidence, here. Make it an agreement between gentlemen."

"Is that all?"

"That's all."

"Well—"

"Mr. Grigio's buying."

"Well." Grey gave Grigio the eye. "Well, okay."

"Waitress," I called. "Name your poison, Grey." I couldn't resist.

Adolph sent a waitress over PDQ. We placed our order and got served, fast.

"To an honorable deal," I raised my glass.

Grigio lifted his glass with a pained grin. Grey held up his drink with a simple, "Yeah." He threw back his head and swallowed hard.

"Grey," I said, "take your money. Mr. Grigio, the package."

Grigio didn't know what to do with his bowler and the packet, but finally managed to place one on top of his head and the other in his breast pocket. He got it right, too. Grey folded and tucked the envelope in his back pants pocket. A quick glint flashed off the revolver shoved into Grey's belt.

"We're through here, Grey. Would you like to leave first or shall we?"

That called for Grey to think again. He came up with, "You two."

"After you, Mr. Grigio." I stood and extended a hand toward the front exit.

Grigio rose and headed out. I gave Grey one last, icy glare. Then I followed Grigio out.

As soon as the door shut behind me, I took up a brisk walk. "Come on, Grigio, we've got to make tracks."

"He's got my money."

I paid Grigio's words no mind and picked up the pace. Grigio fell in behind me with that long-legged, off-kilter stride. We high-tailed it around the corner of the building and made a beeline for the alley. We came down the alley until we gained a clear view of the Columbia's back entrance. We waited, but not for long.

The back door flew open in less than a minute, slamming against the outside wall. Then nothing. No action. Grigio put a finger to his lips.

I told Grigio, quietly, "Wait for it."

Practically on cue, Grey stumbled out. His lean figure stepped once, hesitated, and walked straight into a telephone pole. He rubbed his noggin. He glanced up the pole. He couldn't make sense of it and staggered, weaved and tripped over himself, generally in our direction.

Grigio asked out of the corner of his mustache, "What's wrong with him?"

"I'd say our Mr. Grey's been doped."

"Doped? You mean like a thoroughbred?"

"That's right, Grigio. Like a thoroughbred." I smiled to myself. I hadn't expected the dose to act so quick.

Grey caught sight of us. He stopped in his tracks, offering up a quizzical look. He swayed in place, glanced behind him at the exit door, looked back our way. He reached out for a fencepost, a gate, a bus strap, anything to grab hold of and steady himself—he found nothing. Grey dropped to his knees.

"Ow! Say, what are you trying to pull? What's—Samantha?"

Grey's eyes rolled up, the lids shut fast, and he crumbled like a stale pretzel.

I stepped over to Grey and nodded as I looked down on the heap. My client was simply aghast. I enjoyed a nice, smug laugh. I hate blackmailers.

"Is he dead?"

"No, Grigio. He's not dead. You don't dance the last waltz from a Mickey Finn. He's just cooperating."

I pried the cash envelope out of Grey's pants pocket and tossed it over. Grigio, ever on the ball, watched the packet land at his feet. While he bent down for the package, I rolled Grey onto his back with a nudge of my shoe. I grabbed the pistol from his belt and pocketed that. Going through the rest of his clothes, I came across his billfold.

"Let's see just what we have." I stood up, browsing the wallet for some kind of ID. "Grigio, what we've got here is Mr. Heniek Szary. Ever heard of this mug?"

Grigio kept his distance and his silence.

"Uh-huh. Well, I guess he knew you, all right. Got it. He's on West Roscoe. Right in his own backyard. Very small time. We've got just a short drive, Grigio."

My coupe was parked behind the tavern. We packed up Szary in the rumble seat and made for West Roscoe. Grigio remained quiet, seriously quiet, but Szary was quieter.

We found the small apartment, a second story job, above the laundry at Clark and Roscoe. I hauled out Szary's carcass and slung it over my shoulder. Szary let out a sleepy grunt. We climbed up a terrifically narrow and dimly lit stairway. Grigio carried Szary's keys. When we reached the door, Grigio kept diddling with the lock. I told him I was no fireman and to get on with it. Then a tiny voice called out.

"Hank?"

The lock gave all of sudden and the door swung open fast. The tiny voice welcomed Grigio, crying out, "Ahoy, Vincent!"

"Step aside," I huffed, and pushed Grigio out of the way with my shoulder. I lugged myself across the room and flopped Szary onto a Murphy bed that bounced and clanged under the dead weight. I came about to point at the door. "Close it, Grigio."

I squinted at my surroundings. Everything read dark. The shadeless table lamp next to the bed cast the only light, and not much at that. As far as studios go, this one was large for its kind, a small bathroom just beyond the Murphy bed, and a corner kitchenette on the opposite wall. The wood floor showed dark and worn with a patchwork of bleached spots. In that light you couldn't tell if the walls were tinged from age or if they were meant to be that off-off-white color. Two windows, side by side, afforded a dismal view of the elevated tracks. That view was the only view, and the blue-yellow glow of the streetlamps didn't liven things up any. A small stand by the door supported a vase. The plant in the vase looked more than half dead, and that put it one up on Szary.

In the center of this lavish layout stood the young man. He carried an air of maturity, but his face could've passed for sweet sixteen. He was a short and slight thing, with cropped, blonde hair and pale skin. He wore an athletic shirt and charcoal slacks.

The boy asked, "What's happened?" He looked from Grigio to me. He showed no interest in the bed or its contents. Szary emitted a low, buzzing snore.

"Who are you?" I questioned. "You a friend of Szary's? His partner?"

"He screwed it up, didn't he? He thinks he's so clever." He shrieked at the bed, "You screwed it up!"

"I can't understand this," Grigio said. Lines of pain and anger streaked over his long face. He pleaded directly to the boy.

"Gotta make a living, honey."

"The first time—I thought you liked me," Grigio whined.

"You know how it is, honey. Tough times." The boy placed his hands gently on his hips and quickly shrugged his shoulders.

"Grigio," I busted in, "We're wasting time. I don't know your little history with this one, but the first thing is to make sure there aren't any more photos or negatives, savvy?"

"I liked you." Grigio spoke softly. There was the sound of defeat in his voice. The pencil mustache quivered.

I shot it at the boy, cold and strong, "Give."

"Oh, it's in there," he pointed to the john. "His darkroom. More like a stink hole, if you ask me. He doesn't know what the hell he's doing. It just makes me sick."

I stalked into the bathroom, found the pull chain hanging from the middle of the ceiling. One yank on the line cast the room with an ugly, red wash. Pans of transparent liquid lay balanced on top of the toilet and sink. Two more rested in the tub. I spied three prints taped to the medicine chest mirror—I could've bust out laughing. They were so out of focus I couldn't tell if I was looking at animal, vegetable or mineral. That left just a quick search of the main room. Then we'd be ready to set Szary for a tumble.

I exited the bathroom rubbing my hands and grinning to myself. The last thing I expected to see was Grigio training a gun on the boy. Every once in awhile your own client plays the wildcard.

I stopped dead in my tracks. "What the hell are you pulling, Grigio?"

"He's all pissy because it wasn't love, love, love," the boy said.

"You've got nerves of steel, son."

"There's nothing I ain't seen, mister."

"It was special," Grigio squealed. "It was real, and it was special, and you do this to me."

"Grigio," I said. I went after a gentle, fatherly effect, something along the lines of Barry Fitzgerald. "We can't have any of this."

"Leave me alone," Grigio said.

"I can't do that."

"Just leave me alone."

"Ha!" The boy folded his arms and shifted his hips.

"I can't let you do this, Grigio." I brought out Szary's pistol from my jacket pocket, smoothly, and held it down at my side.

Grigio had eyes only for the boy. He went teary and his whole body looked as stiff as an ironing board. The hand trembled, on and off in spasms. The gun shook. He cleared his throat.

I raised the pistol, aimed the muzzle low, and cocked the hammer. "I can't let you do this."

That metallic click got Grigio's attention. His eyes panned over to mine, then down to my gun hand. He gawked at the rod. He breathed short and shallow. The kid watched Grigio with no hint of emotion.

We made like three statues, and the stillness heightened every sound. Grigio's shortened breaths. The metallic wheeze of the bedsprings expanding and contracting beneath Szary. The light jangling of the table lamp's pull chain. The knocking of chair legs against the floorboards. The salt and peppershakers dancing on a card table. The windows rattled once, twice, and then broke into a non-stop, banging vibration as an elevated train came into range. The heavy, metal wheels on metal rails shrieked louder and louder as it approached. It hit the tracks outside the windows with a bang-bang, bang-bang, and beams of streetlamps shot through the train windows like a strobing nickelodeon. The flashing pattern lit up the room like lightning.

Grigio jerked his head sideways to the boy. His gun arm snapped straight. My trigger finger squeezed. Grigio yanked on his rod at the same time. The deafening noise and pulsating light submerged us into chaos for only seconds. Then it ended.

After the train rumbled passed, I stood poised for the next move. The boy held himself motionless in a semi-crouch, each hand drawn to his face for protection. We both looked down at the sight of Grigio laid flat. A darkened rip tore down his right pants leg below the knee. Splashes of blood decorated the nearby floorboards. A strained pucker creased Grigio's face.

"Thanks for that, mister," the boy stuttered. His startled eyes remained fixed on Grigio.

Grigio's lids fluttered open. He took shallow, panting breaths through his mouth. He looked to the boy and found only cold expression. He looked at me with great worry in his sorry eyes.

I asked the boy, "Where's the nearest phone?"

Grigio exhaled, "Tell..."

"We need a phone, boy."

Grigio sucked in as much air as he could. "Tell my wife—"

"A phone, now!"

Szary moaned and almost rolled off the bed. The distraction caught me off guard.

Grigio sobbed, "Tell my wife I'm very, very sorry."

I turned back to Grigio with an impatient, "What?"

Grigio raised his weapon fast—the sudden swing of his arm had me dead to rights. I raised mine in automatic response. I pumped two shells into his chest. Grigio's tall, slim frame flinched from the impact, almost bouncing. His head pulsed forward then snapped backward, hard against the wood floor. Then he relaxed and went still, like somebody let out the air.

"Jesus," the boy gasped.

Szary rolled over into consciousness, muttered "Samantha?" and passed out again.

We paid no attention to Szary. My eyes held fast on Grigio's motionless form. I watched him for about a minute. I shoved the rod back in my jacket, lit a smoke, and took a deep drag. I stepped to the wall behind Grigio, leaned against it, and let myself slide down to the floor.

"I'll find that phone, now, mister." The boy carefully, delicately, stepped over the lifeless body. He must've discovered a newfound respect for Grigio as a corpse. He copped a sweater from the back of the door and crept out.

I reached over Grigio's bloody form and wrenched out the packets of money and photos. The cash went with the pistol in my jacket. I undid the bundle of pictures and gave them a look-see. The first shot was no better than what I saw in the john. As was the second. And the third. Nothing more than blurs of light and shadow. They read as abstract as Einstein's half-erased blackboard.

My gaze shifted from the prints over to the stiff. A born victim? Maybe so, but that's no longer Grigio's kick. It's all mine, now.

Statement No. 3:
Simeon Von Runck

"**H**ave you ever planned a murder?"

That's some introduction, courtesy of Mr. Simeon Von Runck, the party of interest as you call him. Oddball's more like it. Loony tune. Menace. Lush.

That's what he said, all right. "Have you ever planned a murder?" Right off the bat I'm trying to figure him. Just another eccentric, right? You meet all kinds in this racket. Sure. That's how it played at first.

A little more gab and you take it the guy must have a screw loose. Any of you boys expert in neurosis, psychosis, phobias and whatnot? I don't see any wall plaques around here. You probably have loads of personal experience with dementia. Me, I've never been on the couch, but I had to figure Von Runck popped a circuit breaker. So I watched him. I watched him close. Real close.

Then snap! Things turned dark for good. For all that light, frivolous affectation, a sinister thread weaves through Von Runck's eccentricity. It bubbles up, breaks loose. Von Runck's got his dangerous side, all right. I heard it. I felt it. You can't help taking him seriously. Sure, the manner's light enough, but to ignore the danger is to ignore every gut instinct you're born with. That's why you have to give credit to his menace. You know the guy's not right. You know it in your bones. His lightness of nature is mere camouflage. Frankly, the contrast in his character gave me the willies.

Sure, he impressed me as all those things. But you boys don't give a damn for impressions—if you wanted impressions, you'd catch the stage show at the Panther Room or Chez Paree. No, the bureau insists on only the essential details. The bureau wants facts. You're after evidence, any evidence. You're all hot and bothered for something you can sink your investigative teeth into and put on the record. What have you got so far? My guess? You've got nothing.

I'll talk plenty, but I can tell you right now you'll keep coming up empty. Regarding that night, when Mr. Simeon Von Runck introduced himself? Something along the lines of the truth, the whole truth, and so on? All it'll amount to is so much hot air.

"Have you ever planned a murder?"

We've got Von Runck's question, we've got a few statements, and that's it, brother. As far as anything else, something tangible to pin a rap on? I don't see how you boys have a leg to stand on. I'll give you my account, for what that's worth. Sure, he's as suspect as they come, but what'll you do with that? You'll do nothing. Not unless you've made *suspicion* an offense in Cook County. I didn't see anything or experience anything. Nothing first hand. So I have to wonder what I can tell you. It only adds up to a collection of words, just the conversation of a man pretty well under the influence. If you had some kind of case, any kind of case, someone from the DA's office would be here, right? So you've got nothing. And that's what you'll get from me. But I'll cooperate, all right. We'll sit here and pass the time and go through the motions. We have to go through the motions. Sure, let's go through the motions, by all means.

"Have you ever planned a murder?" I can only shake my head. Sure.

I met Mr. Simeon Von Runck at his luxury penthouse on south Wabash. Any of you boys ever seen a penthouse suite that wasn't luxurious? This one, you right away walk into this jumbo living room. It's even got this sunken area, smack in the middle. There's more than enough space for the full-size, built-in bar. You can make out part of the dining room through an archway, and that's even bigger than the living room.

The joint was swinging when I happened in. A three-piece jazz outfit in one corner—did I hint at the scope of the living room? The undercurrent of syncopated rhythm beat throughout the place. A non-stop parade of guests milled about in endless circles.

See, I got the message from my service late in the afternoon. The message put it simply. Von Runck wanted to see me about a job. I gave him a ring and he told me to drop around. Seven o'clock would be *delightful*—his words. Make a note that he told me to come by, he never asked. A privileged boy, I figured. I didn't know it at the time, but I'll wager he doesn't have a real pal in the world.

Imagine my surprise, expecting to drum up some business, and stumbling into a full-blown shindig. I wound my way through the revelers, stopped at the bar, pretty much took in the scene and all it *didn't* have to offer—I presumed it was a washout, job-wise. That's when Von

Runck showed up at my side. Out of thin air. He looped one arm around mine and led me to a corner. He gave me his name, thanked me for coming, and got right to that question—no way he could hold it in.

"Have you ever planned a murder?" His thin mouth wavered between a smile and a smirk, his eyes wide and full of anticipation.

"One hell of an opener you got there," I said.

"Well, yes, I suppose," he said. Von Runck smiled to himself. "Now as to my question, as to that..."

"Yeah?"

"Actually planning it, that is altogether different from wanting to do it. And then actually doing it, well, I say is again an altogether different proposition. Wouldn't you agree?"

"Sure."

"Of course, one could always hire a killing, couldn't one?"

"If you know the right sort," I said.

"I'd have to say, just as an observation, you understand, that you are not that sort. Are you?"

"But you already knew that when you telephoned."

Von Runck smiled to himself again. "Yes. I suppose I did."

"What I didn't know was that I'd be waltzing into the middle of a party. I thought you wanted to talk."

"Oh, this?" Von Runck eyed the room with an aloof turn of the head. "These people. This isn't so much. There always seems to be so many of these people, endless people, endlessly hanging about.

"I thought you wanted to discuss a job."

"Of course I do, dear fellow. Don't trouble yourself about the peasants."

"You always conduct business in a crowd?"

"It's the only way *to* conduct it. Mind you, I really am a most private individual. Here, surrounded by all these so-called acquaintances, we can discuss anything and everything without fear of being overheard. It's also, most importantly, the perfect excuse to enjoy one's favorite drink. We aren't stuck in the middle of a tired office or some dusty, old boardroom—here we are! Do you see? Do we understand each other?"

"You're saying that as soon as you go off to a private room, you think people take notice. They begin to suspect."

"There you have it. I'm so pleased you understand."

"And you like to hide your drinking problem behind a ready-made excuse."

"Hmm." Von Runck looked me up and down. "You might be quicker than you look."

"Sure. I was born with this pan. So why'd you want to see me?"

"We're getting to it. Aren't you drinking?"

"The moose behind the bar didn't have any coffee."

"You don't realize how funny that is. He's actually a mule."

"Call him whatever species you like."

"Excuse me for stopping you right there, for I must. Mules are not a species, you see? We should classify them as a type, best termed *Equus assinus*—isn't that suggestive?"

"Whatever his breeding, he looked like he was sucking down a whole lot more than he was serving."

"But why coffee, my dear fellow? Have anything you like."

"This is supposed to be a professional visit."

"Hmm." Von Runck eyeballed me up and down. He did a lot of that.

I hitched up my pants and planted my hands on my hips. "So how about it?" I'd grown tired of being strung along.

"How about what?"

"How about getting to the reason I'm here, or do you need to get tight, first?"

"You are a pushy fellow, aren't you?"

"Yeah. Sometimes my line of work calls for it. It also calls for me getting paid. You see, until you offer me some work, and until I accept your offer, I'm on my own nickel." The impression evolved in my mind. Von Runck's stringing me along came by design. The intention was anybody's call. "Do you need a private investigator or not? If you've changed your mind, I can take it on the arches right now."

Von Runck gazed down into his glass and spoke softly. "Have you ever planned a murder?" He smiled to himself, then brought his gaze squarely to mine. "Now before you start making all kinds of faces, we both know the answer. Of course you have. Haven't we all? All of these creatures have. They have wanted to. They have all had the thought, but they never did anything about it."

"Is this your roundabout way of telling me you've done something about it?"

"Hmm. Now we are in dangerous waters."

"Yeah, and me with my lifejacket at the dry cleaners."

"You make me smile. You really do."

"It's impossible to say how much that pleases me, Mr. Von Runck."

"Actually...actually..."

"Get on with it."

"Actually, yes, I have planned a murder." Von Runck nodded to himself.

I stood with my arms folded. Waiting for it.

"Actually," he went on, "actually, I am killing someone." He gazed down into his drink. "At this very moment."

That called for a pause. A whole lot of pause.

"How's that?" I asked.

"Hmm. Isn't this fascinating?" Von Runck shot me the coyest glance he had, and he nodded. He'd gone beyond the point where you could take it as a joke. He knew it. I knew it. Way beyond, where the humorous purpose turns in on itself and grabs you by the throat. Then he knocked back the last of his drink. "Let's have another and talk it over, shall we?"

Von Runck threaded his arm in mine and we strolled to the bar. Without a word the human tree trunk behind the counter shoved a large tumbler toward us. Von Runck retrieved the glass and escorted me across the room.

"Where'd you find him?" I asked. "Ex-prizefighter or ex-wrestler?"

"Right the first time." He took a sip. "You may have heard of The Mule? No? Walter and I go way back."

"Uh-huh."

"Our time together began on the occasion of his very last bout. Or shortly thereafter." Von Runck released my arm in order to gesture without spilling his hooch. "The Mule always had brute force going for him. But he decidedly lacked grace of any kind, you see? The older he got, the more leaden his offense. So on this occasion, there he stood, poised with fists like cement and legs to match, failing to keep up with this Mexican sparkplug. The Mexican simply ran him in circles for three exhausting rounds before proceeding to fairly tear the skin right off the poor soul. Now, I should mention, I'm apt to wager a bit on the fights now and then. Quite a bit, actually. One of my weaknesses."

"I'm having trouble keeping up with them."

"I made an awfully, awfully large killing on the contest. And you know what? I actually felt quite guilty afterward. I had read that the Boxing Commission examined The Mule after the fight. The Boxing Commission ruled that The Mule had been pulverized just once too often. The Boxing Commission ruled that Walter would not fight another day. The Mule was permanently out of the running, so to speak."

"Or put out to pasture. So you put him in harness."

"He's been with me ever since. We've been through a tremendous lot together."

"You mean you've put Walter through a lot."

"Yes, all right. Have it your way." Von Runck threw back a shot from the tumbler.

"But we're wandering."

"I tend to do that. Have you noticed? Please forgive me."

"I'm not in any position to accuse or forgive."

"Hmm. That's really very good. Bringing me back in line."

"Enough tap dancing, Von Runck. What do you mean you're killing someone?"

"Provocative, no? I am confessing to you that I, Simeon Von Runck, am taking a human life at this very moment. Even as we speak." That last line he rendered flat and cold, in slow monotone.

Von Runck tossed a good belt down his throat, then smiled into his glass. He looked me up and down with an ugly smirk. He fed off my response. He must've read it in my eyes.

"I can see you take me in earnest. That truly pleases me, otherwise where would it get us? I should, I suppose, make myself as clear as possible. Just for emphasis, you see? Someone is about to die."

Sure, I could've cracked wise, but not when I saw the look of hot coals in Von Runck's eyes. The heavy lids slanted up at the ends, giving him a serious, deadly somber quality. The small mouth, whenever he stopped drinking or yapping, returned to a thin-lipped smirk. I have to say he could muster a warm smile when he bothered, but his expression always wrenched its way back into that smirk. My gut registered the threat of Von Runck as no laughing matter.

"Have I intrigued you at all?" he said.

"You intrigue me just fine."

"But?"

"It's too early to make you out. I can't decide whether you're just plain evil or just plain cuckoo."

"Hmm." He smiled into his drink. "Nevertheless. Somebody is. Being. Murdered."

I didn't want to give in or let on, but by then we were trapped by his words. We'd gone too far. Von Runck had committed us both. "Why tell me?"

"I should think a fellow like you would adore the opportunity of playing hero. The lone, stalwart knight, riding to do thrust and parry with the dragon. Rescue the princess and whatnot. Wouldn't you like to do that?"

"Sure, sure. Why me?"

"Oh, that. I was given your name by a Mr. Jupiter."

"That crook."

"Mr. Jupiter holds you in the very highest regard. He failed to go into why."

"So I come recommended."

"Without hesitation."

"By a thug who puts on airs. Who runs a gambling house in the sticks where he's safe from any real influence."

"Mr. Jupiter is a bit of a raconteur, is he not?"

"I'll just say I owe him a kiss on the skull with an anvil."

Von Runck tilted his glass into smiling lips. I gave him a long, hard look. The grin grew self-satisfied. I decided to press the situation.

I said, "I think I'll be going."

"I wouldn't. I wouldn't, really. How can you even consider leaving me? With life and death in the balance?"

I knew Von Runck was right. I knew I wasn't going anywhere and he knew it. "I could call the cops."

"Yes, contacting the authorities is one choice. We can entertain that idea. What exactly would you tell them? What could you show them? I, of course, would have to play perfectly innocent. I can do that, you know. They'd be in precisely the same predicament in which you find yourself. Wouldn't that all prove such a terrible waste of valuable time? The wheels, you know, the wheels are already in motion, you see? Tick tock."

"Are you so bored you have to play games like this?"

"The game is already afoot when we first come into this world. We're all born with a death sentence, aren't we, really? After all? I'm merely urging it on. Giving a little push, you see? Yes? Unless, of course," he paused for a sip and emphasis, "unless you can stop it."

Von Runck took his sweet time about it, but we were getting somewhere. "So now we're finally onto it. How exactly do I do that?"

"By finding the victim, my dear!" He smiled with his head tilted to one side. "Your prey is already here. Someone, somewhere, in one of these rooms." He threw back a slug. "I'll introduce you to anyone, everyone. Ask me anything about anyone. I am here to answer your every question."

"Are you telling me this all pans out?"

"With absolute certainty! Do you take me for ah, ah, a senseless killer? Murder on a whim?"

"I can't see any reason why not."

"Let me clear your mind on that count. Please! There is a perfectly justified motive in this instance."

"Uh-huh." My eyes narrowed as I studied his. How do you figure this guy? "I could lean on you, try to make you spill."

"Hmm. Yes, you could. Of course I would try to stall you. Hmm. No, I don't think that's the best use of your time."

"How much time do I have?"

"Not all that much, I'm afraid. Could be any time, now. Really."

"Uh-huh."

"So who would you like to meet first? Tick tock, tick tock."

"How's about meeting the victim?"

"That's good. Yes it is. Very good."

I surveyed the mix of guests in the living room. I gave the adjoining dining room a quick look-see. What about the wait staff? House servants? The musicians?

"Getting the lay of the land?" Von Runck took a sip. "Mm! I do hope you're not counting yourself. Please! That wouldn't be playing fair."

"Let's play fair, by all means."

"Touchy, touchy," Von Runck said.

Von Runck could have skipped that last thought and it would've been jake with me. I felt spooked enough without adding myself to the potential guest list. I let it pass.

It could be anyone in the entire layout? By a quick head count, that made it anyone out of one hundred, give or take. How far are you going to get just yapping? How do you narrow down that field? The idea of interviews sounded like a wild goose chase. No, better skip all that and concentrate on Von Runck. He had all the dope I needed, didn't he? If Von Runck was on the level, he'd be my only clue.

"Do I learn anything else? Any more info?"

"No. I don't think so."

"But your plans are already in motion. Right now."

"Oh, most assuredly."

"And you have a motive?"

"Perfectly plausible."

So what had he already told me? Had he given anything away? I needed to start ruling out options, but fast. Something in the works, in the middle of a party, and the murderer all the time preoccupied with me and his thirst. I dismissed the idea of anything direct like gunplay. I dismissed anything requiring physical violence. Von Runck wasn't that type of kook, he wasn't up for it, and the idea of creating a bloodbath in the middle of a party seemed bizarre even for Von Runck—at the very least it would be in very bad form.

Von Runck gazed into his drink, "Tick tock. I do wonder what he's thinking."

I saw one choice that made sense. That's if you can find any sense in lunacy. Poison. Von Runck could set that up in advance. The catch, of course, is that poison is indiscriminate. A revolver fires where you point it. How do you aim poison? You dump a bag of arsenic in the punchbowl and it'll go after any gink who dunks his glass. How do you control it? Either you find some gag to isolate the dose, or you get someone else to work it for you. I nixed the second option. I couldn't buy the idea of Von Runck taking on a partner. Too much trouble. Too big an ego. Too much risk. Sure, Von Runck had found some kind of scheme. Something he could set up in advance. For all I knew it could turn out to be something deceptively simple.

"Who would you like to meet first?"

"I want to see the bedroom."

"My, my. Anyway, it's locked."

"Off bounds?"

"Entirely irrelevant. At least to this proceeding."

"How about the kitchen?"

That actually caught Von Runck off guard. He turned and swayed lazily ahead. I grabbed him by the shoulder and told him I'd find it myself. He left me to it with a dismissive flourish of his fingers.

I made my way from the living room through the dining room, through a swinging door, and down a short corridor. Another swinging door brought me to a shining, white service kitchen. Uniformed servers and cooks buzzed about preparing various finger sandwiches and the like, arranging desserts, stacking dishes and glassware, unstacking dishes, unstacking glassware.

"Can I help you, sir?"

I needed help, all right. I needed help by the yard-full.

"Can I get you anything, sir?"

I turned to the waiter in the monkey suit. "No thanks. Any of these people regular staff?"

"Most are hired just for the evening, sir. Is there a problem?"

I winked, "No fair guessing."

I threaded my way back through the corridor, the hall, the dining room, the living room. The kitchen didn't fit. I crossed it off as all wrong for this murder plot. Besides, wouldn't Von Runck want to be on hand to take in every detail? The fact that he didn't follow me to the kitchen should have tipped me off p.d.q.

I cornered Von Runck. "I've seen enough."

"I should think you have. Ha! You are an amusing fellow."

"Wish I could say the same."

"Tick tock."

That damn "tick tock" annoyed the hell out of me.

Poison. Control. I tried working backward from that. How else could it figure? I stepped to the center of the living room. The party swirled about me. The guests more animated. The music sped up. Pick out one person. Just one. Isolate a single victim. How is the victim isolated?

I swung around to face my host. He parted his smirk with another shot of rye. I swiveled in the other direction, gradually, until I stood squarely facing the bar. I stepped across to the counter. I pivoted to take in the entire room and all its potential victims, its one potential criminal.

I leaned my back into the wood frame and brought up my elbows to rest on. My thoughts kept spinning.

The Mule leaned in close behind me, "What are you drinking, bub?"

Through the crowd I caught glimpses of Von Runck. He slinked his way along the wall, pausing for a sip from his glass or to nod insincerely to a guest.

"What are you drinking, Mule?"

"Bourbon."

"I'm good. Anyhow, if you don't mind my saying, you're drinking enough for both of us."

That's when it struck me. It started adding up and it started to click. Sure. I forgot about trying to dope out a penthouse full of targets. Nix that. Instead, I turned the whole thing around. What if Von Runck *wanted* me to figure it out? Just suppose, crazy as it sounds, that he meant for me to piece it together. That's why he got hold of me. That's what he had in mind all along. If that was true, call it a tall if, then the solution had to be basic. It had to be plain. Plain and in plain sight. With that lightbulb fully lit, I brought myself around to face Walter, The Mule.

Talk about overgrown in every possible way—large head, broad body, thick limbs. A beer mug looked like a shot glass when The Mule held it in one of those massive paws. The only small things about the Mule, strictly by contrast, were his nose and eyes. His nose looked flat and pinched on one side, and it jutted to the other side where the bridge met the eyebrows. His eyes, tiny and sparkling blue, hid in narrow, sunken slits enveloped by a swollen brow.

"You always drink so much, Walter?"

"I do lately," he shrugged.

"Yeah, I know. It helps, doesn't it?" Sure I was fishing, but with calculated purpose.

"I don't know if I should talk about it."

I jerked my head over my shoulder and narrowed one eye. "It's okay, Walter. Von Runck sent me over"

"Isn't he a swell guy?"

"Swell isn't the word."

"Well, the doc, he gave me a powder for the headaches, but now they're getting real bad. Worse than ever."

"And the booze helps."

"It sure does. Lucky I'm built so big or I couldn't handle it."

He handled it, all right. He handled it with only the slightest hint of swaying.

"I think you're about the biggest guy I've ever seen."

"I'm six-nine. I used to be."

"And you've got your own, special stock. Am I right?"

"Mr. Simeon must a clued you in."

"He wised me up. In his own fashion."

"He's the nicest man I ever, ever met."

"Is that a fact?"

"My only pal. In this whole, stinking world."

"I'm thinking he'll miss you, Walter."

"Yeah."

"How long have you got?"

"It makes me sore to think about it."

"That's better than crying in your soup."

He hunched his oversized shoulders and sighed through his nose. "No one knows. Nobody really knows how much time I've got. Not long, I guess. Not a one of them knows."

"Sounds like a whole group."

"Oh, sure. Mr. Simeon told me to see as many docs as I wanted. He told me you have to see a second doc just to double-check the first doc. On account of it being so serious. You know how that goes."

"Right as rain, Mule."

"I just don't get how a thing like that can grow inside you."

"Me neither."

"Does it make any sense to you?"

"No. No it doesn't. I'll tell you, Walter. I have enough trouble just trying to figure out people."

"Now that's the truth. How about that drink, now?"

"Sure, sure. Whiskey and soda."

"Oak." The Mule prepared my drink with the greatest care, like it took all his concentration. There's no room for casual conversation during such an undertaking. Twice, briefly, he squinted his left eye and a wince overtook his mouth. He fought through it and served me with a kind of delicacy, placing the glass before me using two hands.

The Mule eyed his own glass—empty. "Mr. Simeon put in this awful good stash of bourbon for me." The Mule reached down to a cabinet behind him, then interrupted to bob back up. "Time to break open a new one." He turned away once again, reached down, and came back with a fresh bottle. He poured himself a tall, stiff one. I gave the bottle the once over.

For a moment we stood quiet, dismissing the festival surrounding us, each gazing upon the gleaming pool of alcohol before him.

"What'll we drink to, bub?"

I meant to smile. I didn't pull it off. "Whatever you say, Mule."

"Aw, to my pal." I heard the pride in his deep, scratchy voice. Not an inebriated, sentimental pride, but an honest pride, straight from the gut. "To Mr. Simeon. Who's getting me out of all this mess."

"You really need his help?"

"Can I tell you?" His voice fell low as can be. I leaned in close. "Those docs. They really scare me. They don't mean to. I know that. They can't help that. They told me the headaches are going to get worse. They'll get something worse and then I'll feel sick all the time. You get me? I'll just become weaker and weaker and weaker—"

"Sounds about as bad as it gets."

"I've been slammed plenty in this life. Mostly in the ring."

"Naturally."

"That's the kind of thing I can take. I could always take it. Even when I lost bad I could. I could always take it and hold my head up. Know what I mean?"

I gazed deep into Walter's blues and never broke contact.

"But this other stuff. It's like it won't never stop. So I take another drink. I'm no good at that kind of hurt, see? Aw, that's not how I want to go out. I don't think no one should have to go out that way."

I knocked back a good slug.

"But I just can't do it myself. I just can't."

"So you need a little help."

"You probably find it kind of funny. A big lug like me. I didn't know what to do until I told Mr. Simeon. He didn't say 'boo.' Not one kick. He worked it all out. Told me not to worry about it. Told me not to think about it and he'd take care of everything. He said I won't know it, I won't feel a thing, but there'll come a time when I'll just drop off. I'll just go to sleep. I'll go to sleep and won't have to wake up again. The pain'll be gone for good and I won't go through nothing bad no more."

The Mule's tone grew softer as he spoke, as though he recalled a dream. He wasn't looking at me or anything else in the room. I don't know what he saw.

"Sounds peaceful, Walter."

The Mule drew in a deep breath. "Yeah."

"But it does call for a witness," I thought out loud. "Just in case."

"In case of what?" The Mule made the most honestly bewildered face I'd ever seen.

"How's that drink?"

"Fine, just fine. You know Mr. Simeon—nothing but the best." His lips curled into a smile, but his left eye flashed that odd squint.

My thoughts raced beyond our little corner of the world, beyond that immediate moment. I saw the future, I did. I suspected that The Mule would find his peace later that evening. Later that evening, the police would discover a bottle of the finest bourbon laced with enough poison to knock off a battalion. They'd find traces of the poison in The Mule, too. Of course, they'd also locate a note in his jacket or pants pocket. In Walter's own words. In his own awkward hand. Would the cops come up with more than that? Would they find any direct trace of Von Runck? Would they discover that the vain, eccentric, anti-social Simeon Von Runck was really a pussycat, a diehard pragmatist of the sentimental order?

I shared one more drink and one more conversation with The Mule. We didn't have anything important to say, and we enjoyed saying it. When I left him at the bar, he looked worry-free. I could imagine it, hearing his big-barreled voice crowing, "Mr. Trouble? Never heard of him."

I wound my way through the revelers. Meandered my way to the door. I hesitated before exiting and turned about. Peering through and around the crowd, I spotted Von Runck in a far corner. He stood as still as an owl, an owl with a drunken smirk. He'd been watching.

I motioned to Von Runck with an index finger raised to the brim of my fedora. He returned the salute with a slight raise of his glass, then faded back within himself. His face bowed down to his drink. A crooked smile screwed across his lips, then faded. I exited the penthouse, shutting the door behind me, real quiet. Like I didn't witness a thing.

Statement No. 4:
Johnny Shin

Johnny Shin was gassed. The hour late. One o'clock. It's so hot, so humid, I swear my cigarette's ready to cry. And there squats Johnny Shin. Straight across the desk. In all his glory. Dressed to the nines in full monkey suit and top hat. I'm beat, bothered, and hot under the collar. Shin? Nothing to say. Mum as a sphinx. Doesn't so much as look at me. He waltzes in, parks his can, and sits. He sits and he stares, caressing that absurd topper in his lap. Staring into the great void, he's wearing the expression of a manhole cover.

You'd have to imagine he'd have something to spill. Who stumbles into a PI's office with nothing to kick? At that hour? Not one word from this baby. No "hello." No "allow me to introduce myself." No nothing. Instead, the guy's lousy with hiccups.

If that doesn't beat all for a harmless enough introduction. Feels long ago. Beyond the measure of hours. Didn't take long for those dominoes to fall. Sometimes it's the easiest thing to go wrong, and go there fast. Sure.

I spotted a couple of you boys down at Canal Street. You got a real good squint at the crack-up, the body, the whole stinking works. What you couldn't dope out is how it happened, how it played out. I guess that's where I come in. Sure. Me and my little adventure. That mess we've got down on Canal, that scrambled misery of a scene you witnessed—chalk it up to Shin's indiscretions.

All right, let's take it from the top. For the record. I'll fill in most of your missing pieces. I'm betting it won't fill in nothing where Johnny Shin's concerned. Whoever's stuck getting a line on that baby needs plenty of patience and time and luck. Nine lives' worth. The luck of Lindy.

Roll it back. Last night. Call it twelve thirty by the time I returned to the office. More or less. The stakeout wound up a bum steer. That threw my client for a loop, all right. But let's not go into that story. I figured I might as well get a jump on my report. Why not get it out of the way? It would have been tough going trying to sleep in my oven of an apartment.

I'd been pounding and sweating at the typewriter about thirty minutes when the egg strolled in. Mind you, it was getting on one o'clock, but this gee sauntered in like it's the middle of the day. Business as usual. Most people would've knocked. Some might have gone easy on the doorknob, peeked in first, made with a whispered "hello" or "excuse me" or "gosh, I'm sorry to bother you at this godforsaken hour." Not this gink. He let himself in and throws shut the door just as casual as entering a stall. Not so much as a glance my way. After slamming the door hunched over, he straightens up and adjusts his top hat with one hand, just so—he sported a stovepipe, of all the crazy things. He negotiated the office off-balance, shuffling and weaving, as slowly and deliberately as he could manage. His equilibrium played games with him, and it looked like a winner.

He entered the small circle of light cast by the desk lamp, and I took in the full treatment. Hard to believe anyone would shoehorn himself into a tux on a night like that. He plunked onto the chair on the client side of the desk. Tilted all the way back with his legs stretched out wide. He removed the topper with two hands, carefully, and then placed it on his lap like some delicate bloom. He proceeded to undo his first collar button and loosen his tie. The arm dropped to his side, and he exhaled a lengthy, deep breath. That's when he hiccupped.

My visitor made for a slim figure. Short and slim. Slim all the way down. The thin, tinted face came to a round bottom at the chin. He slicked back his oil-black hair from a part in the middle. His narrow eyes angled slightly, and the skin underneath puffed up in gray pouches. The mouth ran wide with a pronounced, thick lower lip. The bird came across as no one special—no one special enough to be fascinating enough at that hour.

"Pardon me," I said.

No response.

Louder: "I'm talking to you."

Nothing.

"Hey! Rasputin!"

Still nothing, nothing but a hiccup and a stare as blank as plaster. One hand mindlessly stroked the opera hat, like petting a lap cat.

I used a handkerchief to rub the sweat from my palms and wipe my forehead. I swung the typing stand out of the way and felt in my pocket for a smoke. I grabbed a match and pondered the mug. An Asian looking mug. In fancy dress, no less. Stinko, no less. At one in the goddamn morning. I struck the match and the lush came to attention in an instant.

He tipped into a slight bow, in my general direction, carefully placed the topper back on his bean, and tipped the brim. "So very, very pleased to meet." He spoke with a soft tone, a tone small, thin, and nasal.

"So, it can speak, after all."

"I do not get you."

"Got a name?"

He hiccupped.

"I asked if you have a name."

"Yes. I do. My name is Jung Hee Shin."

"How's that again?"

He yanked off the topper, caught himself, and gently lowered it to his lap. "Call me Johnny!"

"Sure. So it's Johnny Shin, is it?" I struck another match and lit up.

"Yes." Shin positioned the stovepipe back on his crown, delicately. He surveyed the layout with sleepy eyes. "This is your office room?"

"That's what I'm doing here. Would you mind telling me what you're doing here?"

"No. I would not mind." He smiled. He hiccupped.

"Go ahead."

"I do not get you."

"What are you doing here?"

"My life!" That diminutive voice turned shockingly amplified. Damn shrill, too. His nose flared out and his forehead bunched up in creases. "My life is in danger!"

"That's what you come stumbling in here at this hour to tell me?"

"My life was not in danger earlier."

"Sure, sure. Okay, let's have it. What makes you say your life is in danger?"

"Paching! Paching!" Shin stuck out his right hand and flexed it into a peculiar, squeezing gesture.

"Paching?"

"Right down street. Outside. In front of bar. Paching! Paching!" Once again his hand signaled with that odd, twinging motion.

"Let's give that a try for starters," I said. "You were in a bar."

"Yes. Bar very, very close to office here."

"Who was with you?"

"No one. I alone with myself."

"Okay. You're at this nearby lounge on your lonesome. So what happened?"

"Oh, very, very nice man at bar. Very, very considerate. He told to me, 'You have had enough. It is time you leave now.' So I go away."

"And?"

"Oh! As soon as I go through door. Paching! Paching! There is a man in middle of street with gun!"

"You don't say."

"No, I do say! I say very, very much."

"How many shots did he fire at you? Paching, paching sounds like two in my book."

"Who know? He try to kill me and I try to not die! I not counting!"

"Take it easy, take it easy. I bet you did count after all. Think for a moment. How much time was there between shots? Did he fire quick and rapid? Or maybe he took slow aim between shots."

"Ah. I get now. Gun man pretty fast, yes. Gun man shoot three times."

"Three shots, three misses."

"I did not wait for number four."

"Was the street empty? Pretty quiet?"

"Except for paching, very, very quiet.

"Uh-huh. Three misses. From the middle of a deserted street, with no distractions, and you sitting pretty. A sitting Peking Duck."

"Peking in China. I no Chinese!"

"Sure."

"I am Korean man!" Hiccup.

"Simmer down. So it's three shots and he comes up with zip. You're a lucky man, Mr. Shin."

"If I so lucky, why he shoot at me?"

"That's an intelligent question, Shin. Did you recognize him?"

"I no wait to find out."

"You ran away."

"Yes, I ran away. I ran like ah...

"Like a drunk gazelle?"

"Oh, that pretty funny."

"Okay, so you ran. Then what?"

"I run some more."

"And then?"

"More paching."

"How many?"

"Just one paching."

"Then what?"

"I come to place of all light and I go in. A drug house?"

"A drug store, Shin. Probably the twenty-four-hour Rexall at Webster."

"Yes, that is place. Find telephone room with big book. All kinds of names and streets and numbers."

"Don't tell me you looked me up in the phone book."

"No, no. Try to find friend, Man-Su Pak. You know Man-Su Pak?"

"Haven't had the pleasure."

"He is living on the side near north."

"You could have called the cops."

Hiccup.

"The police, Shin. You could of phoned the cops."

"No, no. No police man. Do not want police man. Want Man-Su Pak."

"Did you find him?"

"No. I run more, can find no address."

"Any more paching?"

"One more. Out of doors of Rexall. That is right?"

"That's right. Rexall. Then what?"

"I am so much out of breath. So hot. Light in head. Need rest. Door of this building open. Go inside and sit on stairs. Then I see! Up top light." He pointed over his shoulder.

"From my office."

"Holy mackerel! You are home!"

"Sure, I'm home, all right."

"Yes. Maybe, as you say to me, I am lucky."

"Or smarter than you let on."

I got no response to that one. I pressed him on the identity of his would-be assassin—no go. I kept pressing him, but the hiccups got worse. And he lost his place in conversation worse than Gracie Allen. I felt ready for a stiff one myself. I felt ready for bed. Maybe both. The whole thing read screwy on the face of it, and I didn't even know what Shin wanted. If Shin knew what he wanted, it was news to me.

We danced around some more until Shin had to use the toilet. I've got the one office on that floor that comes with a john. When it's working, it saves me the trouble travelling down the hall. With Shin occupied, I grabbed a drink from the water cooler, took a few sips, and splashed the rest on my face.

Back at the desk, I put up my feet. A cool breeze rolled in the open window and chilled the back of my neck. I cupped a match and fired up a cigarette. I burned through the butt before Shin emerged from the bathroom. Framed in the doorway, he painted one hell of a picture in that cockeyed opera hat. Another cool breeze drifted in and I stood up.

"What do you say, Shin, I buy you a nightcap? I'm sure I can find a joint with a late liquor license. Or a place that prints its own. I could use a belt myself—sometimes my line of work calls for it."

"Most pleasing, sir." Shin's thick mouth grinned big, his puffy eyes almost shut. "Very, very please," with a tip of the brim, "why you not call me Johnny?" The request had lost all its steam.

I heard a light sprinkling of raindrops as I shut the window—yeah, like a soft paching. I grabbed my jacket and hat, doused the light, and locked the door behind us. Shin nuzzled my shoulder all the way down the stairs. I told him I wasn't playing piggyback, though I knew he wasn't savvy.

I had to figure Shin's story bubbled forth from a bottle. Even so, I told Shin to hang back in the vestibule while I gave the street a look-see. I pushed open the outside door nice and easy. A misting rain glossed the street like an eight ball and cooled the air. The hum of a lone car driving steady down Clark approached. No other action. I glanced up as I stepped out, keeping one hand on the door. The rain clouds added an extra layer of shadow to the early morning hours. Shin peeked out below my arm.

"I told you stay put," I said.

I leaned out to get a broader view from the recessed entrance. Not another soul. Just the crate rolling down this side of Clark, a green hulk of a Plymouth sedan that slammed its brakes and short-skidded to a fast stop at the curb. I instinctively hit a slight crouch as the driver's door opened. Through the falling sheets and vapor, I made out the silhouette turning my way. The driver's arm swung over the roof of the vehicle, smooth and quick. I wasn't about to wait for any paching.

I spun like a top, sprung back inside the vestibule, and ran smack into Shin as the door swung closed behind us. I took him down in my arms and we hit the stone, tile floor as a blast shattered its way through the glass door. Two more shots buried themselves in the framework. The ringing explosions faded and gave way to the tap dancing of raindrops as they blew into the foyer. We kept still as the pyramids.

I whispered, "You in one piece, Shin?"

"Paching?"

"Sure. Shh."

I began easing myself up, slow and silent—except for the tinkling bits of glass. Three more shots erupted and struck with sharp cracks against the outside of the building. Shin poked at me with little fists.

"Shoot! Shoot!"

"This ain't the Wild West, Shin and I'm not packing any six-shooter. But I'll bet you all the tea in China that our friend is out of pills."

"I no Chinese!"

"Shh!"

I peered over my shoulder, as sly as I could, and spied the figure stepping up the curb. He hesitated, took another step, then another.

"Paching! Paching!" Shin cried.

I pushed up to my feet and wheeled around to face the gunman. I stood just within the blown-out door. The dark figure hung back on the sidewalk no more than ten feet away. He had me cold. I raised my open hands in front of me, palms up. The gunman jerked up the roscoe and aimed at my chest. For a moment we listened to the wind and the rain. Then he squeezed, fast: click, click!

I lunged forward, "That sort of evens things up."

The gunman slid two steps back, then whirled and ran for it. I leapt out of the vestibule and nearly slipped off my feet on the broken glass. As I found my footing, a hard tug jerked me from behind and held me. Shin had snagged one of my belt loops in an effort to get to his feet—he didn't make it.

"Who the hell is this guy?" I barked it out loud, but I was talking to myself.

"Crazy husband," Shin said.

"Crazy who?"

"It probably Mr. Jang."

The triggerman scooted around his car and slid in behind the wheel. He punched the accelerator with the car door still open. The green Plymouth fishtailed out of control as it headed south on Clark Street.

I yanked Shin up by the lapels and hauled him across the street to my coupe. I bellowed for him to get in. I threw myself into the driver's seat and slammed the door shut. Shin hopped in and left his door wide open. I fired up the engine and threw her in reverse to get off the DeSoto in front of me. A rear tire jumped the curb and the passenger door banged shut from the impact. I popped her into first, fed some gas, and barely scraped the DeSoto's bumper as I steered into a tight U-turn.

I spotted the Plymouth one block down, backing off a lamppost with a trashcan wedged in between. The coupe had gained half a block by the time the Plym took off again. We sped down Clark towards the heart of the sleeping city, two machines streaking over the blurred reflections of traffic lights on the slick pavement. An urban ghost town flew by the rain-streaked windows of my coupe. Most of the drunks had already passed out somewhere else, and the wholesale delivery trucks were still in their barns—it was too late for the revelers and too early for newsies and milkmen.

I caught fleeting glimpses of Shin as he took it in, pointing out sights to himself, stroking that god-awful topper in his lap. The chase was on and it struck me—there we were, in the wee hours of the morning, in high-speed pursuit of an assassin on the run, the good guys going after the bad guy, the All-American private detective and his Korean sidekick.

"What do you mean husband, Shin?"

"You know, Mr. Jang probably crazy jealous."

"Who the hell is Mr. Jang?"

"He married to Mrs. Jang."

"Who the hell is Mrs. Jang?"

The Plym barreled straight down Clark as we gained on her. She took a hard right followed by a quick left, cutting over to Wells. I didn't think she'd hold the turns doing thirty-five, but the Plym just made it, almost clipping a traffic light. Now the Plymouth pushed it, flying down Wells at thirty-five, forty, forty-five miles an hour.

"Ah, that Mrs. Jang. She my sweetheart."

"Your sweetheart, Shin? Jesus Christ, are you kidding me? We're getting shot at because you're mousing around?"

"I do not get you."

At times the Plym swerved half a lane to the left or right, quick swerves, then straightened out again. That gave me something to worry about as the coupe kept advancing. For the life of me I couldn't figure what the shooter figured, if he figured anything at all.

"Shin, you're two-timing with Mrs. Jang, and now poppa's trying to kill you? Is that what this boils down to?"

The gunman eased off the gas as we approached the short bridge that crosses the river at Wacker Drive. The Plym hit the ramp and leapt two feet off the ground. It landed hard, scraped bottom on the gridding, and took two zigzagging bounces. Its body heaved side to side before correcting its course one-half block beyond Wacker.

"It's our turn, Shin."

"Call me—Holy mackerel!" Shin leaned over and hugged the topper in his lap.

We hit the bridge doing forty and sailed three feet above the ground. I could feel her kicking up in back, but she leveled off and held steady when she came down. Shin bounced back in his seat, caressing the damn high hat. We were almost on top of the Plym as we neared Lake Street. Through the mist I made out a couple of pedestrians running toward the stairs leading up to the train platform. A white Ford cruised slowly through the intersection.

"Is this Mrs. Jang's husband?"

"It could be."

"Could be? Try to make out his face."

I kept her floored, attempting to pull up on the driver's side. The Plym suddenly faded and careened into a right turn down Lake Street. Her entire body leaned low onto the left side. A hubcap popped off, bounced and whirled onto the sidewalk.

I hit the brakes and we spun halfway around just before the next traffic light. A van entered the intersection from Randolph and screeched to a stop at the sight of my car.

"Did you see him, Shin?"

"Yes."

"Was it Mr. Jang?"

"I not sure, I do not know."

"Why the hell not?"

"Holy Mackerel, I never see husband before."

I hit the gas, worked the steering wheel hard, and headed back up Wells. I turned onto Lake to continue the pursuit. The Plym had a couple blocks on me.

"Is that or is that not Mr. Jang?"

"I don't know what he look like. But who else could he be?"

"How the hell do I know, Shin?"

"You get very, very hot."

We zipped down Lake for two blocks, outpacing the elevated train on the tracks above. At the next bridge we crossed the curving river again, rushing on for another four blocks. The longer we drove, the heavier the mist appeared. The Plym sprayed more water with every swerve of her rear wheels.

The gunman veered left onto Desplaines. I followed suit, lost some traction, but the tires dug in again. From Desplaines we raced to Jackson where the shooter hung another left. The green sedan led us in crazy circles. Where we were headed was anyone's guess. We tore down Jackson and passed Union Station, a dark gray monolith behind the sheets of rain. We came around again to Wacker, and the Plym took yet another left. We followed around to Washington, and that's where our gunman fouled up, when he steered onto Washington to avoid a sedan turning in front of him.

The Plym rolled into a sharp left down Washington, an eastbound, one-way street—the Plym drove westbound, against traffic. A Checker cab slammed on its brakes and came to a dead stop as the Plymouth came out of its turn. The Plym swung wide to the left side of the cab, just shy of a collision. The shocked cabbie didn't so much as tap the horn. The hack held still as my coupe scooted by on its right side.

The Plym fought to correct its path, swerved far right, back toward the left, and straightened out, all without losing speed. The coupe's rear wheels spun out, found their grip, and we sped on.

The block-long viaduct at Canal loomed ahead like a three-eyed, concrete monster. Three tunnels created three lanes of traffic through the structure. Once under the viaduct, it would be nearly impossible to see any oncoming traffic until it was too late. The coupe was coming up fast, in line with the right channel. The Plym didn't adjust its bearings. She held steady, overlapping the left and center lanes.

Shin had been catching the speedometer since we left Desplaines, and he got caught up in the race. He couldn't help narrating. "Forty-one," he said. He glanced quickly through the windshield, then down at the dash. "Forty-three. Forty-five!"

The distance up to the Plym closed quick. Just a car length behind as we flew over the bridge at Water Street.

I held hard to the right lane as Shin cried, "Forty-seven! Holy Mackerel!" The Plym's course was a dead end, headed for direct impact with the retaining wall between the center and left lanes of the viaduct. I cheated one fleeting glance at the gunman's silhouette hunched over the steering wheel. Our cars zoomed past on either side of a yellow Dodge abruptly stopped at an angle in the middle lane.

"Forty-nine!" Shin burst out as we came up parallel with the Plym. We tore down Washington neck and neck. Picking up speed. Holding our positions. One second, five seconds, ten seconds. The shooter's course remained dead set. Shin yelled, "Fifty-one!"

The Plym slammed into the barrier, head on, with a rupturing, buckling contraction of metal against concrete. I couldn't believe it at first. I didn't put on the brakes until well into the tunnel.

My heavy breathing startled me. Shin stared out the back of the coupe. There was nothing to make out of the darkness, so he peered even harder. I eased the gearshift into reverse and backed up, slow and smooth, gliding the coupe until we came to the mouth of the channel. I gave a quick glance at the broken heap to our left, then maneuvered the coupe to the curb. I lit a cigarette and told Shin to sit tight.

I got out and straightened up. My legs felt weak beneath me, on the shaky side, but I ignored that. The rain fell harder, and I ignored that, too. Shoulders hunched, hands jammed in my pockets, I narrowed my eyes in the direction of the mangled Plymouth. No signs of movement. I spat out the soaked butt and took slow, measured steps toward the wreckage.

The front end of the Plym didn't even resemble a car. The impact obliterated most of the hood. Steam snaked up through the shower like hot springs in a rain forest. The radiator gasped and hissed like a dying reptile.

Steady drops of a dark liquid spilled from the jacked up front and created a slick pool on the wet street. The cracked windshield frame twisted wild in different directions. Every window busted clean out. The front tires were blown out. Glass and bits of metal created a haphazard pattern in the glistening raindrops. I felt the crunch of debris beneath my shoes.

I knew the passenger door wouldn't give, but I gave it a go—no soap. I peered through the bent frame of the passenger window. The young man wrapped so tightly around the steering wheel could've passed for modern sculpture. The sightless eyes tilted up and out—the eyes of no more than a kid.

You could read it in an instant—dead. Streaks of blood had whipped across his face. The torso and shoulders crushed deep into the dash with the steering wheel in between. The limp, unnatural posture of the arms and hands. The awkward, snapped repose of the head. Sometimes a dead body says "dead"—this one screamed it.

I lined the window with my jacket and reached in. I worked and inched the wallet from his back pants pocket, and carefully eased myself back out. I stood in the rain and looked through the billfold, a cold, detached summary of a life. Six bucks in bills. A family portrait of the gunman, his mother, a much younger sister. Their stiff pose came off awkward, but cozy. Some scraps of paper, receipts, a ticket stub from The Woods Theatre.

The driver's license provided hard facts and aced it. The name, Min-Ho Jang. His age, seventeen. Shin's piece-meal, hodgepodge of a story had just crapped out.

I marched back to the coupe. Shin had gone out cold on me, dozing like a baby. A baby done up in formal wear. I slid behind the wheel and slammed the door as hard as I could. No answer from Shin. I could've slugged the rat, but didn't want to waste it on any sleeping beauty. Instead, I snatched the damn top hat out of his lap. The topper took me by surprise when it rattled.

Inside the high hat I discovered a black, velvet bag. I loosened the cord, opened the end of the pouch, and picked through the contents. I found a thick wad of small bills held with a rubber band, ones and fives. A tiny, yellowed cameo. One silver earring in the shape of an owl. A short strand, pearl necklace. A small, carved turtle—could have been jade. The other owl earring.

I saved the best for last, lingering over it with a tired stare. An intricately carved gold frame containing one faded still. The photograph captured three people. The same woman from Jang's wallet all right, showing a lot less wear and tear, alongside a young boy and a toddler.

I reached for a smoke, lit up, and listened to the rain. Then I heard Shin rustling awake.

"That mine." Shin leaned over and made a grab for the pouch. "Give it back!"

I brought my right up fast and gave his jaw a sharp, backhand slap. I followed that with a short-throw sock on the button. Shin went lights out in an instant, slumped forward with the crown of his head against the glove compartment. I don't think I'm that good, I think Shin was that blotto.

I gave the photo another look before placing the loot back inside the black, velvet purse. I sat in the coupe in the storm and finished my smoke, a rat in the seat next to me, and waited for the unnecessary cavalry.

That satisfy you? It's supposed to, right? That's the whole story, and that's supposed to satisfy you. You've got the stolen merchandise, you've got Shin in the bag, and you've got Jang on ice. And you should be all nice and satisfied. What else can I tell you? Any of you? Now you know as much about it as I do. Maybe more, if Shin has started to sober up.

Well, gents, I'm not satisfied. Not by a long shot. I haven't been satisfied for years, but what's the integrity of one small gumshoe worth, more or less? If you say it's good enough for you, I'll leave you to it. If not, if you want me to run through it one more time, I'd be happy to. Happy to oblige. Sure. Just as soon as I get myself good and gassed. I can make you one awful good statement when I'm stinking drunk. Sometimes my line of work calls for it.

Statement No. 5:
Mr. North

Three bodies and I don't know how many spent shells. The fireworks started, everything went to hell, and I kind of lost track. I was too busy scrambling clear, diving out of the way. The count didn't matter so much anyway, just that last, most important slug.

I expect I'll never lay eyes on Mr. North again. Or even hear of him. I never even got a solid line on his racket. That speech of his was a pip. But if there's any truth in it, any at all—just think over the backing involved. You think about the apparent longevity of *The Society*. The caliber of men involved, such as Mr. North. It plants a seed in the back of your head to keep you up nights. It ties one more knot in that noose that hangs over our daily lives. It flat out keeps you guessing. Guessing and doubting. Sure.

Let's face it—you know going in you'll never ID these birds. You know it just as well as I do. Comb all the police blotters in every precinct coast to coast from now until doomsday. You'll come up empty. No mug shots. No prints. But go ahead. Put out the word. Put out your feelers on the street. I'm telling you, it's like sucking wind in a vacuum bottle. I know it and you know it. Even your Aunt Sylvia knows it, for Chrissake.

But you'll ignore all that and forge ahead wearing the old blinders, right? Yeah, the hell with the way things really are. Let's make believe the department actually has something to investigate. What say we pretend that my yarn will give you all the leads you need to round up North and any confederates he has left. Let's waste each other's time because due process is bigger than all of us, is the savior of all us.

Sure, I'll give you my account. Why not? Even a wild goose chase can make a good story. It began with the wire, see? The yellow slip arrived a little before ten o'clock. That was Tuesday morning, June second. I'd just wrapped a job, filing the paperwork, when the boy dances in. I signed for the cable and the kid cuts out.

The telegram originated in San Francisco, and that meant zip to me. It read plain and spare, like most telegrams do, bordering on the obscure if you weren't in the loop—I wasn't.

"KEEN INTEREST IN YOUR SERVICES STOP. WISH TO MEET RE CRITICAL AND PRIVATE BUSINESS MATTER STOP. WILL BE IN AT 3 PM FRIDAY JUNE 5 TO DISCUSS STOP. URGENT AND CONFIDENTIAL STOP. MR NORTH END MESSAGE."

Simple as it read, that telegram gave me pause. Who'd cable me from clear across the country? That's assuming the sender didn't call it in from another locale. Why bother sending a wire at all? Why not pick up the telephone? Why three days in advance?

I'm not the professorial type when it comes to telegrams. Sure, I've sent plenty of cables, but I never made it a habit. I bet there's a whole department of G-men down in Washington. Analyzing, charting, cross-referencing. Making a goddamn science out of it. All I'm saying is that this one gave me the itch. And what really stood out was this: you recall ever seeing a sign-off that dropped the given name? There it was, in black and white: "Mr. North." It stood out like Sparkplug at Pimlico. I wondered, that's all. Simply wondered. I wondered if I was the only private eye in the city who received that telegram. Sure.

The whole set-up rubbed me the wrong way. It just plain felt wrong, but what are you going do with that? I tossed the wire on top of the in-basket overflow.

Wound up a slow week. In between cases. Very in between. On Thursday I skipped the office altogether. I checked in with my service a couple times during the day. They logged a single call in the afternoon. I'd won a free dance lesson. I took a pass.

Friday, June fifth rolled around and I hadn't given the telegram a thought. Then my eyes fell on the yellow slip in the basket. I read it over and gave it some thought. Then a bit more. Maybe it wouldn't have proved such a distraction if I'd been on a job. It's tough to say. What I do know is that it got me going. The curiosity grew like a wild vine. Two o'clock found me at my desk waiting out the final hour. The telegram worked, all right. I'll admit it. I was suckered. And I knew it.

The solid rapping on the door sounded at three o'clock on the nose. The frosted, glass panel revealed a dark silhouette. A tall one. Tall and still. I called out to come ahead.

My gentleman guest entered. Could have been a gentleman, the way he conducted himself. His body glided with a smooth quality, a kind of distinction, if you know what I mean. You could call it polished or suave, all right, not like he picked it up, but like he came into the world that way. He was a natural.

My mystery man closed the door behind him, pivoted my way, and removed his hat. "Good afternoon," he said. His words carried the thickest Russian accent this side of the Urals. "I thank you for receiving me."

I kept to my chair behind the desk, told him to take a seat. He nodded, graciously, approached the desk, and chose the chair on his right. He sat straight as a plumb line, but he made it appear relaxed.

Those eyes—the most striking thing about him. Set off from a lean, clean-shaven face. Light gray, baby-blues they were, ringed by a crown of short and precise eyelashes. That gaze at once arrested and imposed. My caller had the makings of a regular Svengali.

I'll tell you the queer thing. Here was this debonair gent before me, like I said, but the way he dressed? Completely against the grain. From his heavy, cloth work shirt to the dungarees, the outfit screamed "workman." From the suspenders over his shoulders down to the cap held in his hand. One of those caps you might see on a ranch hand or a baseball player.

He glanced down at himself then back at me, amused. "My appearance does not meet your approval."

"You don't add up. You enter a room like royalty, but you're decked out to go ditch digging. And I'm sure you'd just hate to ruin that beautiful manicure."

"You have failed to mention my accent."

"Forgive me. It's the Russian-est Russian accent I ever heard."

"Perhaps the reputation is true. I have been informed you are a man of *shrewd* perception." He grinned as he said that.

"Shrewd? I like that. Shrewd, sure. I'll have to put that on my business card."

"There is also wide agreement that you are decidedly insubordinate."

"That's true, that's true. But it's got nothing to do with my personality, see. Sometimes my line of work calls for it."

"I trust you received my telegram."

"That's why I'm here. Mr. North, is it?"

"Yes, you may call me that."

"I figured as much. What can I do for you, Mr. North?"

"I need you to perform a service for me."

I watched him while I pulled out a cigarette. He watched me watching. I struck a match, lit up, and waved out the flame. "What do you have in mind? Smoke?"

"No, thank you. I require you to act as my agent and accept three deliveries."

"Three."

"Yes. You will receive three messengers."

"This doesn't have anything to do with Dickens, does it?"

"I will need you to safeguard these deliveries."

"Are they bigger than a breadbox? And for exactly how long?"

"Perhaps as small as a business envelope. No larger than a small parcel. I expect to conclude my business within one week. Do you have any way to protect such items?"

"I see you're eyeballing the safe in the corner."

"It appears quite formidable."

"It sure weighs enough."

"It appears very old."

"Came to me by accident. It's the old man's safe. Maybe you passed the jewelry store on the street, two doors down. The owner kept his office up here, on this floor. When the old man passed away, his boys decided to close the office. I took the safe off their hands. That saved them the cost and annoyance of lugging it somewhere else."

"Good. Do you have room to accommodate my deliveries?"

"I may have to stow my lunch elsewhere, but I can probably swing it."

"Good."

"Let me get this straight. You're asking me to receive three parcels on your behalf, and put them in safekeeping for one week."

"Yes."

"But you're not asking me to store anything like smuggled goods, or act as a go-between for you and your fence, or anything else nefarious or otherwise not on the up and up?"

"Ta ta ta. Nothing of the sort, I assure you. Your position will not be compromised in the least." Mr. North smiled like he'd just won on a bluff.

That got us through the easy part. The tough part was ironing out the details. It was tough because there weren't any. My fee presented no difficulty. After that, it got downright murky.

Regarding the contents of the three deliveries, North insisted there would be no need to worry my pretty, little head. Just confirm they arrived intact, and lock them away. Nothing more, nothing less. In any case, per North, their substance would prove meaningless to me. Once all the surprise packages arrived, should Mr. North be contacted? Where should the parcels be brought? Neither action would be necessary, he said. The deliveries should remain in the safe and that's all there was to it. Mr. North said he'd know when they arrived. Mr. North would personally oversee all the necessary arrangements.

I knew it meant spinning my wheels, but I kept pressing. "You don't need to know when each one arrives?"

"I will know."

"So you'll know when I've got all three."

"Yes, I will know."

"Uh-huh. How exactly will you know they're all here?"

"I will know."

"I'm to do nothing about it."

"Nothing."

"Nothing."

"That is correct—nothing."

"As simple as that?"

"Yes, as simple as that."

That's the kind of flack I ran into, and North gave me all the time I wanted to consider his non-answers. He remained perfectly at ease in that regal posture of his. Like he had all the time in the world. I fired up another cigarette.

"When will you be back, exactly?"

"Within one week's time. I will make arrangements."

"How will I know your arrangements?"

"You will be informed."

"What if I need to contact you? How do I get in touch?"

"You don't."

"What if something comes up?"

"Take care of it."

"What if I'm called out of town?"

"Don't go."

"What if there's a fire?"

"I suggest you telephone the fire department."

"So it's like that, is it?

The more I asked, the less I got, and the more North's regal grin got on my nerves. In this racket, I'm used to being broadsided. Sometimes my line of work calls for it. But this felt like stumbling blindfolded into a mineshaft. It didn't roil North any. He played it smooth as silk, all the way. But the biggest play of all he saved for the big exit. That proved the topper.

North lingered before the door. He faced the exit and said, "There is one final matter. This I must make absolutely clear. There must be no mistaking this." He hesitated and brought a long finger to his lips. "I fear I have you at a disadvantage," he continued, still with his back to me. "You have a reputation. You are known. Your work is a matter of record with clients, the police, and with the newspapers. On the other hand, I am the great unknown. Of me you know nothing, so it is imperative that you fully grasp the gravity of my business. I must be fully satisfied in this respect."

"Uh-huh."

North paused, turned to face me, that imposing, gray-blue stare working overtime. "Do not tell anyone anything about me. Mention nothing to anyone about our preparations." He put up a long, slender hand. "I am fully aware that this should, of course, go without saying, that confidentiality is a matter of professional ethics in your industry. I know this. So, you must appreciate, it is not from a matter of ignorance or disrespect that I mention it." He bent forward. "I simply need it understood, comprehensively, that anyone who interferes in my business affairs will be dealt the most severe reprisal."

For the moment I let it pass. I made North a present of my best poker face.

"If, under these circumstances, you prefer to cancel our arrangement, I will, regretfully, respect your decision. But you must tell me now."

"You're not threatening me, are you Mr. North?"

"I do not threaten. I inform."

"Sure."

"I'm informing you of my position."

Fancy talk, all right. A sideways threat, all right. But, like I said, it was a slow week. I nodded. "Fair enough, Mr. North. I get you."

"Good!" North's head tipped slightly in my direction. He pivoted smoothly and slipped out the door.

I've had my share of odd meetings, but talk about taking the cake. This ranked right up there, kit and caboodle. One of the queerest arrangements I'd ever taken part in. Almost as screwy as the guy you're tailing coming up to you and asking for directions. In my time I've heard plenty of threats, but none quite exactly like North's. None nearly so eloquent. No, I had to figure you didn't toy with Mr. North. Not more than once. And not for long.

I waited for North to catch the elevator. The clang of the iron grate slid open and shut, the bang and hum kicked in as the machine lurched and began its descent. I hopped up, cracked the door, and made sure the coast was clear. I strode briskly to the rear exit and quick-stepped it down the fire escape. I wheeled around the building, down the alley, and spotted my target. My client hailed a Checker cab, aimed south on Clark Street. I trotted back to my coupe parked in the alley.

Traffic proved a snap to navigate. I gave the Checker a half-block lead until we hit North Avenue. The taxi pulled up to a curbside newsstand. I passed the Checker and parked it by a fire hydrant. North stepped out, paid for a daily, and returned to the cab. He stood for a moment, lingering by the passenger door, glancing at the rag in his hand. Maybe the headline was a honey—a wide grin stretched across his pan. His long form stooped into the back seat. The Checker swung onto Clark Street.

I tailed the hack through sluggish traffic. The Checker had managed as much as a block up on me, twice, but most of the time I kept her within view. After we reached the Loop, the driver grabbed a spot in the Greyhound station taxi line. The coupe fit the corner tow zone just fine. I fired up a smoke and kept watch in the side mirror. The Checker sat tight. No action. I smoked the cigarette all the way down, flicked the butt in the curb, and stepped out of the coupe.

I waltzed toward the Checker with my brim pulled low. Nearing the hack, I made out the empty back seat. I spun on my heels, checked up and down the storefronts. I didn't know how, but North had flown the coop. I rapped on the front passenger window. The hack reached over and rolled down the glass.

"You want the first cab in line, Mac."

I leaned in. "What happened to your fare?"

"What fare, Mac?"

"The fare you picked up on north Clark Street."

The driver shrugged his shoulders.

"You stopped at the newsstand at Clark and North."

"You got me, Mac. I don't know what you're talking about."

I straightened up and swept the sidewalk. Moms with kids in tow, businessmen and briefcases, college joes lugging grips and duffle bags. No North to be had, in any direction.

I bent down to the cab. A neatly folded newspaper lay on the back seat. It looked untouched. The cabbie's pan wore an expression as blank as a pillowcase. I noted a five-spot stuck in the visor above him.

I chewed it over, the whole dizzy affair. It annoyed me and it amused me. North's game was anybody's guess. I had no line on the mug whatsoever. He'd left me as empty as an abandoned taxi, sure. I'd been stuck but good. Call me bothered, bewitched and etcetera.

Bang! Sure enough, I got the first delivery Monday morning. A little after nine. A flat, nine by twelve, plain manila envelope. Sealed, of course. Brought in by an older egg, done up in complete messenger uniform right down to the white gloves. He wore the messenger cap low on the forehead. His Chester Conklin mustache masked the bottom third of his face. He made for a tall fellow—it struck me you don't often see birds his age that tall. I signed his pad, he handed me the parcel, and he bowed to me with a tip of the shiny black rim of the cap.

I locked the door after him and took the delivery straight to the safe. You've seen the type of strongbox before. The length and height of a small bureau or credenza. All a deep, lusterless black. On the inside, one half set up in into shelves and cubbyholes. The other half wide open. I kept one small file of documents in it—most of the safe sat as empty as Comiskey Park in January. I used the top for a bookshelf.

I dialed the tumbler right, left, right, I released the silver handle, I heaved wide the heavy door. I balanced the envelope in my hand. Damn light. Couldn't have contained more than a few sheets of paper. The packaging itself probably outweighed the contents. The outside of the envelope appeared as plain as plain gets. No extra markings on it. Just the address label, made out to my office. No return address, save for one word: *South*. That's it. I slipped the packet onto a shelf, shoved the door closed, jammed down the handle, and spun the tumbler. One down. Two to go.

The next day I read the paper front to back without interruption. No deliveries. No callers. I closed shop at five o'clock.

Wednesday started out just as quiet. I filled the morning digesting *The Daily News*. I debated whether to skip out for lunch. The set-up got to me, spooked me, so I went out for lunch after all, though I didn't feel terribly hungry.

Minnie Murphy dropped by the office late. Minnie did time for the employment agency down the hall, City-Wide Secretarial. When jobs thinned out, like during summers and holidays, some of the regular girls camped out at the office hoping to cop an assignment on the fly. A sweet enough kid in her early twenties, Minnie displayed all the sunny innocence and pep that goes with her age. Sometimes a little too much pep. She also nurtured a romanticized idea of the whole private eye game. She enjoyed pumping me about recent cases, and I always played it cagey. She made a cute distraction for the eyes, though, and I was primed for a distraction.

Minnie and I were shooting the breeze going on about four when the second delivery showed. A heavy, tall mug strode in with a small bundle under his arm. He reminded me of the toughs who drove for transfer companies. His leather cap appeared a size too small and leaned awkwardly on his head. The gut of the denim shirt hung a ways over his belt. He also sported denim pants and leather work gloves. He placed the parcel on the desk, a package wrapped up in plain, brown paper, tied once around with white string. My office address had been scrawled by hand in bold, block letters in the center of the bundle. In the upper left corner read the word, *East*. Nothing else on the package. The agent's stained kisser gnawed at a chaw of tobacco as he handed me a clipboard. My eye ran down and across the rows of companies, addresses and piece counts. Most, but not all, had signatures. I spotted my office address listed on line ten.

"Number ten," the agent said in a low, tired drawl.

I signed the log on line ten and handed back the list. His wrists were surprisingly thin for such a big guy. The man swung about and strode out of the office.

Minnie's big, brown eyes chased back and forth between me and the bundle. I read her mind as easy as reading a headline in *Variety*—she practically buzzed with curiosity, so I cut her off fast. No, I confirmed, the Chinese laundry delivered my shirts yesterday.

She said, "Something important?"

"Could be."

"Are you working a case?"

"Yeah."

"A whopper?"

"Aren't they all, kid?"

"You know who it's from?"

"Uh-huh."

"So give!"

"It's from a client."

"A matter of life or death?"

"Nothing quite so melodramatic."

"So spill it!"

"There's nothing to spill."

"You're not going to tell me about it, are you?"

"Nope."

"I should mind my own beeswax."

"That's right, sugar."

"And I should take a powder, shouldn't I?"

"Sure."

"If you ever need to dictate anything—"

"I'll call for no one but you, angel."

Minnie smiled, winked, and bugged out. I listened to the sound of her giggle as her heels clacked down the hall. I shut my office door and locked it. The parcel felt near empty in my hand. I crossed over to the safe, contemplated the bundle, got nowhere fast. I dialed the tumbler, yanked the handle, and pulled on the door. I compared the address labels on both pieces. A different hand addressed each label. One abbreviated "street" and the other wrote it out. That big discovery told me a lot of nothing. I deposited the packets, shut the door, flipped the handle, spun the tumbler. Two down. One to go.

Thursday was a washout. No delivery, no action, blanksville. Friday was Thursday all over again. I gave the safe a long, tired glare before I locked up, some time after five. I headed to Barney's Market Club on Randolph. I dropped into Barney's every week or two for a hunk of red meat. I recommend their Roast Prime Rib of Beef Au Jus. That night I was digging into a Broiled Butt Steak when someone nosed in from behind.

"Excuse me, Senator. Someone dropped this off for you."

A tapered, manicured hand held out a number ten envelope. I put down my cutlery, took the letter, and just about tore into it. I froze mid-chew when I caught the word in the upper left corner: *West*.

I spun about in my seat, but the waiter or messenger or whoever had evaporated. I tucked the envelope in my inside jacket pocket and went back to work on the steak. On my way home I stopped by the office to lock up the third delivery.

A sealed message awaited me Monday morning, June fifteen—this missive from North crawled under my office door. The typed note informed me that North and his compatriots planned to wrap up their business that evening, at the stroke of midnight, in my office. The three surprise packages would, of course, be required.

I'm used to working odd times in this racket. After hours the building gets quieter than City Hall in August. The retail shops on the street level close up for the night by seven. The insurance offices on the third floor lock up at five. So do the outfits on my floor, the second. The vacant, silent halls feel evacuated, like somebody's put out the word to clear out and stay out. North wanted to play invisible man, all right.

I lit only the desk lamp. The ceiling globe remained dark and the blinds closed. I tilted back in my office chair and checked my watch: half an hour to go. I fired up a cigarette and kept my eye on the thread of light streaming through the door—I'd left it cracked two inches.

North turned up at quarter to. His darkened silhouette hung in the doorway and cast a lean shadow. He must have seen me clear enough. I'm guessing he was scoping out the room. I'll guess even further than that. I'm willing to bet he already knew the building was deader than the pyramids. I'll bet he knew my office was clean, too.

North's rich voice inquired from the darkness, "The packages?"

"In the safe."

"Good." North glided into the room, leaving the door as he found it. "My colleagues will arrive directly."

North sported a full suit and tie. In the dim glow of the desk lamp, I'd say it was a light, linen fabric. Top-drawer linen, of course.

"I see you dressed for the occasion."

One corner of North's mouth curled slyly. "The time for charades nears its conclusion."

That declaration carried some oomph to it, but I let it go.

North said, "I expect you are filled with immense curiosity."

"Brimming with it," I replied. "I find you and this whole set-up curious beyond the pale."

"Prepare yourself to witness a most astonishing evening."

"Astonishing. Imagine that."

"Though I fear you will be left with more questions than answers."

"Is that right? You, afraid?"

"As an outsider, you are in a most rare and privileged position."

"And me without my diary."

I watched North's flat expression as I lit up a cigarette. He watched me watch. He said nothing else. That was fine with me, and I took his cue.

North's associates filed in just before midnight: Mr. South, Mr. East and Mr. West. I guess Mr. South-By-Southwest got held up. North invited them to take seats while he closed the office door. Mr. South and Mr. East took up positions on the small sofa against the same wall as the safe. The third board member, Mr. West, claimed a client chair in front of the desk.

Mr. North threw the lock on the door, then approached the far end of the desk. He posed, as if standing at a podium, as though about to give a great oration. I couldn't help but notice that he faced all three directions at the same time.

Mr. West sat closest to North. Short, heavy set, pale. I'd peg him for forty-five years old. A wide-faced mug with pellets for eyes and a cork for a nose. His hands thrust deep into the lightweight trench wrapped tight. His mouth twitched to one side of his face. I didn't care for it. He probably wouldn't have cared that I didn't care.

Mr. South, the youngest chicken in the roost, occupied the far end of the couch. A man of about thirty years, he presented the All-American nondescript. South's the kind of jasper you could overlook in a crowd of one. Average build, simple face, crowned by a fedora with an oversized brim. I didn't see anything to mind in him. I didn't see anything to him at all.

To his left, Mr. East. Fifty and then some. A big man, a strong man. His glasses used the thickest lenses I've ever seen. Peering in his eyes was taking on an aquarium through a fog. Those tank lenses made him a tough read.

I glanced down at my wrist as I lit a smoke. My watch showed twelve o'clock, sharp.

"Gentlemen." Mr. North's eyes fell on all three men in turn. He smiled warmly, like a district attorney with a confession in his hip pocket. "As you know, The Society is counting down to its next evolutionary cycle. Every ten years we renew our pledge to The Society, its ruling council is realigned, and our sentinels are reassigned and replaced by a new guard. For more than nine years each of you has served admirably in protecting one of our critical reserves.

"The reserves are only one instrument within The Society's financial structure, an organization of funding as varied as the members themselves. Over time The Society's holdings have grown, methodically, beyond the crude and simple forms of shielded bank accounts and secreted safety deposit boxes. In the last several decades its holdings have increased threefold every year, diversifying into financial and business investment, underwriting, foreign trade, international loans. The Society's wealth has outgrown and outpaced The Society's activities, overshadowing the founding principles of The Society itself!"

Mr. West hunched his shoulders and his lips quivered. Mr. East laced his large fingers together in his lap and rolled his thumbs. Mr. South kept still as an oil portrait. All eyes fixed on Mr. North like permanent glue.

"This is a crisis, gentlemen, as you all recognize. This is a crisis that strikes at the very core of The Society. The emergency has arrived in the form of The Society's own subversion. The cause of The Society has become fatally, irreversibly flawed, and men such as we can no longer abide its policies and actions. That is why you three men, strangers before tonight, have come together."

Mr. East nodded in a jerky fashion.

"I have watched this change progress, and I have watched this change subvert leaders of The Society away from the cause. I have watched. I have waited. I have waited for you." He lowered his head and eyed his audience. "I have waited year after year for this evening to become possible, to bring you men together, men of just the right character, to do what needs to be done.

"My good comrades, you have been protecting the Fifth Reserve, safeguarding a stockpile with an estimated worth, I say *estimated* worth, of no less than five million dollars."

I choked back a whistle.

"The evolutionary cycle dictates the transfer of each stockpile to a new location under the assignment of new sentinels. Before that transpires, we will relocate the stockpile ourselves. For ourselves alone." North beamed at his colleagues.

South remained stone-like. West blinked behind his fish lenses. East fidgeted. They exchanged glances.

"Gentlemen," North raised his arms, "the time is at hand to bring together the three keys which will locate the reserve for us. We shall draft a plan for reaching, procuring and securing this reserve. In short, gentlemen, after nearly ten years of waiting for the right men, after years of waiting to bring you together, the opportunity is upon us. The time has come, my friends, to make ourselves exceedingly rich—as the saying goes, rich beyond our wildest imaginations."

North's gaze bore into his three associates. He braced his arms and bent forward, his eyes hard and his tone as solemn as a death sentence: "If you will be kind enough to retrieve the packages."

I stubbed out my smoke, pushed back from the desk, and rose. I gazed upon the faces of that little circle. What a serious looking bunch. Crouching at the safe, I worked the tumbler, the handle, the door, grabbed the three parcels, and deposited them on the desk.

North came around to the client side and broke open the packages with great aplomb. He was aplomb, all right. His associates crept around him, cautiously, without a word. The quiet magnified each tear, each rustle of paper. I watched from my side of the desk as North produced three documents. They looked like maps to me. He lined them up, side by side, with the greatest care, pushing the wrapping to the side.

Each page played like a city grid as far as I could dope out. I spied notations of longitude and latitude, compass symbols, a key for measuring distance in kilometers. Two aspects of the docs threw me for a loop. All of the street names and other locations appeared to be penned in some mumbo jumbo foreign language. The characters ran cursive-like, heavily scrolled, accented by one or two dots. Three triangles created the other odd feature. Gold triangles with a circle in the center they were, one on each of the three sheets, pointed in three different directions.

North spoke without looking up. "I now require a ruler."

I fished out a ruler from the middle desk drawer and handed it over. We all leaned further over the papers. North adjusted the lamp to suit him, then centered the ruler over the first triangle. He drew a line against the ruler in red ink. He repositioned the straightedge across the second triangle and created a second line in red ink. He repeated the process for the third triangle. The procedure reeled us in, mesmerized us. We were hooked.

The four men stepped back from the desk. They pondered North's handiwork, then leaned forward again in unison. You could see it clear as anything, the point where the three red lines intersected. Looked to me like X *marks the spot.*

"Gentlemen!" North proclaimed and overwhelmed the room. "We have it!"

Someone whispered, "Five million bucks," but I didn't catch who. North's three associates registered smug satisfaction on their smug faces.

I couldn't tell where the hell we were looking—the city, the country, let alone the continent. But Mr. East and Mr. South seemed well satisfied, their greedy lips warped into broad curves.

"Now, now," North spoke as he returned to the far side of the desk. "We have numerous arrangements before us. The undertaking, while simple in principle, will not be an easy one in the physical sense."

Mr. South and Mr. East bent in close to the maps. They scrutinized the red lines with the assistance of South's index finger. I lit another cigarette, folded my arms, and considered the charts with one eye squinted.

Mr. West backed off from the desk a couple paces. "Don't put yourself out, North, arrangement-wise. I'll take it from here." Mr. West held a long-barrel revolver. He must have had a special holster under his topcoat to secure a rig like that.

"Where'd you find that," I asked, "the circus?"

"You," looking at me, "put everything back in the large envelope. Be *extra careful* about it." His mouth spasm gave the words a peculiar twang.

"Everything?" I asked.

The end of the barrel flicked up twice, fast. I took that as a "yes." I cheated a look-see at North and the other two, then I did like West instructed. I gathered up the charts, deliberately and slowly. I moved awful slow. No one else budged. No one else made a peep. We all held our breath.

"You're no Mr. Speedy, are you?" West's pan broke out a nervous, ticking grin. The gun hand held steady. "All right, all right. Bring it here—"

"I know," I said. "Extra careful."

I walked the long way around the desk, beyond North, around to the front, and stopped next to Mr. East.

"Give it here," West spat and ticked. He extended his free hand.

I made a flip of the wrist and flung the package toward West. It fluttered short and landed six inches from his feet.

West breathed deep, sighed big, and brought up the barrel in line with my eyes. He cocked the hammer. "Smart guy. You're the most expendable one of all."

"My good Mr. West." North held one hand to his chin. His head cocked to one side. He exhibited the calm of a contented camel. "We have all seen the maps. Each one of us knows the precise location of the cache. Do you intend to murder us all?"

"Sure," I said. "He's played his hand. What choice has he got?"

West kept the rod trained at my head. His eyes darted between North and me, back and forth. South didn't shift one hair. East eased his right hand behind his back, beneath his jacket, ever so gradually. Something was going to break, all right, and I was first in line.

North asked, "Are you actually prepared to take the lives of four men?"

I said, "I don't think Mr. W.'s figured that far ahead. What's it to be, gunslinger?"

West shot me a puzzled squint, and that afforded East his opportunity.

That moment before all hell breaks loose is a funny thing. We've seen enough of them. It's a snap of the fingers, that moment of great clarity, a frozen, tolling bell, an image as perfect as a still photograph, a sweep of the second hand you know is about to be lost forever. Then it cuts loose and busts wide open into chaotic whirlwind, a blur of motion and sound that your conscious mind can't keep time with, a swirling mayhem where actions can only play on the gut level, where everything happens at once, in a flash. Everything's pop goes the weasel.

East and West faced off. West swung around to aim and fire. East dropped to one knee while drawing out an automatic. North shoved South out of the line of fire, then lunged for me as I twisted and spun toward the other end of the desk. West should have had the drop on East, but East worked fast and smooth. I couldn't tell who's shot came first. The blasts lit the dim room like instant lightning and the reports pounded our ears. West took one in the throat while his slug went wild and caught South in the foot.

North slung my arm with such force that I went tumbling backward over the desk. I caught my forehead on the center drawer. South stumbled in pain, knocking East to the ground. West reeled backwards, clutching his throat, and fired freely without aiming. East recovered, rolled over, and pumped shot after shot into West. South recovered himself, pulled a snub nose from a shoulder holster, and he squeezed more rounds into West. East spun around toward South ready to fire, but South kicked over a chair that tumbled onto East's arms. East couldn't free himself before South fired multiple shots at will, smashing two slugs into East's skull.

A matter of seconds. Sometimes that's all it takes for life and death to play out. It got quiet again. It felt hot. Gun smoke swirled like a gray fog that burned.

I hauled myself up, supported by the desk, used the back of my wrist to feel the small wound on my forehead. The scrape stung to the touch. I grimaced and felt the smashed cigarette that dangled from my mouth. North appeared untouched, standing tall and straight at the end of the desk.

West lay motionless, wedged against the couch, his clothing and body shredded into a mass of black and red pulp, like a storm of blood had rained across him. East's crumpled corpse butted up against the front of the desk. Scarlet streams oozed from the deep holes in his forehead and temple. The fish lenses had been thrown off, and a blank agony registered in his still eyes.

South propped himself against the overturned chair, just beyond East. He strained forward to nurse his foot, working to unlace his shoe with awkward delicacy. He winced with every breath.

Mr. North approached South from behind, lowered himself to one knee, and placed a hand on the man's shoulder. "Mr. South," he said softly, "You conducted yourself quite admirably."

South wrenched his head over his shoulder and forced a pained grin for North's benefit. He returned his attention to the bloody shoe.

"Amazing, is it not?" North murmured. "It is just as I warned you. The greed of men is like a vile plague. You have witnessed the virus of evil that is within all men. The seeds of man's own destruction. Even now you are weighing the fortunes of mistrust. You are at once shocked by the duplicity of your comrades, yet equally encouraged. You find two less shares to account for. Two less exposures. Your own fortunes have risen two-fifths in a mere matter of moments."

The hard click of a gun hammer stilled South's hands. North held the cold barrel against the base of South's skull.

"The money belongs only to The Society. No one else. I must inform you that you have risked your life to no end but your own."

Mr. South's eyes narrowed. His lips uncurled and his mouth popped open and shut like a goldfish. He must have had something to say—he couldn't manage the words. He lowered his head and looked at the gat in his right hand. Smears of blood covered the tips of his left hand. The shoe propped half off his bleeding foot. Those were the last things the sentenced man saw. And there was nothing I could do.

"Mr. South, the cycle of evolution has begun."

Mr. North squeezed the trigger once, the cartridge burst and sang, and the shell cut through the base of South's skull like an axe through butter. South's body flailed from the impact, slumped to the floor, his eyes squeezed shut. A tiny gurgling sound bubbled up from his throat. The life faded out of him as we watched.

North rose to his feet. He held the gun easy, its muzzle aimed low. He straightened his tie and cleared his throat. I noticed he wore a gold triangle tiepin. He gathered the papers with one hand, folded them, and slid them inside his linen jacket. He turned to me. I hadn't moved, leaning on the desk, supporting my weight on my hands. North removed the crushed stub from my mouth. He speared a cigarette from my shirt pocket and placed it between my lips. He struck a match and brought it to the end of the cigarette. He blew out the match and dropped it in the ashtray.

"That," Mr. North said, concludes my business."

Statement No. 6:
William Sykes

I've got a story about William Sykes. Not that blathering epitaph in the papers, either. Let's talk about Mr. Sykes and breaking the bank. How to get rich quick in three easy lessons. The overnight success story. Every little boy's little dream. The all-American dream. On one side you've got Henry Ford. On the other, Willie Sutton. Mr. William Sykes pictured himself somewhere in between. Sure.

William Sykes was a conman. Coming and going. A man who thought he hit upon a shortcut to paradise. Thought he had it handed to him, Sykes did. Had it right there, in his tight, little fist. William Sykes hungered for that dream. Its taste teased him, wetted his lips. Sykes needed that dream. Sykes needed it like the thermometer needs a fever.

Sykes thought he had it knocked. Had it rigged for floating. All ways around. I'm not privy to the inside operations of the Costopoulos organization. Or the Stronzate organization for that matter. But Sykes must've worked it pretty good. Must have really nursed it. Maybe you need a loose screw in order to take on Konstantin Costopoulos and Vittorio Stronzate in the same whack. Maybe you do. I'll give Sykes credit for nerve, anyway. Plenty of nerve. Like the prisoner showing the hangman how to tie a noose. Sure.

I'm getting ahead of you. I can see it by the dazed sets of peepers around the room. To fill you in on the great Willy Sykes, let's back it up. Start things off with Flint Mundy. That's where I came into the picture. Sure, the bureau doesn't know any Flint Mundy, yet. Keep the wires open, boys, just to stay on the safe side. Bunko and vice will be keen on it. There's maybe even a little something in it for homicide. But save that one for later.

Mundy's phone call caught me at the office. That was late morning on the eighteenth. In the middle of surveying the repairs. Most of the bullet holes had been plugged, but the bleaching had a ways to go. A long way. Mr. North and his trigger-happy colleagues did a real number on my rooms, all right—but that's another yarn. So I informed Mundy the office was strictly off bounds, and we'd best make it elsewhere. I suggested he join me for lunch at the Belden Deli.

Patricia laid down my usual: corned beef on rye with Swiss. She served it up with a smile that could take the cold out of cold potatoes. Mundy hadn't bothered with the menu, too busy fidgeting and sweating. A regular bundle of nerves, Mundy. Daily nourishment became trivial for a guy like that. I winked to Patricia and ordered Mundy a cup of joe.

"Or maybe you don't need any caffeine," I said.

"How's that?"

"You've got more jitters than a con parked in Old Sparky."

"Yeah.

"Sorry about the office being out of commission and all."

"Yeah, well, repairs have a way of coming up—"

"Just a matter now of cleaning up the blood. The landlord's seeing to it."

"Did you say blood?"

"Uh-huh."

"Blood as in...blood?"

"I cut myself shaving."

"And the landlord's got to clean it up?"

"It was a nasty cut."

Mundy didn't merely miss my drift, he missed the launch, the sailing, and the return to port. He had these restless eyes. He peered around the restaurant non-stop, paying especially close attention to the front door. He must've caught my amused smirk.

"Is there a back door to this dump? I can't say I fancy being caught out in public right now."

"No fooling."

"I guess it's safe enough. You come here regular, right?"

Mundy adjusted the round specs that lent him an awkward, bookworm appearance. He rolled his shoulders, swung his head, and snuck a peek behind the booth. Pivoting back around, he reached for the coffee mug with a jerk. I saved the cup just before it went over. I slid it to the far end of the table.

"I think this will be safer over here, Mundy. I know I'll be."

"Yeah, okay."

"Settle down, Mundy, for chrissake. You're making me jumpy."

"You have no idea."

"You want to switch booths?"

"No, no, that's not it." He craned his neck to steal a view beyond the cash register.

"They tell me it's possible to wean yourself, Mundy. Cut back a little bit at a time. You should consider it—the dope's got you paranoid."

"Don't be a bunny. I'll be all right in a minute."

"I doubt it, Mundy, but let's have it—what's on your mind?"

Mundy faced me squarely. He leaned forward and dropped his voice just above a whisper. "I'm in big, big trouble."

"Big trouble?"

"Loads."

"Exactly how is that, Mundy?"

"Gangsters." The narrow eyebrows arched. "Gangsters are after me."

"Gangsters. Is that a fact?"

"I owe them a whopping sum."

"What is it? Loan sharks? Gamblers? Protection money?"

Mundy winced. "Playing the ponies."

"If you placed a bet you can't cover, there's nothing I can do. You want J. Paul Getty."

"It's not as simple as that."

"It never is."

"There's this guy I know."

"A guy?"

"William—" he stopped himself. A glance to the left, a glance to the right. He lowered his voice further and spoke precisely. "William Sykes."

"Okay," I shrugged. "William Sykes."

"We met in school."

"College?"

"No, nursery school. Of course, college."

"Just trying to paint the full tableau, Mundy."

"For a while now he's been hustling for Konstantin Costopoulos."

"Costopoulos I've heard of. Some boy. One serious operator."

"Yeah."

"Dangerous, as a matter of fact."

"Dangerous as in—" Mundy drew an index finger across his Adam's apple.

"That's what they say. Sure."

"Sykes makes book for Costopoulos, okay?"

"All right. Sykes and Costopoulos and making book. What's your game, Mundy?"

"Sykes set this up a few months back—"

Mundy froze, made like a Popsicle, dipped his head, concentrated hard, braced for something out of place. Anything. Ready to jump out of his skin. He nearly did when a boisterous laugh boomed from the rear of the room. He snapped his head and raised his eyes above the back of the booth. He scrutinized every customer in sight and found nothing irregular. I could've told Mundy the Belden clientele had stopped by for food rather than our gab. I could've, but he wouldn't have listened, so I didn't.

I said, "Mundy, you're going to throw yourself into a seizure."

Mundy swiveled back around. He bent over the table and waved his fingers for me to come closer. I brought an elbow onto the table and planted my chin on the palm of my hand.

"First off, we pool together a couple hundred, right? Seed money? And I start placing a few bets with Sykes. Nothing too big, nothing too little. But that's only a stall, get it? That's just establishing me as a customer. Setting things up, okay? What we're waiting for is a big-ticket race, when the fix is on and Sykes is put in the wise—he gets tips, see? He'll feed me the name of the winner, I place a big daddy wager, and we all clean up."

"So you're telling me that while Sykes worked for Costopoulos, he also played footsie with the racketeers running the race tracks."

"Uh, yeah. Yeah, I guess that's about right."

"So this Sykes, your pal, mapped out the whole thing."

"That's what I'm telling you."

"Lined up the entire deal and set it up for the big payoff."

"We had The American Derby knocked."

"Uh-huh. Don't tell me. It blew up in your face."

"Kerflooey!"

"Sure."

"The nag didn't come through. I don't know what went wrong."

"Nothing went wrong, Mundy. You were had."

"Nothing went wrong?"

"Tell me," I said. I had a notion percolating. Quietly percolating. "Was anybody else in it with you?"

"Yeah. We had another partner. Another school friend. Herbie Colgate? Willy set the whole thing up with both of us."

"Where is Colgate, now?"

"Beats the heck out of me."

"Sykes?"

"The bum was supposed to ring me up after. Nothing. I waited by the phone for two hours. Two whole hours. No word. And I can't find him anywhere. Nerts."

"I suppose Colgate could be in it with Sykes, but I don't see it."

"Don't see what?"

"Would you say Sykes always stuck to himself?"

"You mean like a loner?"

"Yeah. That's what I mean."

"I guess he always was. So what?"

"So you can stop trying to locate your Mr. Sykes. You're not going to find him."

"I don't get you. I mean, what happened? I just don't get what could of gone wrong."

"Like I said, nothing went wrong."

"You keep saying that!"

"That's only the second time, but I could say it a third time if you like. Mundy, you've been duped. You and your buddy Herbie have been hung out to dry."

I didn't know it, not for a fact, but that's how it figured. The mark, the set-up, the play. I could see it adding up real smooth, outlined and typed up nice and pretty, like a bad Monogram script. I had ideas about our Mr. Sykes.

"You can take the dopey look off your pan, Mundy. Let me spell it out for you. Sykes, your bosom buddy, is a grifter."

"I knew he pulled a couple gags in school."

"How's that, Mundy?"

"While the rest of us were delivering groceries or working in the library or what have you? For spending dough? Willy sold advertising for a magazine."

"Uh-huh."

"Only the magazine didn't exist."

"Sure."

Mundy fingered his lower lip. "I'm a dead man."

"Sykes was ahead of you on this one. Way ahead of you and Colgate. And I'll lay odds the two of you weren't alone. I'm thinking Sykes had a long line of suckers out there. I'm betting you've got a whole lot of company you know nothing about."

"I don't get you."

"Skip it. The point is, Sykes sugared you in, set you up, and took you to the cleaners. And now you're the one stuck with the tab."

"The son of a bitch."

"Only it's not a simple dry cleaning bill we're talking about."

"I'm a dead man."

"All right, all right. Maybe it's not as hopeless as all that. How much are you and Colgate in for?"

"Five."

"Well, five hundred's not exactly a small amount, then again it's not exactly a large amount, either."

"That's five thousand."

"You're kidding."

"I haven't got five thousand. I don't have nearly that much. I'm no where close to having that much."

"That's what we call a real situation, Mundy."

"Situation? Cripes! You call this a situation? I'm a dead man!"

"If you scream a touch louder I bet it'll carry all the way to the delivery boy having a smoke out back."

Mundy muttered in a low croak, "I'm a dead man, I'm a dead man." His face turned white and wax-like. Tiny pellets of sweat dotted his forehead. His fingers got the tremors. Mundy tightroped that line between bawling and spitting up. I didn't care to see either.

"You're not going to swoon, are you?"

Mundy worked a glass of water to his lips with shaky hands. He spilled less than I expected.

"So how about it, Mundy?" I plucked a napkin from the dispenser and pushed it at him. "What exactly do you want with me?"

"Maybe track down Sykes, maybe?" Mundy dabbed around his glass.

"No, I don't think I'll take that on. I doubt you've got time for that. He may have already taken a powder."

"Then tell me what to do. Tell me." He kept wiping at the same dry spots on the table.

"That's one hell of a request."

"You've got to tell me what to do. I'll do anything."

Behind Mundy's dodo glasses loomed the fear of all time. He'd made an interesting choice, calling a private investigator. As he wrestled out a new napkin, two thoughts struck me, two ways of batting around Mundy's fix.

The first way, hard and straight: stiffing a bookmaker's one of the flat out, worst moves you can make. Even my Aunt Sylvia knows that. Mundy lost his head. Like spitting on the queen, or jaywalking on Lake Shore Drive. Sure, he made his own call, but he didn't savvy the kind of the hole he was digging. Or how deep it could get. Or how it could turn into quicksand. For a jasper like Mundy, the setup was a laugh, wasn't it? Just a gas? Gambling without the risk—he couldn't miss, Sykes told him. In a pig's eye. Costopoulos had no choice. He had his operation to run and a reputation to protect. Bookie protocol dictated that Costopoulos make an example out of Mundy. A permanent example. That's to be expected.

On the other hand, try this on for size: through a series of unethical, dishonest and otherwise naive circumstances, not to mention bonehead, Mundy got himself took. Instead of taking Costopoulos to the cleaners, he wound up a two-time victim. He already played chump for Sykes. Now he's about to play bull's eye for Costopoulos. All on account of the unattainable sum of five thousand bucks. For that fatal, numbskull screw up, Mundy wound up setting a value on his own life—a crummy five grand. Looking at it that way, five G is peanuts.

You couldn't see Mundy as blameless. But he was also part victim. That went for Colgate, too. That went for I don't know how many others.

"I can't say there's anything I can do for you, Mundy. I'm not sure if there's anything anyone can do."

"Nothing? You're going to leave me hanging?"

"I leave people hanging a lot. Sometimes my line of work calls for it."

"Leave me hanging. Isn't that some joke?"

"I'll tell you what—I'll talk to Costopoulos, Mundy. How's that? I don't know what good that'll accomplish. Probably a kick in the pants for my trouble. But I'll see him. That much I'll tell you."

"Okay." Mundy choked out the word like a last breath.

"In the meantime, you're down to one last move."

"Okay."

"Do a vanishing act."

Mundy's index traced his warped reflection in the napkin dispenser. He spoke soft and low, from the bottom of a barrel. "Disappear, you mean?"

"I mean like you were never born."

Mundy's face went dumb as a dead herring.

"You put as much distance as possible between you and everyone you know. Your friends, your family. Mom, dad, women, the works. You wipe out every trace of yourself. You make yourself invisible, Mundy. Coming and going."

"Invisible?"

"You think you can make yourself invisible?"

"Invisible."

"You work on it, Mundy."

I left Mundy working on it.

After settling up with Patricia, I hoofed the three blocks back to the office. The bloodstains showed improvement, but called for another couple rounds of bleaching. I checked with my service for messages then headed back out. I meant to hit the Randolph produce market, to look up one Konstantin Costopoulos, but an inkling led me on a little detour.

Driving south on Clark Street, a notion sprung to mind. Spinning on Sykes and Costopoulos and ponies got me wondering. Anyone taking on the likes of Costopoulos better make it worth his while. We're talking going for broke in the largest way possible. But was that the only play Sykes made? As basic as that and no more? What do you say—any takers? That's an awful big show for just one mug. I decided some calls had to be made—it looked like I was going to burn through a lot of nickels.

I popped into the Rexall Drug and grabbed an open booth. I placed my first call to Eighteenth District headquarters. Sergeant Tom Polhouse snickered over the wire. I caught him in a good mood. My mentioning William Sykes tickled the heck out of him.

Of course Polhouse had heard of William Sykes. They'd all heard of William Sykes, he told me. Everyone knew Three-Card Willy, alias Willy Six, alias Willy Sky. Small-time confidence man. Always on the make, whether dealing the shell game on an L-train or selling make-believe ad space in *The Police Gazette*. Those ad sales sealed his reputation. Citywide. That scam made a name for Sykes in every police station across the burg. Polhouse confirmed that Sykes was never known for pulling a big con. He'd never done hard time. Always seemed like a harmless enough fellow, Polhouse said, considering.

Must have been a slow day down at the old Eighteenth because Polhouse wanted to keep chinning. I got him off the line with a promise I'd tell Sykes that the boys at Larabee and Division sent their best.

Next up, I took a flyer and put in a call to the sticks, to one Mr. Jupiter. Ran a gambling house up north on River Road. A questionable operator, that guy. Nothing but class from the close-cropped hair on his noggin to his jeweled fingers, and all of it low. I figured he owed me on account of a run-in a ways back. I wondered if he'd figure the same.

A rasping wheeze told me Jupiter had come on the line. Sure, Jupiter told me, he'd be glad to do me a favor. I told him I didn't see it like that, but I was on a payphone and didn't have time to two-step. Call it as you see fit, Jupiter delivered the goods. He dictated a list of second-tier moneymen, most of them working territories in The Loop and throughout the North Side. Jupiter said I should feel free to toss his name around, if I like. Anything to help a friend, Jupiter said. The notion of Jupiter as a friend is enough to make anyone consider taking the pipe.

I got a fistful of nickels from the cashier, settled back into the booth with my list, and started dialing. That directory of small-potato loan sharks came up with a few hits and loads of misses. Those hits were enough, though. More than enough. Each one in bed with Costopoulos, one way or another. I couldn't get exact numbers out of these gents, but my calculations put Sykes into these boys for plenty. Thousands, easy. More than enough to bankroll all the bets for all the joes in the entire grandstand on Derby day. Sykes must've made the play of his life.

So what do you suppose Willy did with all that scratch? He could have bankrolled a special trust for the local orphanage. Sure. Or he could have laid down bets on the American Derby with every two-bit bookie who'd take his action. I would've started up that round of calls, but my sundial ran low on juice. I still had a visit to pay on west Randolph.

Costopoulos kept his offices on a small side street in the heart of the produce market. Maybe he fancied fruit and vegetables. Maybe he went nuts for a good whiff of day-old fish. More likely than not he maintained an interest in a produce or meat concern. I made my way through the nondescript entryway and up a narrow flight of stairs. A plain plaque adorned the plain door at the top: "K. Costopoulos Ent." I stepped through to find a crummy, little office set-up comprised of two folding chairs, one cramped and cheap looking desk, and one very platinum secretary. The secretary looked cheap, too.

Light bounced off her coif like off a chromium hubcap. She had blonde eyebrows, watery baby blues, and lips redder than a stop sign. A beauty mark accenting her upper lip bobbed in place as she worked a wad of gum. A tight fitting angora sweater emphasized her secretarial attributes.

"Is the boss in?" I smiled. I spied a heavy looking door just beyond the secretary's desk.

"Who the hell are you?"

"Now what kind of greeting is that? I walked in nice and polite, didn't I? And with just about the sweetest smile you ever saw? Everyone says my smile is aces."

"It don't make no never mind to me."

I leaned on the desk. "Now what if it turned out I was the boss's brother?"

"The boss ain't got no brother."

"What about a sister?"

"You can't fool me, bub. You ain't *nobody's* sister."

"You got me there."

"So who the hell are you?"

"I'm a friend of Sykes. Willy Sykes told me I could drop by anytime."

"Sykes? Sykes don't run this office." She chewed the chewing gum double-time. "Sykes don't know nothing about running this office."

"Is that a fact?"

"Besides, Sykes ain't in today."

"Under the weather, is he?"

"He had a death in the family, if it's any of your business."

"I could give you the business, sister."

"I don't even know your business."

"There's always mail order."

"What kind of runaround is this?"

"Just tell Costopoulos I want to see him regarding the Derby race at Washington Park."

"For your information, there ain't no such Derby race, today."

"You have read a racing form, haven't you? I'm referring to yesterday's card, sister. The American Derby at Washington Park. You accept wagers on horse races, don't you?"

"I'm not allowed to say nothing that might infer, or is it entrap—that ain't it. That might in any wise imply or imperil our legal, uh—

"Monkey business?"

"I wasn't going to say that. Hey, just who do you think you are?"

"I told you. A buddy of Sykes."

That's when the phone rang.

"You'll excuse me," she said. Her eyes rolled, "I'm so sure." She plucked up the earpiece and leaned her breasts into the candlestick. "Hello? Momma. I can barely hear you. Hold the line." She placed the earpiece on the desk like a half-chewed appetizer. She tore a corner of paper from her steno pad, meticulously, and wrapped up the wad of gum like some veteran at the Brach's plant. She plunked the wad into the wastebasket, adjusted her hair, and resumed her call. Momma's tale about a gasman proved so riveting that I casually skated by Gal Friday undisturbed. She never batted an attribute.

Behind that heavy door I found one of the ritziest and dizziest layouts I'd ever seen. Done to the point of overdone, and should've been done in. Every stick of furniture and every slick lick of bric-a-brac looked newer than new. Like a showroom catalog fabricated by a dope fiend. Nothing was too overpriced or too gaudy for Konstantin Costopoulos.

In a far corner, not near as ritzy, stood a human gorilla. His thick arms folded tight and his eyes bugged out mean. He wore a fedora too small for his mammoth head. I guess they don't make them that big.

Costopoulos popped up from perusing his *Esquire* centerfold. A heavy man, but light on his feet. Below average height, with thinning black hair and a short, thick mustache. He carried off the sharkskin ensemble like Fatty Arbuckle carries off a wetsuit.

"Who the hell are you?" Costopoulos's voice boomed without being loud.

"You should be at the Civic Opera."

"Don't screw around, will you buddy? I ain't got the time."

"Well I sure ain't the gasman."

"Smart guy, huh?" He turned to the torpedo. "What you think, Henry? We got another smart guy."

Henry sneezed. Costopoulos frowned at Henry.

"Actually, I'm this here private investigator nosing around on my own time." I reached into my jacket. Henry unfolded his arms and leaned forward. I flipped a business card across the desk. Henry resumed his take on a cigar store Indian.

"On your own time, eh? You ain't got no client?"

"Nope. A little bird put me wise to something. That something gave me such an itch that I had to find a way to scratch it."

"You think maybe you'll find calamine lotion here?"

"I might."

Costopoulos chortled and swiveled towards the torpedo. "Pretty good, eh, Henry?" Henry did not respond. "Calamine lotion." He gave my card the once over. "Hmm. I'll be right with you in one moment."

Costopoulos flopped into his seat like a wet mop, picked up the handset, and dialed a local exchange. "Iggy? This is C. Give me J.J." Costopoulos drummed his fingers on the centerfold while he waited. "Yeah? Oh. Can he call me back, maybe? Oh. I'm trying to get a line on a private gumshoe. No, he's here right now. He says he got the itch."

Costopoulos recited the details off my business card and hung up. He gave me a one-eyed squint, and went back to the centerfold.

"So what's it to be, Mr. C?" I asked.

"We wait, smart guy."

So we waited. Costopoulos licked his second finger and leafed through *Esquire*. Henry must've figured I had something up my sleeve, the way he glared at me. The phone jangled less than two minutes later. Costopoulos snatched it fast.

"Iggy? Yeah, so quick of you. You got the word from J.J.? That's a good one. I got it. Good. My warmest bygones to J.J."

Costopoulos hung up the receiver. His dark eyes narrowed. He raised his glance to me, cocked his head, a huge grin plastered across his mush. "I got the whole lowdown on you from J.J. Take a seat, smart guy."

"J.J.?"

"No one you should know about, smart guy. But he says you're A-okay."

"Does he, now? Tell him I asked how was every little thing."

"He says you're all right and that I should trust you like a throat trusts piano wire."

"Nice image."

Costopoulos shrugged his shoulders. "So what do you have in mind that I can do for you, Mr. No-Client Dick?"

"I came for a little intelligence."

"I got little."

"In abundance."

"Personal or business?"

"Strictly business."

"Such as?"

"Such as, did you make heavy book on Whirlaway?"

"There's always plenty of action on the American Derby."

"Heavier than usual?"

"So what is it? You know something I don't know about?"

"Could be. Could be hearsay."

"What hearsay have you heard?"

"There's talk going around concerning a series of bets fixing to break the Costopoulos Bank."

"You looking to irritate me?"

"You looking to be irritated? No, I might have some information you'd find of keen interest."

"Hmm. Information of any kind is always very welcoming."

"Sure, sure. I'll tell you how it is. I'm just small potatoes. I try to make a reasonable living, and I try to keep my nose reasonably clean while I'm at it. Boys like you? You're the big leagues, Costopoulos, the mean leagues. Your kind plays for keeps. The wrong word in the wrong ear can lead to broken bones and broken necks. I wouldn't want to put any innocent bystanders in the wrong."

"You say what is true enough. And I applaud your, your diplomatic senses. You have tact!"

Henry sneezed again. Costopoulos spun around. "We are trying to have polite conversation, Henry." The gorilla didn't stir.

"Let me tell you a story," I said. "It's the story about a real slick operator. This operator, he makes book for a going concern. A well-heeled concern. Our boy makes out okay, as far as it goes, but he's got bigger plans. Plans for himself and plans for his boss's bank account. First thing he does is line up backers, a group of investors, if you will. A sort of consortium."

"Like a cartel?"

"No. He pulls together maybe ten guys. Or twenty. They could be relatives or old school buddies. Doesn't matter. What matters is that none of them are wise to the others in the group. Get me?"

"I got you so far," Costopoulos said. Then he grunted.

"Our hero starts things easy. His boys place reasonable bets and build up credit."

"Good."

"Sometimes they win, sometimes they lose. Our hero uses his cut of the winnings to cover some of the losses in the short run. Eventually, our boy is ready for his big play. He tells everyone about this money race coming up. Not only is this a top-drawer race, so he tells them, but the fix is in, and our boy claims he's got the inside dope."

"But there is no dope."

"Of course not—our boy's lying through his crooked teeth. He's already calculated the odds and knows the spreads he wants to cover. So he divides the wagers across his group. They don't know any better and lay down their bets. Heavy bets. *Very* heavy."

"As heavy as a piano? As an elephant?" Costopoulos grinned.

"Sure. Heavier than Soldier Field. The day of the big race arrives. Some bets come in smelling like roses. Others crap out. Our hero's only interested in the winners, natch."

"Hmm. That goes without saying so."

"He'll collect his cut from the winners and blow town p.d.q. The losers he'll stick holding the bag."

"You arouse me." Costopoulos ran a thumbnail across his lower lip.

"Savvy the set up? He's stuck the bookie but good—he's stuck with a huge outlay to the winners, and he'll never collect from the losers. He'll wind up bust or run out of town."

"This ain't no fairy story, is it?" Costopoulos said. "I take it this slick guy works for me."

"That's right."

"So why peddle this here? What's in it for you, smart guy?"

"Men like this operator, and men like you, skew the playing field for the rest of us."

"Are you trying to get my goat?"

"Your goat doesn't interest me, Costopoulos. I'm pitching it straight. No curveballs. My interest is manicuring the playing field. Constructing something a little less lopsided."

"Yeah? How do you come by that, smart guy?"

"I feed you the name of this hero in exchange for your word."

"Oh yeah?"

"Yeah. Give me your word, Costopoulos. Promise you'll give the guys on his sucker list a break. I'm not saying they get off scot-free, but you find every way possible to go easy on them. You don't turn this into something personal. That's my proposition."

"Oh yeah?"

Costopoulos's soft face looked at me hard. He stretched his neck, then toyed with the large rock in his tiepin. High on the wall behind him hung a clock fashioned from a schooner's wheel. The mechanical ticking of the second hand counted off as Costopoulos chewed over my proposal. I lit a cigarette and listened. I counted twenty-five clicks before Costopoulos placed his palms flat on the desk and leaned over them.

"All right, Mr. Gumshoe Smart Guy. You give me the name, and, if I can find the rat, I give you my word of honor that I'll go soft on his...pals. We got a deal, smart guy? You got a name for me? Henry, tell him I want that name!"

Henry sneezed.

When I got back north, I found a couple goons camped out in front of my office building. Enormous fellows. Regular linebacker types. One buried his hand in a bulging suit pocket.

"George Halas send you?" I asked.

"Who, us? We're from Western Union."

"Is that right? I don't see any bicycle."

"We got a message for you."

"Where's your bicycle?"

"It's parked in the alley, Mac. I'll show it to you."

They prompted me past two storefronts to the alley. It didn't require *Good Lousekeeping* to know what to expect. It's not like they gave me much choice. Either they made their play, or I made mine.

"Not a Schwinn in sight," I said. I was turning to face them when a heavy fist landed on the back of my neck. The wallop sent me to the ground. They graciously stood by as I peeled myself from the asphalt.

"I remember," I huffed between breaths, "when Western Union sent telegrams."

"We don't care for the likes of nosies. We don't like private dicks sticking their nosey noses where they don't belong."

I worked back onto my feet, crawling up the brick wall like it was a close friend. "I got that impression, all right. You boys come to this conclusion on your own, or did somebody draw you a diagram?"

The first moose leaned in, "The message was signed by Mr. Vittorio Stronzate."

I threw a jab to the gut while he was winding up, but the other mug caught me a quick rap across the chops. He followed with two shots to my kidneys, and the first lug kicked the feet out from under me.

"You got the message, shamus?"

I would've answered, but I was busy not breathing.

"Yeah, I'd say you got the message!" A sharp boot to my gut got his point across.

The thugs stole away and left me sucking hard for air. You ever try inhaling in a vacuum chamber? Light turned into fog, and I remember the pavement felt cold. The next I thing I knew, one set of footsteps entered the alley.

"If it ain't Mr. Private Detective hisself."

I rolled over in the direction of the voice, as gently as cement allows. A hazy figure stood just a few feet in front of me. I could make it out, in an out-of-focus sort of way. I called, "Friend or foe?"

"Don't you know me, Mr. Private Eye Man? You should know me. You been grilling everyone and their mother about me all day."

Of course I knew him. Who else could it be? It had to be the one and only Three-Card Willy, alias Willy Six, alias Willy Sky.

"Mr. William Sykes, I presume."

"Damn right."

"You with Stronzate's men?"

"Yeah, sort of. Well kind of, but not exactly. We didn't all ride down together, if that's what you're asking."

"I didn't take you for part of any goon squad. But you do work for Stronzate."

"So what if I do?"

"So who else you're working for?"

"Number one Willy Boy. I always come first."

"At least you're honest."

"And what about you, Mr. Big-shot Detective? How come you're picking on me? I ever done anything to you?"

"Personally, not a thing."

"So what gives?"

"You're a pestilence, Sykes."

"What'd you call me?"

"A disease. A virus, cancer. A walking, talking piece of filth. I can't begin to guess how many germs I'm exposed to just from your yapping."

"You calling me names? Me? How's about Costopoulos? How's about Stronzate? I'm just taking them at their own game. Don't go telling me that Costopoulos and Stronzate got clean hands."

"We're not talking about them, Sykes. This is all about you. All about you bringing in friends. Bringing in strangers. Suckering the bunch. Setting them up to take the fall. Whose idea was that? Yours? Stronzate's? How many necks exactly did you put on the chopping block? Ten? Twenty? More?"

"Plenty!" He said it proud. "I conned them all."

"I'll bet you did. You even hoodwinked Stronzate—he must of bankrolled you in the first place."

"Sure, Stronzate laid it all out. His play was all about an old beef with Costopoulos. Goes back five years, maybe. I don't know. Stronzate's kick is that Costopoulos stoled the fish market from him."

"And before that, who'd Stronzate steal it from?"

"With these birds, you're asking me? Go read a book."

"So it's got everything to do with payback for Stronzate?"

"Big time but big. He wanted to break the Greek bastard for good."

"Clever. Without gunplay."

"Stronzate's had his fill of that."

"So the idea was to cripple Costopoulos."

"Stronzate's got the smarts. You gotta hand him that."

"And what about you? Working both ends against the middle."

"Why not? I saw my chance to make a killing, a real killing. Know what I mean? Stronzate hands me the set-up. On a silver platter, practically. I got all these guys placing bets with the Greek, each one of them owing me a cut of the winnings. So I figure to ratchet it up, see? I borrow from every small-fry loan shark I can talk to. Then I place every bet under the sun in the American Derby with every bookie gullible enough to take my action. I could place all these bets and clean up a hundred fold. A thousand, even. It was a thing of beauty! Then, while Costopoulos don't know what hit him, and before Stronzate starts moving in, I blow town with all those winnings."

While Sykes yammered, I got to my feet in easy stages. I kept bent over, hands on knees, working for every breath.

"Everyone's looking out for themselves, see. But no one's looking out for Willy Sykes. So I looks out for myself."

"And the hell with the rest of the world."

"It's dog eat dog."

"I hope you choke on it."

A Gene Krupa solo pounded between my temples, but the fog started to clear. I straightened up and got a look at Willy Six. Turned out a pipsqueak of a thing. A cheap dandy in cheap duds. The pencil mustache completed the effect. He stood less than twelve feet off, his legs spread wide and his hands thrust deep in his pants pockets.

"So what is it, Sykes? Why do you want to see me?"

"I got a message."

"Everybody's sending me messages."

Sykes brought out his right with a snap of the wrist. The switchblade danced in his hand, back and forth, nice and obvious.

"Why'd you want to go crabbing the works?" he said. I was going to shoot the moon. For the first time I was really going to pull off something special."

"Sykes, you're nothing but a punk. You think like a punk and you operate like a punk. I've just been worked over enough to be feeling real mean. If you want me to take it out on you, I won't argue. Just give me an excuse, Sykes. You'll be eating your own switchblade."

Sykes' shoulders pulsed a couple times. I took one lunging step forward and stopped. His eyes shut tight and he dropped to his knees and the blade made a thin, metal ring as it bounced on the pavement.

"I'm not so tough," Sykes whined.

I stepped up to the trembling figure. I stooped over, picked up the knife, and threatened to slap the little creep. He cringed when I snapped off the blade and tossed it down the alley. Even the switchblade was cheap.

"What now? What are you going to do to me?"

"Just leave you to the wolves, Sykes." I leaned in close and his little eyes blinked as I hissed, "I'm going to leave you to the wolves and let the nature of man take its course."

I spat on the ground as I shambled past Sykes. I left him as he was. I left him as easy as you walk away from a lost race. What's not so easy to leave behind are those poor suckers, the Flint Mundys. Hard to forget them. Harder to save them from themselves. Sure. So you call it a day and get some rest and let the bruises heal.

That's about all there is to it. I guess that's pretty much everything I have that's worth mentioning—except maybe for that newspaper account. Sure. I almost forgot about it—that's what brought me here in the first place. Ain't that a laugh?

It just happened to catch my eye. I wonder if any of you boys caught that one. Some of you must have seen it. It was in all the rags, but I think *The American* covered it first. The bureau's going to love this one.

I read in the paper where a stable boy, early yesterday, discovered this body. And what do you think? Turned out to be the body of a Mr. William Sykes. The body was a dead body. People never seem to discover live bodies. The article went on to say that the stable boy also found the head. Also quite dead. The head and the body must not have got along very well because they were no longer attached. This happened all the way down in Homewood. As I recall, if I'm not mistaken, they keep a racetrack out there in Homewood. Doesn't that beat all for one hell of a coincidence? That's one for the record books.

But before you call Ripley—wouldn't it be a pip if the racecourse and that head and that body and my story were all somehow tied up together? You want to bet on it? Sure.

Statement No. 7:
Anna Burgle

Sometimes people just plain vanish. That bucks the cliche, all right. The old Indian rope trick. You ask Anna Burgle, if you can get a thing out of her. Anything at all. But you'll manage it. One way or another. You'll make something out of it, you will. The department can't just leave it alone. Can't let it just sit. You boys never do. Sure.

I wonder how a roomful of alienists gets along with that lady. What's left of her. Headshrinkers—that's what the department's going to throw her up against. Am I right or am I right? First you trump up some charge, lay on any charge, so you can justify the mug shots, the prints. After that, bombs away. Reflex tests and personality tests and Rorschach tests. The IQ tests and free association tests. Lots of luck to all of them, and they can keep it.

Mr. Burgle. There's the real odd man out. He's the one screwed over but good. And then, of course, there's Goldie. A real question mark, that one.

Okay, skip it. I'm ready to dish it out. See if you boys can keep those ears from flapping. In the end there's probably nothing to my yarn. But I couldn't just bring in Mrs. Burgle and walk away, could I? Dump her off like a sack of wet cement? Cut out like that on Mr. Burgle? Go ahead, take it all down, make out of it what you will. Then you can take a good look in the mirror and see where that and two bits get you.

People don't just vanish. That's what Mr. Burgle had to tell me. That's what he told me, and that's what he asked me. In one and the same breath. I straightened him out on that one. I straightened him out on a lot of things.

Mr. Emeric Burgle, mortician's assistant. Married thirty years. Father of one—mark that one completely unexpected. Short, stout, a regular bulldog of a mug. The kind of build like he'd been inflated inside his clothing with a bicycle pump.

Burgle hung onto this black derby. Never left his grip. Not for one moment during the appointment. He stroked it, gestured with it, spun it in his hands and played with it in a thousand ways. Maybe Goldie gave it to him, for all I know. Sure.

Mr. Burgle deposited himself in the client chair, gave me that loneliest bird in the world look. All balled up and small in the straight-back, he was. No friends. No real family left. Desperate, you could call him, in an unspoken kind of way. He took to sighing a lot with his eyes closed.

In this game, you never stop getting a read on clients. Some play it foxy and put on a dodge. Those are the dangerous ones, the ones to keep your eye on, the intriguing ones. The rest are mostly everyday types. They put up the strong front, like the reason they're there doesn't hardly matter. The read on them is cake—they're trying to bluff it out, bluffing themselves as much as anyone.

This Burgle jasper? I've read deeper baseball cards. Strictly a second-stringer. No personal life to speak of. No joy in Mudville for this guy. Nothing to look forward to. The hung head and the rounded shoulders said plenty. His voice dripped with defeat. All the injuries of the past, the ones that wouldn't go away, could never go away, showed through that flat, vacant look slapped onto his pan. And now he was asking for my help, but he really knew better. Burgle couldn't admit it, but he'd given up long ago. I wonder if he'll ever realize that. Maybe he's working up to it in easy stages.

"My daughter is missing." The words escaped in wisps of breath.

"What's your daughter's name, Mr. Burgle?"

"Golda. Everyone knows her as *Goldie*. That's what we all call her." Burgle sighed with closed eyes.

"Did you go to the police about Goldie?"

"Yes, of course I did."

"And?"

"They couldn't do anything."

"What did the cops make of it?"

"Nothing. They didn't have a thing to tell me. Nothing at all."

"Tell me what they told you."

"They spoke with me, of course. And they spoke with my wife. They said they stopped by Goldie's apartment. They checked up on all the area hospitals and the emergency rooms." Burgle's throat contacted. "They even told me that they followed up at the morgue."

"All sounds pretty routine."

"I suppose so."

"What about her job? Her friends?"

"The police officer, the one who would speak with me, said they made the rounds." He paused, stared at the derby. "My daughter's missing and they made the rounds."

"I get you, Mr. Burgle."

"People don't just vanish. Goldie didn't just vanish."

"Sometimes they do." I let that sink in while I pulled out a cigarette, tapped it on the blotter. "Mr. Burgle, I'm not going to soft-soap you. You deserve the truth—you want the truth, don't you? I don't accept money from people who want to pay for the privilege of being lied to. Truth's an iffy commodity. You at least deserve not being lied to. Get this straight, Mr. Burgle—people vanish every day. The sooner you stomach that one, the better. That's not the Sunday funnies truth or the Burns and Allen truth or even the truth according to City Hall, but that's a fact. That's the world we live in. Sure. Maybe we don't always know how it happens, or why it happens. But it happens that folks just plain vanish, and that's the truth."

"Goldie?"

"Maybe she did, maybe she didn't. Don't go fooling yourself. We may flat out never know. Get me?"

"Yes."

"People sometimes just vanish. Period."

"But they come back."

"It's possible."

"Possible?"

"Let's you and me kick it around. Let's see what we come up."

"Yes. Please."

"Uh-huh. When's the last time you saw Goldie?"

"She's been gone five months."

"That's some stretch of time."

"I can tell you it's a long stretch. Five months is a very long time. It is to a father. Do you have any children?"

"And the last time you saw her. Do you remember that?"

"Of course. Lunch at the Berghoff. We had lunch together on her twenty-fifth birthday. Goldie cherishes the Berghoff, so that's where we went. She had a corned beef sandwich and a root beer. No dessert." A smile crept out, slipped quickly across Burgle's lips, and crept away.

"How did she strike you?"

"That was the last time I saw her."

"How did she strike you?"

"Goldie looked beautiful."

"How was her mood, Burgle? Was she happy? Sad? Did she show any signs of being in any kind of trouble?"

"No, not what you think of as trouble."

"Uh-huh. But there was something."

"She told me that she was supposed to come by the next day and see my wife. That's her mother. That's Anna."

"And?"

"She never went."

"Goldie never went."

"She never showed up."

"Was there trouble between Goldie and her mother?"

"You could say there was."

"What do you say?"

"This isn't the kind of thing you just mention casually." Burgle adjusted his shoulders. "I don't like talking about it. I have never told anyone anything about it."

"We can't put it off, Mr. Burgle. It's going to come back around."

"Yes, I see that."

"Then cut to the chase and get it over with."

Burgle's gaze traveled upward. He held the derby with both hands, standing it on its brim in his lap, rotating it like a baby steering wheel. Spinning slowly to the left, left, left.

"Go ahead, Mr. Burgle. Spill it." I lit the cigarette. Burgle didn't smoke. Wearing his wounded heart on his sleeve was the only vice he needed.

"Goldie and her mother never really...they haven't been close for a long, long time. Not like a mother and daughter. Goldie came along very late. You understand. I've always said that made all the difference. I've always said that."

"An only child?"

"That's right. She is." Burgle paused, his eyes went blank and drifted off. He kept drifting out like that, drifting out and drifting back in again.

"Mrs. Burgle, Anna, had this little job at Hart Schaffner Marx. When we were first married? She liked to sew, and she liked visiting with the other ladies at the factory."

"Of course she gave it up for Goldie."

"Of course she did. And they were close at first. Terribly close. They really were inseparable. For a time. Her mother never left her."

"Anything else?"

"Yes. I suppose I'm obliged to mention *the accident*." Burgle's jaw flexed, he swallowed. His voice came way down, all *sotto voce*. "When Goldie was still very small, there was *the accident*. Goldie narrowly avoided being injured. Seriously injured. But she was very lucky. Instead, it was her poor mother. Her mother is the one who suffered the injury. All the nerves in her right hand—completely crushed."

Burgle studied the back of his hand. His face wrenched up and the fingers contracted and froze, like paralyzed talons. I watched the blue smoke curl off the end of my cigarette, rise slowly into a widening loop, melt into the air.

"It was very bad. They were able to save the hand, but it turned into this useless thing. This ugly, useless thing. It was very, very bad."

"That's tough."

"Mrs. Burgle always blamed Goldie for the accident."

"Does she say Goldie did it on purpose?"

"I think Mrs. Burgle thinks so. She doesn't say so, but that is what she thinks."

"Was it really the kid's fault?"

"No, it was not. Of course not. But that's what her mother believes. Mrs. Burgle never discusses it with me."

"Uh-huh. As far as your wife's concerned, she sacrificed her job and her hand on account of Goldie."

"Yes. By her accounting of things."

"And she's been sacrificing ever since."

"It's so difficult. To explain about people. I see that a lot at the home." Burgle raised the derby and cleared his throat again. His eyes shut. "What I'm trying to say is that she doesn't hate the girl. Do you understand?" The eyes opened. "That's not it at all. Mrs. Burgle just never could show any affection for her. Do you see? They've never been like a mother and daughter are supposed to be. She was never really loving or warm with Goldie. Isn't that what a mother's for?"

"Sure."

"That's what a mother's for."

Burgle gawked at me, a young boy coming through Burgle's washed out expression. Mostly around the eyes. A hurt look. The lost look of a lost, little boy. What the hell do you say to that?

"What you said before. It sounds like Goldie has her own place."

"Yes. She took up her own apartment. Not all that far from the house."

"How long ago?"

"Oh, she ran away from home many times. I don't know how regular that is. I never ran away from home. She got her own place two years ago. That's when she was twenty-three. I brought the keys with me."

"You've got the keys?"

"Yes. I'm honoring the contract. When I first notified the police—" Burgle's eyes narrowed. His mouth formed a silent wince. His eyes avoided mine. "It's my way of pretending." He smiled meekly. "There are only two months left in the lease. I've paid up through the end. Her mother knows nothing about it. We never discuss anything concerning Goldie."

"Who knows, Mr. Burgle? It could prove helpful."

"Could it? Really?"

"Sure. Maybe. Maybe not. I don't know at this point, but let's say we keep it on the table. What about her friends?"

"She never said a word about her personal life."

"Girlfriends, boyfriends."

"Goldie never spoke about it. We used to talk about other subjects."

"Okay, no dice on the social front. What about work?"

"Hart Schaffner Marx. The same factory where her mother had been employed."

"Sure."

"It's easier for a girl that way. When she has an *in*. That was the best we could do for her."

"Maybe she had some friends at the factory."

"I don't know about that. Are friends important?"

"Don't you have any friends, Mr. Burgle?"

He drifted out and in again. "No, I guess I don't. Not outside of the home." A confused wrinkle fell across Burgle's wide forehead.

"You were young once, weren't you Burgle? Didn't you ever tell things to your buddies that you never mentioned to your parents?"

"I see. Of course. I expect she never told her mother anything at all."

"Uh-huh. Friends unknown. Okay. I have to bring up one other matter. I'm afraid I'm not making it easy for you."

"All right. I understand you. Go ahead."

"Has it crossed your mind, Mr. Burgle, that maybe Goldie doesn't want to be found?"

Burgle shut his eyes and sighed. "Yes, I have thought of that. I've had to think of that." Burgle drew a deep breath through his nose. "I've tried not to think about that."

"It's a real possibility."

"I know."

"But you want to go ahead anyway?"

"I have to know she's all right."

"Sure."

"You don't have to tell me about what misfortunes can happen to a young girl. I'm accustomed to such things. Death doesn't scare me. I work with death every day."

"Sure."

"But I have to know, you see? Can you understand that? Five months and no word...without my daughter..." He wagged his head, the voice trailed off, his eyes followed.

"I get you, Mr. Burgle."

"I have to believe her mother wants to know as well."

"Uh-huh."

"Goldie is still her daughter, after all."

"Two possibilities are most likely, Mr. Burgle. You ready for it?" I took his silence to mean he was ready for it. "In the first case, Goldie ducked out on her own. For whatever reason, she dusted. Probably for something we wouldn't savvy if she tried to explain. If that's true, the trail is pretty dried up."

"Yes. I understand." Burgle dropped his eyes to the derby.

"If something untoward happened to Goldie, the second possibility, I expect the city's finest would have come up with something. But they didn't, did they?"

"They said they didn't."

"They came up blank, sure. So we're up against it, Mr. Burgle. You shouldn't pin hopes on such a long shot."

"But you can do something, can't you?"

"It could turn out to be one terrific waste of my time and your bank account."

"It's not a waste of time! It isn't. It's not a waste of time." Burgle's lower lip quivered like a loose bumper.

"All right, Burgle, all right. I'll tell you what. Let's take it a step at a time. Give me seventy-two hours. I'll see what I can turn up."

"Seventy-two hours."

"That's right."

"That's three days." Burgle covered his eyes.

"Let's see if I can scrape up a lead or two, if there are any. Seventy-two hours should do it. If I come up empty, we'll call it quits. I'm not going to string you along, Mr. Burgle."

"Is that enough time?"

"Most likely. My hunch is we can wrap it up a lot faster than that. If there's anything to find, we should stumble across it pretty quick."

"Oh."

"Mr. Burgle, you ever place a classified ad?"

"No, I didn't. Should I?"

"That's all right. I'll take care of it."

"I never thought of that."

"Did you bring a photograph?"

"Yes, I did. I have it here."

Burgle reached into his inside jacket pocket, tenderly. He brought out a small envelope. He held it up for me on the palm of his hand. He forced a smile. I took the packet and slid out the print.

"Goldie."

"Yes. That's Goldie. Just last year."

She stood in front of some jalopy. Leaned her hips into the hood, arms folded. She sported a heavy, knit sweater and long, plain skirt. She wore mittens. Her dark hair hung long and straight. Dark eyes shone big and bright. Her oval face ended in a square jaw and chin, hard and strong. A big-time laugh lit up her face. Looked like a good enough laugh. Maybe she got it from her mother. She sure as hell didn't get it from her father.

While I contemplated the photo, Burgle remained fixed in his seat, a worn man, a tired man. A man frozen in time. Like a forgotten knickknack, one you're so used to that you don't even notice.

"You have a beautiful daughter, Mr. Burgle."

"I thank you." His gaze floated away, he began rocking in place. His gaze snapped back. "Can you return that, please? When you're done with her?"

I said, "I'll take good care of Goldie."

Burgle's eyelids shut tight for a moment. I saw light glistening in the corners.

I placed a few calls after Burgle slunk out of the office. Maybe I played the sap, sure, but what did that make Burgle? I figured I must of have been his last hope—I didn't care much for the idea. In any case, I made some calls.

I placed a personal ad in *The Trib*, *The American* and *The Daily News*. That blanketed the burg and then some. There were plenty more papers to choose from, that's if any real leads developed farther out. The ad was strictly boilerplate stuff. *Goldie, are you okay? Dad misses you. Reply to box etc., etc.* You guys know the routine. Just enough detail so any Goldie out there would know if she was the *right* Goldie. Just enough and yet keep it short. Just enough without making any reference to her mother.

I dropped by the Eighteenth District the following day. You boys know Sergeant Tom Polhouse? A pretty good egg. He played it short and sweet with me, but damn thorough. I asked to see the report on Burgle. He asked for a cigarette. Once I appeased his tobacco habit, the sarge ran me through the prelims, a list overdrawn on the negative.

Name: Burgle, Golda U.

Nickname: "Goldie."

Aliases: None.

Single white female, 25, five-two, brown hair, brown eyes.

Physical peculiarities: None.

Friends, none. Male acquaintances, none.

Hobbies, none.

Employer: Hart Schaffner Marx. Cleared.

Bank account: First National. Cleared.

Physician, none. Subject presumed in good health.

Apartment: cleared.

Polhouse gave me the goods, all right, long on detail, zip where substance was concerned. Not that I expected any different. The Eighteenth District had thrown up its hands, called it quits, and moved on. They should've added a line to that report. Leads, ideas, hunches: fresh out.

Next I looked up Charles Crank at the Hart Schaffner Marx factory, crew one manager for "the finest bunch of gals you'd ever want to put you in stitches." Another washout.

Goldie signed on at Hart Schaffner Marx going back better than two years. Crank summed up Goldie as the nicest, quietest girl. Imagine that.

"She was a good little worker. Good enough, I always said. Not the best, mind you, but serious. You know what I mean? She took it serious, and that's something the company appreciates. And that's no bunk."

"Uh-huh. Was she steady? Did she miss a lot of days?"

"Very steady. You could always see Miss B. at counter fourteen."

"When did counter fourteen go vacant?"

"Gosh, it's been months. The whole thing was so unsettling. I could check with accounting. You know, look up the payroll dates."

"That won't be necessary."

"It's no trouble. It's all so mystifying."

"No, thanks. Did she make many friends here? Maybe she was seeing somebody at the factory."

"Beats me," he grinned.

"I see. Did she leave behind any personal items?"

"We don't go for that."

"Uh-huh."

"I could give you a tour, if you like."

I skipped the tour, and I skipped out on Mr. Crank. My checklist was running awful short, awful fast. I headed over to Berteau and Damen. The yellow brick four-flat made for a peaceful building on a peaceful block. A few ash trees peacefully sprinkled along the peaceful parkway. Tall wire fences helped maintain the peace. Mildred Landau, the ancient, feisty concierge, met me in the lobby.

"She was a soft, little thing," Landau said. "It's a shame. Never gave us no problems. Never did see or hear that much of her. None of that carousing like some tenants I've seen. Now you take Mr. Bleeker—"

"You can keep Mr. Bleeker."

"You can say that again. What a ruckus! But Goldie? Now there was a nice, quiet girl. I don't think she even had no radio. It's just a shame. Go on up with you, if you like. Go ahead. I don't know what you'll find that the coppers didn't find."

"Thanks, Miss Landau." I started up the stairs.

"If it's all the same to you," she called after me, "that's *Mrs.* Landau. He left years ago, but it's still *Mrs.* It's a shame!"

The tag on the door read "2-B." I worked the key I borrowed from Mr. Burgle and entered Goldie's apartment. It felt still as a museum, the little Goldie Burgle Memorial Museum. The place had been kept real tidy. A light layer of dust had settled across every surface. Otherwise just as neat and preserved as a hospital chapel, or a mortuary, maybe. And just as sterile.

The under-sized living room nailed that antiseptic mood, something cool and impersonal. In the center of the room, a plain, wooden coffee table surrounded by a two-seat sofa and two drab sitting chairs. Nothing on the seats, the tabletop clear. A planter stood by the front door. Nothing on that, either.

While we're at it, just for the record, a sizeable console radio stood in the far corner. Looked newer than anything else in the room. Our Mrs. Landau had been misinformed. Ain't that a shame?

The dining room preserved that purely impersonal quality. A wooden table, four wooden straight-backs, a buffet, a built-in china cabinet. The glass doors on the cabinet revealed a simple collection of dinner plates, salad plates, cups and saucers. The numbers didn't jive. I counted enough pieces to cobble together a service for five. A worn tablecloth and two placemats filled half of the first cabinet drawer. I found the bottom drawer as barren as Mr. Burgle's hopes.

An empty, inexpensive platter lay on top of the buffet. I popped open the two large doors. As bare bones as everything else in the joint. I fingered an abridged dictionary, a Hemingway novel, a windmill music box. Nothing more.

Call the walk-in kitchen understated. Spare approaching bleak. I found a jumbled collection of glasses, mugs, silverware and utensils in the various cupboards and drawers. Very few of the pieces matched. Three pots, two pans, no baking sheets. One colander. A handful of cooking spices and condiments, if your hand's on the small side. Nothing in the refrigerator—still plugged in, and empty as a balloon.

The bathroom sat just off the kitchen, a pipsqueak affair by any standard. I'm no expert on female toiletries, but the stash I hit upon struck me as minimal. Almost to the point of ridiculous. Toothbrush, toothpowder, lipstick, cold cream, soap—that was all of it and all of it showed use. Maybe she carried more stuff in her purse. Maybe. One white bath towel hung on the back of the door. A dingy hand towel hung on the bar above the toilet. Everything bone dry, including two more bath towels stowed below the sink. A single tissue lay in a wrinkled ball at the bottom of the wastebasket.

A six-foot hall brought you from the john to the bedroom. The plainest of rooms. A double bed and nightstand. Lamp and alarm clock and photo on the nightstand. A horizontal style dresser made of dark, cheap wood. A petite jewelry case on top of that, set with inlaid floral design. One wooden chair with a gray cardigan thrown neatly over its back. The bed was made. The white linens didn't appear new, but not terribly worn. Likewise the brown, wool blanket.

Two sets of earrings parked in the jewelry box. The first pair diamond shaped, made of black glass. Half-inch silver hoops made up the other set. I found a plain, silver-plated necklace, a chipped cameo pin, and a deep red heart pendant. The box also contained a short and thick key, rounded, the kind used to wind a clock or music box.

Not a whole lot of stock in the dresser drawers. I combed through the usual suspects: bras, panties, stockings, nightgowns and so on. Not enough to get through one week. Nothing buried in the clothing.

You could count the blouses, dresses and skirts hanging in the closet on both hands and have fingers left over. Simple stuff. Nothing flashy. For my money, I'd say her style approached dull. On the floor of the closet I ran across two pairs of flats and one pair of black pumps. I'm no Coco Chanel, but I couldn't picture those high heels going with any of the dresses.

I caught sight of myself in the full-length mirror nailed to the outside of the closet door. Rust had developed in spots along the mirror's edge. Then I caught the reflection of the photograph on the nightstand. The positioning of its slim, gold-plated frame faced away from the bed. A fairly recent shot of Goldie and Mr. Burgle. They sat snugly on a couch. The furniture and background didn't match anything in Goldie's digs. Not a hint of a smile between the two of them.

I took out the shot of Goldie that Mr. Burgle gave me. The same girl, all right, the one on the nightstand a couple years younger, the hair shorter, the mouth more serious. Mr. Burgle appeared a whole lot younger. Age has a way of coming on like a race. And it never loses.

I retraced my steps in the bedroom. I wanted to find personal effects—long-term, immediate, it didn't matter. I wanted to come across anything that might, in some way, any way, express that a living, breathing thing actually occupied the joint. So far I hadn't come across any kind of investment that makes it your home. Most women are plenty big on that, or so Clare Booth Luce tells me. Sure.

I double-checked under the bed, the shelf in the closet, behind the dresser. No clues, no hints. The boudoir was a bust. I left the bedroom and started again. I gave the whole apartment the once-over, and then I tried again. I gave her digs the once-over three times.

I've turned up some real goose eggs in my day, but Goldie's apartment took the cake. The biggest find at Goldie's was that I found nothing. And I don't mean "nothing" as in "nothing suspicious." I mean *not one thing*. Searching her rooms felt like searching a blank canvas for a spot of paint.

Just the single photo in the bedroom. That was it. No artwork, no collectibles, nothing decorative. No plants, no flowers. No bankbook, documents, files or letters. No mail, no bills. No extra purses or handbags or luggage. No raincoat, no umbrella, no winter coat. No booze. No medicine. Not even a lousy bottle of aspirin. The joint was cleaned out but good. No bodies, no skeletons. You don't need the DA to show you how all that fails to add up.

I took my time coming down the stairs, chewing on everything I *didn't* see. Who the hell was Goldie Burgle? Her father sure didn't know her. And you could forget about the mother, at least according to Mr. Burgle. Either Goldie Burgle lived a double life or no life at all. Go figure which.

I caught up with Mrs. Landau on my way out. I asked if the building kept anything in storage for Miss Burgle.

"No, we aren't storing nothing for Goldie, mister."

"Do you know if the police removed anything from her apartment?"

"No, I don't remember seeing them take nothing."

"How about Mr. Burgle? Did he take anything of Goldie's?"

"That I couldn't say, mister. He came and went a few times in the beginning, but I never paid him no mind."

I thanked Mrs. Landau for her help, got back in the coupe, drove towards the office. I kept spinning on that empty apartment. Searching someone's rooms is like breaking into a private world. Go in with all the brilliant guesses you want, because that's all it is—guesswork. You never know what you'll run across. Except for one thing, maybe. You can almost always count on something throwing you a curve.

Sometimes you run into Cracker Jack and get a cheap little prize for your trouble. Sometimes it turns out to be a possessed jack-in-the-box with all hell about to spring loose. In Goldie's case, the curve ball came in its negative form. Goldie's rooms were an empty shell stripped clean of life. No box of wicked spirits there. No Cracker Jack, no prize.

I rang up Mr. Burgle on a long shot. I wanted to know what he took out of Goldie's place. I wanted to know, but I expected to get nowhere fast. Burgle told me he took care of the trash and removed all the food items. That was it according to Mr. Burgle—nothing more, nothing less.

"We don't want any vermin," Burgle said.

I pressed him as far as any personal items go and he played dumb. He was anxious to learn if I'd come up with anything. I put it to him bluntly. All I could see ahead of us, I said, was a dead end. I had one final lead to follow up, I added, and I'd get back to him the next day. I didn't mention that the one thing more was Anna Burgle.

The Burgle house occupied a small lot on Sawyer Avenue, a strictly residential section about a block north of Addison. Small sidewalks, small trees, small houses. The few cottages blessed with garages accessed them off the alley. I arrived in the morning around ten, handed a cool greeting by the lady of the house. Despite the frosty attitude, Anna Burgle invited me in. She led me to the living room and offered me coffee. I declined. She sat down on the couch. I took a spot opposite on a broken in easy chair. We ran through the intros, including what I was up to regarding her daughter. I purposely left out the part about her husband hiring me, but how else could she figure it?

Mrs. Burgle said, "Go ahead." She spoke hard and jerked a nod of the head. "Take a good look at me."

I did just that and took in two people at once. Anna Burgle had one of those strong, tapered, oval faces, a real Modigliani. Her dark, almond eyes opened bright and wide. Her thin, long nose led to a narrow-lipped, short mouth, creased at the corners by lines drawn down to the chin. I could've held up my hand and divided her face into two ages: above the hand, a good looker of forty or forty-five with a severe gaze; below the hand, the face of an elderly existence, mean and bitter.

"You're avoiding my hand," she said. She sounded defiant and proud, as icy as January winds off Lake Michigan. I expected a thaw no time soon.

The bent and gnarled hand rested in her lap, more like a frozen claw, the fingers narrow and curled. Her other hand appeared unusually youthful, well manicured and polished.

"That must be tough for you, Mrs. Burgle."

"We all have our dues to pay in this life."

"Some more than others."

"I know what you're thinking."

"Then you're one up on me, sister. Sometimes I don't know what I'm thinking, myself."

"I don't go in for witticisms."

"Uh-huh. I can see that. It's not my intention to come here and be witty, but sometimes my line of work calls for it."

Her eyes narrowed, her lips pursed and "hmm" came from the back of her throat. Anna Burgle tottered on the fence—had the interview just begun, or already ended? Seemed even money to me.

"I'll speak with you after all," she said. Then abruptly, "I've been expecting you."

"You have."

"I knew you would come."

"I find it hard to believe anyone said anything."

"My husband's a fool." Anna Burgle spat it out as sour as they come. "No, my husband hasn't said anything. He knows better than that. He has provided well for me. Beyond that he's a small, stupid creature."

"I enjoy a good waltz as much as the next guy, Mrs. Burgle, but I'm not here to dance or chit-chat. Do you want to tell me about your daughter or not?"

Mrs. Burgle snorted and a twisted smile rose up one side of her face. Her good hand rubbed her chin. "Tell me, are you a religious man?" I couldn't stop my lips from snaking into a wry smile. Anna Burgle pushed the question. "Do you consider yourself a man of faith?"

"That's just a lot of hocus-pocus to me, Mrs. Burgle."

"Yes, I read that plainly. Very distinct. It's so curious that you were chosen."

"Chosen. Uh-huh."

She continued rubbing her chin while I took out a cigarette. I began wondering about that accident to her hand—I wondered if, by any chance, she also cracked her noggin. Her eyes widened as I lit up and blew out the match.

"I'll tell you about my daughter."

"Go ahead, sister."

"That's why you came here, isn't it?"

"Uh-huh. I sure didn't come for any floor show."

"Though I can see you aren't the type of man to understand. I wonder why you. Why *you* were sent."

The old gal sounded off the beam, sure. "I'll play along. Try me, Mrs. Burgle."

"Hmm! Well now, my husband. He considered himself a devoted and loving man."

"You must have gone for him just a little, once upon a time."

"My dear, sweet husband wanted children."

"What did you want?"

"I served as the dutiful wife. I submitted to my husband's wishes. I was an ignorant girl and didn't interpret the signs. There was good reason I didn't become pregnant, but Mr. Burgle insisted and sent me to doctor after doctor. So-called *specialists*. He refused to accept the opinion of our learned men of medicine, that my body was incapable of bearing children."

"Yet you had Goldie."

"Yes. Years later. When I better understood and it was too late. The pregnancy truly terrified me. At first, I couldn't even tell Mr. Burgle. When at last he found out, do you know what the oaf actually had to say? Shall I tell you?"

"I can't possibly imagine."

"The fool proclaimed it a miracle! A miracle. The reality was more likened to a curse. I knew that and had to live with that for the entire term. Did Mr. Burgle tell you I almost died?"

"No, he didn't mention anything about it."

"No, he wouldn't. The pregnancy put me through a terrible hardship, and the birth a difficult one. I suffered the worst complications and lost an immense quantity of blood. But we both survived. It lived."

"And you blame your husband for this? Or Goldie?"

"Ahhh. This is where you misinterpret me. I am not speaking of Goldie herself. I refer to a spirit. An unnatural thing, an inner evil."

"Evil, sure. Are we talking about Old Nick? The Prince of Darkness himself? Real fire and brimstone stuff?"

"That was the first time the evil attempted to take my life. In my heart I knew what was happening, but I didn't have the courage to admit it consciously. I became drawn to it in the way we become drawn to destruction. The only thing I could do was watch her. Constantly watch her."

"And then came the accident."

"It compressed all the nerves to leave me with this." Mrs. Burgle raised her right arm, slow, dangled the lifeless, stricken hand. "Thereafter I knew. I knew and I understood. I could never leave Goldie out of my sight. My stupid husband and the stupid neighbors. They thought me such the devoted mother. Do you see? That was the only way I could protect myself, to protect anyone. I remained on watch. It became my vigil."

"Sure."

"There were more attempts on my life."

"Goldie tried to kill you?"

"Your small beliefs. Your small, limited mind and limited beliefs. I'll tell you once more. It wasn't Goldie, not Goldie herself. I'm talking about an infinite darkness within the child. A depraved spirit flowered inside of her. It struggled to burst free. It knew I was the first obstacle it needed to overcome, before anything else. It's that wicked force that fought against me, not the child, not her. Can you possibly comprehend that?"

"Uh-huh. Kind of a like a human Pandora's box."

"Dismiss this, if you can. On her last birthday, it tried again. The spirit made another attempt on my life."

"Your husband said Goldie planned to visit you, but she never showed."

"I lied to him! Of course I lied. She came to the door and I let her in and walked ahead of her. When I turned, she flourished a dagger from beneath her cape."

"She actually wore a cape?"

"I was taken aback at first, but I shouldn't have been. Her eyes were the eyes of the dead and she came toward me with the knife as if cast under a spell. She thrust the blade at me, but I was stronger and faster and I caught her and stopped her.

"I realized it, then and there, that only one choice stood before me. That thought maintained me as we struggled over the blade—I knew that only I could end the evil. I forced her to drop the knife and she fell to the floor weeping. My will proved stronger.

"She continued sobbing, wailing, but I did not allow myself to be moved. My spirit prevailed and I swiftly braced one arm behind her neck and grabbed her throat as tightly as I could. I began to squeeze. She struggled against me and tried to speak and her tears fell on the skin of my hand, my dead, unfeeling hand, but I shut my eyes and squeezed harder and harder and wouldn't let go until the evil was gone for good. I didn't stop until the evil was dead."

"You're telling me you murdered your daughter."

"Will you understand that I *freed* my daughter? Evil has been vanquished. The darkness has left us."

"Sure."

"What other choice did I have? To let the evil flourish within my only daughter? Allow it to grow? No, only one path lay before me, the right path, and I have done what must be done. I had no choice in that, just as I have had to confess to you. The time had come."

Sure. There's always the unexpected, that curve ball. And then there's just the plain off-the-wall unbelievable. Mrs. Burgle—mad as a hatter and leaving Mr. Burgle holding the bag. That was the capper, that nothing she told me revealed the slightest hint about the disappearance of Goldie Burgle.

"Would you like me to show you the body, now?"

"No, that won't be necessary, Mrs. Burgle. We can leave all that to the police."

"As you say. I don't know about such things. I'll get my hat and my coat and you will drive me to the station."

Mrs. Burgle offered one last comment, her final statement, as we got in the car. I held the door for her and she stared hard into my eyes. This is exactly what she told me:

"The darkness is gone for good. Goldie and I are free. Now Goldie can be with me forever."

Mrs. Burgle's almond eyes narrowed and the creases from her mouth curled into a grin. Her gaze drifted, downward, fell to the ground, and the smile faded clean away. She dipped down into the passenger seat calmly, deliberately, almost serenely—yeah, as if under a trance. Anna never spoke another word.

During the ride in I brought up a thing or two, asked Mrs. Burgle a couple questions. No go. I even tried to bait her by mentioning her old man. No response. Anna Burgle had gone completely incommunicado. She kept still as a sphinx, gaping listlessly through the windshield, as if she envisioned the empty future. She sat beside me in the coupe, expressionless, motionless. As though she was a non-person. As though every emotion and trait of character had gone just as dead as the twisted claw in her lap. Anna Burgle was nowhere to be found. Sometimes people just vanish.

Statement No. 8:
Carlo Spinetti

Five minutes. Five lousy minutes. That's all it takes. The difference between a pat on the back and a snapped neck. Sure.

Timing. It played with me all day. Strung me along like a cheap windup toy. Chalk it up to kismet, crossed stars, good luck or bad luck—whatever flips your pancake. Me? I tag it all as coincidence, and that's saying something. Good old blind coincidence. You ever know coincidence to have twenty-twenty vision?

Can't say I envy you boys. You've got one hell of a mess to sift through on State Street. Heaps of bodies. Oodles of carnage. Plenty to go around. And think of all those witnesses. Contemplate that mass of paperwork ahead of you. The precinct's going to be up to its nightsticks in interviews. For weeks. You'll probably go through more pulp than a Sunday edition of *The Tribune*. Sure.

All right, let's move along with this one. I've got the whole story. Most of it, anyway. I'll set you wise to more of the puzzle than anyone else.

It always starts simple, doesn't it? Nice and plain. Pumpernickel and cream cheese. Downright innocent, it does. In this case, you could say my stomach kicked off the whole thing.

Your stomach ever talk at you? A low growl and a quiver told me I'd best be grabbing some chow. I'd gotten an early start at the office with a plan on catching a late breakfast. Maybe eleven o'clock or so I locked up, took the stairs down to the front exit, pushed through the door. It went downhill from there, but fast.

A couple minutes' difference and I could have missed them. Just a couple minutes' difference and I wouldn't be parked here dictating my statement for the venerable Eighteenth District. But no such luck. A pair of suburban torpedoes stopped me in my tracks. Two gorillas I'd had the displeasure of meeting a ways back. I knew them in the employ of one Mr. Jupiter. You know this lowlife? Runs a gambling joint in the sticks. A regular gangster of the big fish, small pond variety.

The lead goon, a moose called Geoffrey, stepped right up to me. Nice and close. Close enough to give me the full treatment of his cheap cologne. Both barrels.

I said, "Any closer and you'll be trying on my suit."

Geoffrey's smile swallowed his upper lip. "Say, you remember us?" He sounded like a bear with a cold.

"How could I ever forget Tweedledum and Tweedledee?"

The second goon chimed in, "That's Geoffrey and Angus, sharpie." Angus sounded like a bear with a two-pack-a-day habit.

"Angus? Really?"

"Mr. Jupiter wants to see you," Geoffrey said.

"What a revolting thought," I replied. "A reception with Jove himself. I wouldn't expect you boys to pick up on the obvious, so I'll spell it out: I'm on my way somewhere."

"He's waiting for you."

"Is that a fact? Been waiting long?"

"Naw, we only just got here."

"Just now? Figures. Let him wait."

"You don't keep a man like Mr. Jupiter waiting."

"Is that so? Maybe you don't. Me, I keep people waiting all the time. I've made a personal study of it and I've gotten darn good at it."

"This way, sharpie." Angus snagged my arm in his large paw.

"Easy boys, easy. Sudden moves make me jumpy."

"Let's go, flatfoot."

"Now you've done it. You've gone and got the lingo all bollixed up."

"Move," Geoffrey said.

They attached themselves to me like a set of goon bookends and escorted me to the curb. They pressed me towards the crate parked in front of the fire hydrant. It had to be one of the largest automobiles I'd ever laid my peepers on, a flamboyant, black number no longer than Navy Pier.

I said, "You see, a flatfoot's a policeman."

"You hear that, Geoffrey? A flatfoot's a copper."

"That's right, Angus. Maybe what you meant is gumshoe or PI or dick or shamus."

"Get in, sharpie."

"Shoofly, bloodhound, sleuth, Sherlock."

Geoffrey opened the rear door and Angus gave me a shove. I stooped into the bus and found myself across from Mr. Jupiter. The short, round man sat bundled up with scarf and lap blanket. He fussed with a cigarette holder. Geoffrey shut the door.

"Mr. Jupiter, as I live and wheeze."

"Jibes already? Must you always mock my asthmatic condition?"

"Yeah, I do. What else have you got?"

"You'll find me not in the best humor for your usual banter."

"That's a shame. My unusual banter's at the cleaners and won't be ready until next week."

Jupiter raised his eyebrows, squeezed shut his eyes, and tugged at the collar of his coat.

I said, "You must be dying under all those wraps. It's a beautiful spring day outside in the real world."

"I'm doing battle with a terrific head cold. And I have places to be."

"Maybe you should take a little something for that. I hear rat poison's a great cure-all."

"I thought we were on friendlier terms. I thought we had achieved an understanding."

"I'll tell you what I understand, Jupiter. I understand it takes a lot to make up for getting cold-cocked, for having a thirty-eight purloined out of your mitt while your brains are out for lunch." I copped a glance at the legroom between our facing seats. "Cripes, this rig is larger than my sitting room. Aren't you going to offer me a drink of something?"

"It's only transportation after all, my dear, Mr. Detective. Not a gin mill for the working class."

"Oh, is that what this thing is? I thought we were in a viaduct on wheels."

"This," pausing to wheeze, "this is a Daimler Double Six 40/50 Sport Saloon. There is only one other in the entire metropolis."

"Couldn't get them to move, huh? You must've got a good price on it."

"You're becoming annoying. More so than usual, I must say. Without so much as a civil hello."

"I have that tendency. Especially when I'm force fed an audience. Look, Jupiter, I didn't ask to see you. You didn't even have the decency to call. Instead, you send Mutt and Jeff out there to practically shanghai me. Still having trouble growing out your hair, I see."

"Shall we keep this on a purely business basis? I require your services. Are you interested or not?"

"I don't do delousing."

Jupiter let out a sighing wheeze. "I'm offering you employment. I have need for some assistance and thought the least I could do was afford you first refusal."

"Sure, sure. First refusal. Very deluxe. What's your pitch?"

"This assignment is in regards to my girlfriend, Miss Geneva French."

"Girlfriend? I thought you were hitched, Jupiter."

"As of this moment we are speaking only about my girlfriend. We aren't involving anyone else. Do we understand each other?" Two rasps came and went. "Her name is Miss Geneva French. I have not seen her for five days."

"Frenchy's playing hard to get, is she?"

"Her name is Miss French. Remember it." Jupiter closed his eyes and rubbed the center of his forehead with the tip of his stubby ring finger. "You worsen my headache."

"You should take something for that."

"You would propose, perhaps, strychnine?"

"I can recommend just the doctor for you. Sure."

Jupiter endured my smart remarks like a green warden at juvie hall. I kept up the pepper, but he managed to give me the rundown on his tootsie. I guess the old boy felt pretty riled. He worked up a lather just filling me in.

Jupiter made the acquaintance of Miss French at the Aragon Ballroom. I tried to picture Jupiter tripping the light fantastic—I tried and gave it up quick. One thing led to another until another thing led to French relocating to the Metro Beach Hotel. All the way down in Kenwood. Jupiter the sheik footed all the bills, of course—French knew a good thing when she saw it, all right. They developed a cozy routine. He popped by her digs once a week. Sometimes twice. Just to chin about culture and current events, I'm sure. Once or twice a month they'd run out to supper and maybe catch a floorshow.

"How long you two been keeping company?"

"It has been almost one year."

"That's a pretty long clip for a gold digger."

"We maintain no pretenses. I provide Miss French what she wants, she provides me what I want."

"The less said about that the better."

"You obviously don't care for me very much."

"That doesn't mean I can't work for you. So you want me to track down the dish. Then what?"

"*Dish.*" He worked his forehead again with his thumb. "My primary interest is to learn whether or not she's in any sort of trouble. I simply mean to find out that Miss French is all right. That must provide a shock to your cynical nature. The discovery that I have a heart?"

"You'll have to show me the x-rays."

"I want you to make sure that Miss French is not in any kind of difficulty, and then bring her back to me."

"But you're not telling me to force her to do anything against her will, are you?"

"I would never dream of such a thing. Besides, Miss French has very little will. Just make sure she is safe and sound, and bring her back. Nothing more, nothing less. Surely you can achieve that, can't you?"

Sure. Nothing more, nothing less. Cut and dried. It's all black and white when it comes down to people. We're the simplest creatures on the planet. Locate the mistress of a local racketeer? Simple and easy. Easy as shooting yourself in the heinie. Sure.

Fifteen minutes later found me in my coupe tooling south on Jefferson. A snapshot of Miss Geneva French fit snug in my jacket pocket, a healthy retainer burned a hole in my wallet. A quick detour led me to Manny's for that overdue early lunch. At least my stomach felt satisfied as I continued south to the Metro Beach Hotel.

The original Metro covered two square blocks, a regular lakefront fortress. It sprang up in the wake of the Columbian Exposition. As the smart set spread out to the South Side, resident hotels like the Metro fit the bill for those who wanted all the domestic services without the trappings of a house. The hotel provided guests with the lap of luxury. A big, fat lap at that. We're talking luxury with a capital *L*. Just the joint for Jupiter's ritzy love-nest.

Getting up to French's rooms proved a breeze. The pipsqueak guard dog of a deskman regarded me with a smile. He set to work on his huge console switchboard complete with headset and mouthpiece. He got the okay, gave me a nod, and wagged a finger towards the elevator. I tipped my brim.

The maid showed me in. As if I couldn't of figured it out myself. I knew right off she was the maid by the uniform straight out of central casting, right down to the feather duster poking out of her fist. So I said to her, "I take it you must be the maid."

"That's right," she replied. "I must be."

I flipped her my card and swept past her. I tossed my fedora on a white cushioned chair. The whole joint reeked in white. The sofa, coffee table, throw rugs, the works. All very swank. All ultra modern. All very soft. Everything done up in white. Like living inside a cotton ball.

"So you're a private detective man?"

"Just as the card says. You normally let just anyone drop in, sister?"

"All kinds of people comes and go at all hours. We're used to it." She dropped her head to look at me from the tops of her eyes. "And I ain't your sister."

"If you're used to all kinds, then maybe you don't mind answering some questions."

"I sure don't."

"I'd hate to break up your routine."

"I don't mind. I usually does the shopping right now, but the boy who drives me is fixing a flat."

"That's a break for me."

"C'mon, snoop. What're you selling?"

"I'm just looking for your mistress."

"Don't matter to me."

"Maybe you know where I can find her?"

"I sure don't."

"Well, when's the last time you saw her?"

"Oh, it's been days, mister."

"Is that regular?"

"With that one? Nothing regular about her. You never know what she about."

"She got any hobbies?"

"Mm hm. There's that Jupiter man."

"I know all about him."

"He give me the willies."

"Me too, sister. Not to mention a pain."

"Kind of low down? On your backside?" A faint smile crept over her sweet lips. "I tell you her most favorite hobby in the world, though."

"What could that be?"

"Spending the money."

"Spending the money."

"That her most favorite hobby. She just loves it." She waggled the duster.

"Don't let me stop you from your chores, if you don't mind talking as we go."

"I don't mind. I likes it when she vamooses—alls it takes is a little tidying here and there. When she's around, she's something of a little piglet."

The maid gave me a cook's tour of the place, dusting a knick-knack or two as we shuffled through. French's boudoir, white on white of course, bowled me over.

"Do you know," I said, "I could fit my entire office in this bedroom?" The maid folded her arms and leaned against the door. "A round bed, huh. You don't see that every day." I glommed onto a line of doors running the full extent of one wall. I pointed. "The closet?" The maid nodded. I whistled. "Do you mind?"

She shook her head. I proceeded down the line and swung open every door. "I'd say your mistress is in monumental trouble. She's down to her last couple hundred evening gowns."

"Mm hm. That's The Twenty-eight Shop, mister. That girl's just mad about The Twenty-eight Shop."

"Marshall Field's, am I right?"

"Uh-huh. Each and every Monday. Come rain or shine, hell or high water. Just like the postal man. The new dresses comes on Wednesday, and they're ready to model Saturday. But some whosit or other told Miss Geneva that the finest ladies never do the shopping on Saturdays, so she don't do that."

"She don't."

"No, she don't. But she down there the first thing every Monday morning."

"Every Monday like clockwork."

"Mm hm. That's right, mister. Lickety-split."

"Now isn't that a coincidence?"

"How so?"

"Today's Monday."

"Mister, maybe you just found her. Maybe that's where she been staying nights."

"You might be right, sister."

I left the maid with a wink and another card. I asked her to call if she thought of anything else regarding her no-show mistress. She said she didn't think all that much about her mistress. I told her one never knows. She told me one never do.

I paused by the desk to pump the clerk on my way out. Had he seen Miss French in the last week, etcetera? First, he apologized. Then he refused to divulge any information whatsoever regarding the guests. The milquetoast recited that with a broad grin that he must've been keeping in a drawer. I tipped my brim and pursed my lips.

When you've only got one lead, you might as well play it like one hell of a lead. Play it for all it's worth, if anything. Isn't that the same for you boys in uniform? Sure.

So I drove back north to the loop and hopped into Woolworth's. I shelled out for a single pack of Wrigley's Doublemint gum. I *insisted* on a bag.

"Yes sir!" The cashier's enthusiasm almost knocked my socks off.

Merchants are plain service happy. You can tell them you want to buy a single toothpick, from the middle of the package, you want it gift wrapped in the clerk's tie, and you want the floorwalker to spit in the bag. And have it delivered, too. They'll do it for you, all right, along with a dopey grin and jovial, "Come back real soon!"

I entered Field's with the Woolworth bag in hand. Went in the special elevator entrance at twenty-eight East Washington. Rode up to the main salon. Salon my eye—amounted to nothing more than a wide-open loft and a lot of ceiling to floor curtains.

The hostess greeted me, laying on the smarm like she percolated it. Call it contemptible effervescence. She kept her hands clasped together in front of her bosom. Her torso maintained a permanent tilt to one side. The poor thing never straightened up.

"Sure, you can help me," I said, dangling the Woolworth's bag nice and high. "I've got some toilet water here for Miss Geneva French. I'm supposed to deliver it."

"Thank you so, so much, my good man. You may leave it on that table, and I will see that Miss French gets it without any unnecessary delay."

"I'm to hand it over in person, get me?"

"I see, I see. That does pose a problem, now, doesn't it? Yes, it does."

"I don't see any problem with that, honey."

"I am afraid Miss French is not here. You see?"

"Ah."

"I'm afraid—"

"Gee, that's nothing to be afraid of, honey. But that is kind of raw. I was specifically instructed to meet her here. Has she already been?"

"No, Miss French has not visited us today. Not that we like to talk about our customers..."

"But you're so good at it."

"She is one of our dearest, dearest regulars. She never ever misses a Monday morning."

"Except today."

"Perhaps Miss French is running late from an earlier appointment. These things do come up."

"Running very late."

"If you'd care to wait? I could offer you a Frango Mint."

"No thanks, sister. They make my nose bleed."

That nixed the interview. I kept my Doublemint, she kept her Frango Mints, and I exited the joint.

Maybe the hostess was onto something. Maybe French simply got held up, legit. That would be the easy, simple answer. Maybe I'd get lucky after all. Maybe if I hung around long enough. Maybe it was a shot in the dark. Maybe it was the only shot I had. So far, my timing put me out of win, place and show. Even so, I decided to stick.

I took up a post across the street from The Twenty-eight entrance. I wore a hole in the sidewalk for an hour. Nothing to show for it. I lit another smoke and rang up my answering service from a phone booth. No messages.

After two hours, still no little Miss French. I picked up the afternoon edition of *The American*, checked in again with my service. Sergeant Drummond had called. Something about my deposition regarding Flint Mundy and Herbie Colgate—but that's another story. A screech of brakes and the wail of a car horn interrupted my note taking. I jerked around toward the sound of the ruckus. I caught sight of a young miss and a Yellow Cab. The taxi had stopped abruptly in the center of Washington Boulevard. The dame dashed around the taxi, hiking up her skirt and scooting her heels. The girl on the fly was Geneva French, in the flesh. I dropped the receiver like a sales pitch.

French scurried down the sidewalk in a beeline for The Twenty-eight Shop. I zigzagged across Washington in time to hold the door for her. I made her a gift of my choicest, wry smile. French glanced about, threw me one of those furrowed brow looks, twisted one corner of her mouth. She walked in, I walked in. I hopped on the elevator first and held that for her. We watched each other as the lift climbed to the main salon.

Something of a doll, Frenchy was. Marcelled, blonde hair, blue eyes— no surprise there. Long, narrow nose. Small, fat mouth. Pointed chin. Maybe not the prettiest face, but striking for its strength. She appeared quite a slim thing, definitely on the tall side compared to Jupiter. Doubtless on the young side compared to Jupiter, too. No surprise there, either. Textbook gold digger.

I stepped out first and made sure the elevator grating didn't bite her in the accoutrement. I stuck to her as she scuttled into the salon. The hostess approached us, toot sweet, as rigid and bent sideways as before.

"Miss French? This gentleman has been looking for you. He has."

"*Moi?*"

"*Oui*," I said.

"What can I show madam today?"

"Tell you what," I beat Frenchy to the punch. "We'd like to see something in a frou-frou."

Frenchy wedged a fist against her hip and rolled her eyes. "I bet you would," came under her breath. Then she smiled to the hostess, "Evening wear will do awful fine, thanks."

"Very, very good, madam." The hostess spotted more suckers on their way in. "If you'll have a seat in the fifth salon..."

We followed the beckoning, sideways remonstrations of our hostess and buzzed over to the fifth salon forthwith. Frenchy took a seat and crossed her legs. I paced the floor.

"Okay, bub, are you following me?"

"I've been waiting for you."

"Why's that?"

"I wanted to see you."

"What'd you want to see me for?"

"I wanted to talk to you."

"Are you trying to mix me up?"

"Why, is that difficult? Before you try to make heads or tails of that one, I know what you've been up to for the last week. You've been playing hide and seek and it's got your boyfriend all concerned and nervous-like. Daddy misses baby and wants to know what gives."

"Boyfriend? Which boyfriend are you talking?"

"I don't have time to play cat and mouse, sugar. *The* boyfriend. The one with the gambling racket. That money machine stuck out in the sticks. The guy what pays for the fancy digs and the clothes and all the extravagant paraphernalia."

"Paraphernalia?"

"The boyfriend with the heavenly name."

"Oh. Him."

"Yeah, him."

"Poor Jupy."

"So what gives, angel? You been stepping out on Jupiter?"

"Actually..."

"Yeah?"

"I'm all kind of jittery about it."

"I'll just bet you are."

"No, I mean it. I'm so hinky I don't know what.

"You're talking the new boyfriend?"

"That's what I'm saying."

"Has your new Lothario got a name?"

"Of course he's got a name. And it ain't Lothario."

This was going to take a while. "So tell me his name, already."

"Carlo."

"First, middle or last?"

"Carlo Spinetti."

"Carlo Spinetti."

"I don't know if he's got any middle name."

Let me cut to the chase here. Frenchy considered Spinetti pretty vavoom at first. Until he recently began pumping her about Jupiter. You

know, like he was working up some kind of dossier for his files. What
were Jupiter's habits? What were his routines? What's it like running a
casino? Worrying about security must be an awful headache—how does
that work, exactly? You get the drift.

At first, Frenchy found Spinetti's curiosity an amusing diversion. The
questions sounded innocent enough at first. Then, bit by bit, the
questions turned more specific, more pointed. He pressed her. He flat
out grilled her. Then he threatened her but good. He meant business. She
better not squeal if she knew what was good for. Etcetera. He scared her,
all right. Spinetti plain scared her out of her wits. She couldn't possibly
go to Jupiter about it, she said. That's how bad Spinetti gave her the
heebie-jeebies. And she had no one else to turn to. She got agitated to
the point that she feared being seen anywhere. She'd spent the last few
nights with an old friend from the Aragon.

"Male or female?"

"Jealous?"

I asked her what changed.

"Whaddaya mean?"

"I mean, here you are."

"Well, after all, there's some things a girl just can't give up."

"Uh-huh. You should've told Jupiter."

"I couldn't possibly!"

"You should have gone to him first thing."

"Don't you get it? Carlo said if I said anything it'd be curtains!"

"So what do you know? What could you tell?"

"Beats me."

"We're getting nowhere fast, angel."

"Looking back, I think—ain't that dreamy!"

A lilting figure flowed by, dripping in layers of chiffon. Like a well-
tailored moth.

"Sure, it's a pip. Now about Spinetti—did you hear any of his plans?"

"Can't say I did."

"Some kind of heist, maybe?"

"Mm mm."

"Maybe he let slip about knocking over the casino or hijacking Jupiter."

"Beats me."

"Aw, you don't know which side is up."

"He did talk on the phone a couple times with a man he called Zim. Or Zimmer, maybe. Something like that. Does that help?"

"Sure, it's a big help, baby. We may be sitting on a time bomb, but at least we know that a guy named Carlo Spinetti knows a guy by the name of Zimmer."

"Or maybe just Zim."

"Sure. Just Zim. Maybe he's an insurance agent. Or sells magazine subscriptions for *Casino Quarterly*."

"Now you're getting sore."

"Think, angel, think. Do you have any clue at all about Spinetti?"

"I did overhear him mention something about fireworks."

"Fireworks?"

"And it ain't even July."

"Does that make any sense to you at all?"

"Why should it? The rest of this conversation doesn't make any sense."

"We better go have a talk with Jupiter, pronto."

"But I can't! I told you!"

"You don't have a choice, angel. Don't you get it? Something's cooking and you're the only link."

"I don't want to be a link."

"That's why you should have come clean before. But you're going to talk to him now."

"I can't. I mean we can't. I mean Jupy's temporarily unavailable."

"What the hell is that supposed to mean?"

"He's probably at his hood convention by now."

"His what?"

"Jupy and a bunch of his old cronies hold this powwow once or twice a year. Get it? They put on the feedbag and put away a lot of hooch and swap yarns and who knows what else, you know? These are Jupy's pals, get me? Guys who run rackets from Lombard to the lakefront. I ain't crashing that kind of action."

"Are you telling me this is happening today?"

"Yeah. So?"

"You dizzy dame!"

Timing, sure. Everything kept adding up. I was heavy on equations, and the answers would have to be filled in later. I grabbed Frenchy's hand and yanked her in tow. I called out to the hostess as soon as we hit the main salon.

"We need a phone. An outside line. p.d.q."

"Oh, Oh. Well, that would be the payphones outside."

"You telling me you don't have an outside line?"

"We're not allowed, sir."

"Swell!" I pitched the Woolworth's bag onto a small table. "You can keep the toilet water."

I pulled French toward the elevator. She yanked back when she spotted a model whirling by in some billowy ebony number.

"Black is for funerals, Frenchy."

"You trying to scare me?"

"Just keeping you honest, sugar."

I got as much as I could out of Frenchy in the elevator. I'm talking info—some of you cops have awful dirty minds. The name of the restaurant: Chez Raconteur, at State and Cedar. The time: Jupiter's hood fraternity started meeting up, and boozing up, anytime after three. My watch said we were fifteen minutes past.

We hit the street. I shoved Frenchy into the closest phone box, slapped coins into her hands, ordered her to start dialing. Call the restaurant, I barked. Get Jupiter. Tell him to get the hell out of there now. She fumbled a coin into the slot.

Spinetti must've had something in mind, all right. Two and two still make four, don't they? It might've helped if I'd known anything about Spinetti, but I had no more line on the mug than I had on Edward G. Robinson. It sure felt like something was going to pop, but what did I have? I couldn't bring in the bulls on the basis of coincidences, a hunch and Geneva French. My hands were tied and time kept marching on.

Or just maybe it was all a false alarm. Much ado about nothing, and nothing to get bent out of shape about. Later I'd have one, big fat laugh over the whole thing. Sure I would. And my Aunt Sylvia is really the king of France.

I zipped across Washington and ducked into another phone booth. I nudged in my coin and rang up my pals at the Eighteenth—sure, we always come home. I wanted a line on Spinetti, fast. Sergeant Polhouse sympathized with me. He was real good at that. He said he'd like to help, especially in light of my past cooperation, but my request could take some time. That's what I was afraid of, I told him. He'd call back on my office line as soon as he came up with anything.

I hung up and peered across the street at Frenchy. I hunched my shoulders and threw up my hands. She hunched her shoulders and shook her head. I ran to her, dodging traffic all the way.

"Well?"

"Well nothing. I only got some dumb cluck of an immigrant who knew from nothing. He could barely understand me, and I was born here."

I crammed another coin into the box and told Frenchy to dial the number again. The joe that came on the wire knew nothing from Berlitz, that's for sure. He spoke with the thickest Italian accent this side of Taylor Street. A cliche straight off the boat if there ever was one. I couldn't get him past, "Who is a'speakin' please?" I tried. I told him that there was danger, something bad was going to happen, get me anybody who can speak English, tell Mr. Jupiter. I spun my wheels with the gee for several minutes when he finally summed it up rather neatly: "You talka craze." He rang off, I rang off. No soap.

I grabbed Frenchy by the shoulders. "You said State and Cedar, right?"

She nodded with open mouth. I turned and began a brisk walk east to my car parked on the other side of Wabash. Frenchy's heels clacked right beside me. I could've said something to her, tempted as I was, but I figured she could do as she liked.

"Where're we going now, for Pete's sake?"

"I have to catch up with your boyfriend. Something's about to pop, see? Big time. I don't know what, I don't know when, but it sounds to me like daddy Jupiter's about to make the hit parade."

"On the level?"

"That's how it adds up, baby."

We hopped into the coupe, I fired her up, and we took off down Washington. I hung a fast, hard left on Michigan and tried to gauge the traffic.

"I been thinking I don't know what got into me," Frenchy said.

"That makes two of us."

"I mean, why I fessed up to you like I did."

"What are you getting at?"

"Why I spilled, know what I mean? Told you everything about Carlo? I've been scared to death, but you asked and wham! I melt like lipstick on a radiator. I filled you in on just about everything, practically."

"Sure, you did. Sure."

"Maybe I oughtn't have said a word, but..."

"But what?"

"But I guess I couldn't help myself."

"And why is that?

"Anyone ever tell you you're kind of cute?"

"Are you kidding, sister?"

"I could sure go for you. In a big way."

I'm tearing down Michigan Avenue, speeding, weaving through traffic like nobody's business. The other crates are like moving pylons on some crazy test track. I'm on a life-and-death mission for all I know, and I've got some hot-to-trot moll giving me the eye.

"Admit it," Frenchy said. "You do like me, don't you? Just a little?"

"I'd rather have a Frango Mint."

We hit a snag without warning, traffic-wise, slowed to a crawl as we neared Cedar. I could see the cars ahead getting boxed in. At the Michigan-Oak intersection I punched the accelerator as the light turned yellow. I laid on the horn and snaked the coupe between the through lane and left turn lane, jogged over fast, and cut to the inner drive. About one block from Cedar, I slammed on the brakes, short-skidding just shy of a Packard's trunk.

"Take it easy, honey!" Frenchy checked her hairdo.

Three cars sat bumper-to-bumper in front of me. Beyond them a tow truck angled out from our lane into oncoming traffic. Three mugs stood next to the tow truck in heated conversation. I waved at the Hudson on my tail, threw the coupe into reverse, and backed into a ninety-degree turn. I popped her into first and forced my way through the opposite lane of traffic. I gunned it and spun out, fish-tailing into the curb. We made it in one piece, to my surprise, so I figured we were parked.

"Looks like I'm walking," I said.

"Looks like *we're* walking, honey."

"Suit yourself."

I hopped out, slammed the door, hoped for something brilliant along the lines of inspiration—I had zip. I took off in a fast trot toward Cedar. I left Mademoiselle Frenchy waiting for me to open her door.

At the next corner I ducked into one of those fancy, greystone apartment houses. You know the type, those exclusive, lakefront joints that employ short elevator boys like organ grinder monkeys with white gloves. I rushed up to the front desk, flipped open my wallet, flashed the concierge a peek at my private investigator's ticket.

"A phone, Skippy. Now!"

The egg stood dumbstruck. I darted around the counter. The gink backed way up, almost tripping over himself. I spotted the instrument and dialed my service. Frenchy peeked inside the doorway just as Veronica picked up my call.

"Hello, angel. Yeah, it's me. Sorry to cut off before. Couldn't be helped. You take any message from a Sergeant Polhouse? Uh-huh. Give it to me quick, angel. Uh-huh. No ordinary criminal? Oh, an agitator, I see. What do you mean, a Bolshevik? That doesn't make any sense. When's the last time you heard of a Bolshevik named Spinetti? Okay, sugar, if that's what he said, that's what he said. Anything else, angel? Okay. Gotta run. You're aces."

Frenchy did her best Harlow pose, one palm pressed against her torso, high above the waistline. "You had to stop to phone the girlfriend?"

"Thanks, Mac."

"Where you running off to now?"

"I got a date with a radical."

"What you mean, rabbit hole?"

I hightailed it out the door, flew around the corner and took off down Cedar. Frenchy hiked up her dress and scurried after me. A half-mile lay between Chez Raconteur and me, and I didn't know how much time I had—if I wasn't too late already. Should I mention I'm not exactly cut in the Ralph Metcalfe mold? I'm more of a Jesse Owens type. Not bad in a short sprint, see? I just don't have the wind and stamina for distance. I hit a good gallop and kept it up for three blocks.

One short block off I could see where Cedar came to a dead end at State Street. Chez Raconteur ran along the t-intersection on the other side of State. At two hundred feet I could see the big gathering on the restaurant patio.

There was no mistaking Jupiter, front and center, Geoffrey and Angus hanging on the wall behind him. In all, twelve men filled the seats down the long table. They made for a lively bunch. The party yapped and passed bottles of spirits and raised glasses. Jupiter kept popping up and down and bowing. Waiters came and went, serving and clearing, clearing and serving. Everything appeared as right as rain. Nothing out of place.

Between my gasps for air I heard the scuffling clicks of heels a ways behind me. I glanced over my shoulder. It was Frenchy, all right, one arm working like a pump organ, the other jacking up her dress beyond the allowance of etiquette. The burning in my lungs kicked in, looking for a deeper breath that I didn't have in me. I ratcheted down to a half-run, a brisk walk, and then a tired walk. I peered, slow, left to right across the intersection. Everything looked regular. Very regular.

I had no more than maybe one hundred feet to go when the oddest vision threw me for a loop. Maybe chalk it up to my light-headedness, but it appeared to float into view like an apparition. It drifted real easy down State, as though coasting on the slickest of blacktops. It rolled into view on the restaurant side of the street and I shuddered. I caught sight of the back windows covered in black curtains, and I gawked at the spectacle—a Daimler Double Six 40/50 Sport Saloon, one of only two in the whole metropolis.

I didn't take time to think about it. I broke into a fierce run down the middle of Cedar, headed straight towards the car. At the same time I reached beneath my jacket for the thirty-eight. I got off one round in the air, a warning shot to the patrons. All hell broke loose from there.

The party began to scramble as the explosion of a Tommy gun erupted from the backseat of the Daimler. The Thompson scattered its lead as the vehicle continued rolling past the diners. Glasses, plates, cups and saucers shattered under the barrage. The guests and wait staff scattered, ducked, clawed at the table and chairs, clawed at each other. The heavy slugs burst through cloth and flesh. Geoffrey reached for Jupiter as Angus jumped in front of them.

Pistol shots flashed in my direction from the driver's window, but the aim was wild and the slugs sailed by me. I returned two blasts and one must have found its mark—the car careened sharply to the left, jumped up a curb and took out a fire hydrant. The man with the Tommy flew from the car, low and fast, skirted the trunk, and brought the muzzle around in my direction. I was ready and emptied the thirty-eight without missing a beat. The shooter spun and recoiled from the gunshots, stumbled twenty feet from the momentum, and toppled over to land with a skid on the pavement in front of Chez Raconteur.

The sudden quiet fell heavy. Smoke from the Tommy drifted away like rising fog as water from the fire hydrant backed up in the curb. The scene played like a frozen piece of time. Still as a picture. As ugly a picture as I've ever seen. Then sounds of men in pain and the clatter of broken china rose as the targets attempted to recover themselves.

Restaurant workers began scurrying about with water and towels, sorting out the dead from the dying, the dying from the living.

I spotted Jupiter at the end of a side table laced with bullet holes. He dragged himself up and busily picked debris from his clothing.

I pocketed my rod and looked behind me. I made out Frenchy a couple hundred feet back down Cedar. She laid face up on the hood of a parked Mercedes. Her arms reached out to the sides and her legs crossed at the ankles. Two black holes had been ripped through her torso. Her dress was doused in red, and a kaleidoscope of crimson painted the auto and the street. She looked peaceful, all right. Take away the gunshots and the blood and she could have been sunbathing.

Just a couple minutes' difference, sure. A little heavier traffic, a little lighter traffic. If I hadn't called Veronica. Or hadn't waited two hours on Washington. If I would've grabbed a lousy breakfast just five lousy minutes earlier. If you found yourself in that position and you got the chance, would you swap one life for another? Sure.

I caught the driver's profile, pressed against the steering wheel, still as rust. I walked on. I passed the gunman's corpse as I approached the restaurant patio. Dead as prohibition. His eyes had the cold stare of the blind. Maybe that was Spinetti, maybe Zimmer. It could've been Alf Landon for all I knew. I left that one for the cops to sort out.

I headed straight for Jupiter, this absurd figure engulfed by an even more absurd surrounding. Encircled by assorted debris, mayhem leftovers made to order, the center of a macabre tableau—chewed up bodies of dead men, wounded men in agony, friends and colleagues who'd been raising glasses to him, smiling. This little, round man in the midst of a massacre's remains, stood preoccupied with the state of his attire.

"You look unscratched," I said.

"A bit soiled, perhaps. Nothing more. I trust these stains will never come out."

"Yeah. Blood always throws my laundress into a tizzy."

"Glass. There's nothing I detest more than tiny bits of glass."

"You know of a guy going by the name of Zim or Zimmer?"

"Should I?"

"I don't know. I'm asking you."

"Never heard of him."

Jupiter caught me looking down at his feet. Geoffrey and Angus hugged the floor, cold as concrete. One slug caught Geoffrey in the throat, another in the left cheek. The chopper did a number on Angus, chewing up his torso into dark oatmeal.

"Your little men played it straight down the line, Jupiter. I'll hand them that."

"Yes, didn't they?" Jupiter discovered a tear at his left shirt cuff. "They did what they were supposed to do."

"Uh-huh. They did, did they?"

"Yes, they did. That is what I paid them for."

"You really buy that, don't you? That's a hot one. You're going to stand there in the middle of all this and try to put that one over. That's the breaks and that's how the cookie crumbles. Angus and Geoffrey paid their dues and they took their chances. But all of that's jake because they were on the payroll. Is that how this pans out? Is that what you really think? You really believe you paid them enough for that? You think you can pay anyone enough for that?"

Jupiter stopped fussing. His little black beads gave me a hard, hard look. The wheeze became amplified, uglier than usual.

I shoved my hands deep into my pockets, spun on my heels and stalked away. Thirty paces off I caught myself and pivoted three-sixty to face Jupiter. I called over to him.

"By the way." I almost smiled. "You'll want to know I found Miss French." I stopped to light a cigarette. I pulled a deep drag. "She's back there, Jupiter." I motioned with my thumb. "By the Mercedes." I walked off without another word. Sailed right past Frenchy down Cedar.

Bad timing, all right. It was the height of rush hour. And there'd be ambulances and black and whites to contend with.

Statement No. 9:
G-Man

Stick me on a Chinese menu, scrambled as anything. Can't make out if I'm going out or coming in. Probably something they slipped me. Something damn strong. Potent as Turkish coffee spiked with a Mickey Finn. Do I look like I swallowed a Mickey? I feel like I swallowed a Mickey. Sure I do. I could do a loop-the-loop flat on my back.

Jokes keep springing to mind. A fine how do you do in my state. Bum jokes, and I can't for the life of me see what's so funny about them. I'll tell you what's really funny. See, if I cut to the chase, you'll miss half the story. Get it? The chase? Before that—I remember before that. Sure. That old bird came before that.

The old bird and the valise and the snow. Heaps of snow. Thick, wet snow. And gunshots. Wounds, blood, death. Thick, wet death. The left side of my face's still numb. I got cuffed, you know. I remember that.

You fellas in the habit of taking statements off of gurneys? This'll be my first. That's something to write home about. The old man won't be volunteering any statement. Now there's a punch line that's wanting. He could tell us plenty, but he's got nothing to say. Never had the pleasure of a formal intro. But I met him, all right. Just shows up, out of the blue, just like that. No name. No *how's every little thing?* Did I tell you already? Came in like a sneak attack, he did.

The door sailed, like to come off its hinges, flung open as if walloped by Joe Louis himself. It slammed against the inside office wall, *bang*. The frame shook, the frosted glass panel rattled. Nothing chipped, nothing shattered. *Bang.* That's when the old boy shambled in.

Those pants legs. They fell an inch short of heavy shoes that scraped across the floorboards, caught and bunched up the thin rug. The cuffs soaked, and I mean but soaked. The plain, black overcoat wore out more than a cocktail waitress's honor during happy hour. Shoulders, damp. Fedora, soft and black and sloped far over his gaunt face. The brim and crown of the hat good and doused, too. His neck bent, head forward, chin dropped to the chest, the dry mouth working for every breath. Yeah, the guy's in a state.

The bird's shaky arms squeezed tight this small duffle job to his body, just above waist level—it must've weighed plenty by the way he hunched over. One of those rich brown valises, all in leather with two straps wrapped short ways around, cinched hard along dark, brass buckles. A thick padlock secured the bundle.

The jasper hauled it as far as the customer side of the desk. He coughed, a weak, thin spray of a hack, collapsed hard into the library chair like a dropped anchor. And that bag clattered. Screwy thing. Low and metallic.

His ancient face twisted my way, turned upward, gray as the late edition. The dull, blue eyes wandered about, the searching gaze of a deserted child—then they lit on me.

"You know." His frail rasp made you strain, lean in, listen harder. "The—the—"

His chin sunk to his chest. The narrow shoulders slumped and his arms relaxed. The duffle sagged and slipped onto his lap. His eyes fluttered shut. The mouth cut loose two more breaths and went still.

I pushed up and out of the swivel chair and dashed around the desk. I fingered the old man's throat. Folds of skin registered moist and cool, with as much beat left as busted timpani. The old boy'd had it.

I dug out a butt from my breast pocket, struck a match and took a picture through the sulfur's flare. His drained pan, a dark stain caked up on the side of the duffle next to his body, shredded cloth where a couple slugs must've ripped through his overcoat and dug straight into the gut.

It's sure that even the crustiest of mugs couldn't have hiked too far, not with a couple pills pumped into them. Not slinging around that curious package. The old bird hadn't seen sixty for some time. An easy candidate for seventy. And maybe then some. You'll have to check with the county on that. Death has its own way of toying with age.

"That was downright peaceful," I said. "Considering."

My guest looked up from the couch, tossed me a tight-lipped sneer. "Yeah. That was damn peaceful, like anybody gives a goddamn." He wrenched his jaw, flicked his chin. "Now close that door and keep your hands off the bag like a good little man."

"Sure, sure I will." I stared into my guest's wide-set eyes without losing track of the nickel-plated forty-five automatic he trained on my pump. "You mind telling me what's in the package?"

"Yes, I would mind."

I threw the door shut, swiveled back, and stood with my hands on my hips. "Now what?"

"By any chance are you acquainted with the deceased?"

"Uh-uh. I could say a few words over him, but my heart wouldn't be in it. Maybe you'll do the honors, if he was a close pal of yours. Of course a mug like you probably doesn't make many friends, close or otherwise, what with your lack of social graces and all."

"Yes, I know him. That's none of your beeswax. Nothing for the likes of you to worry about."

"I'm glad you said that. I was getting all nervous like, you strong-arming your way in here and pulling a gat, and then this old-timer croaking in my chair. But that's all okay, now. As you say, I've nothing to worry me. Everything's copacetic. I haven't a thing to kick about."

The thug's wide mouth curled into a thick, pained smile. His lackluster eyes conveyed the soulless quality of a mannequin. His hushed voice pressed out every consonant, a disturbing sibilance that struck a cross somewhere between the hiss of a snake and a porterhouse sizzling on a grill. "You're an amusing fellow, for a shamus."

"Sure, that's me. I used to fill in for Martin and Lewis at The Palace. What do you do for an encore?"

"We have places to go. You'll need your hat and coat." He jerked the gun barrel towards the rack by the door.

I stubbed out my smoke in the chromium floor stand next to the old man. He must of lost a lot of blood along the way. Even in death the knobbed fingers dug into the side of the bag. I grabbed my hat off the hook and pulled on my topcoat. "Want to leave the thirty-eight? If you don't mind?"

"No," my guest said. He calmly toyed with the revolver in his left hand. "I don't mind one teensy bit."

He rose unhurriedly from the couch—that was kind of hard to make out on account of his height being all of five-one. He presented a well-pressed little figure, clean and neat, like a new ironing board. With a personality to match. Every stitch on him in black except for the white socks. From the back, he could've been a kid playing dress up. Short, sideways steps led *the kid* behind my desk while the forty-five kept its bead on me. He yanked open the center drawer, dumped the rod, shoved closed the drawer, careless.

Little Lord Fauntleroy hoisted the duffle out of the old man's lap as he swung by. Lifeless arms drooped to the side and the body sagged to the left. Some kind of weight in that valise caused my visitor to rear back with his upper body. I led the way out and hung by the door.

"What are you doing, fella?" he said. "Have I forgotten something?"

"Mind if I lock up?"

"Ah, yes. You do that, shamus. By the way, where is your car parked?"

"I'd be delighted to take you for a ride, if that's what you want."

"Enough falderal. Let's depart. And strive to remember that we're both professionals, isn't that right? Keep in mind I've always got you covered. If you blink funny, I'll thread one through you faster than sunlight. Just like that. Without a second thought. It will only take one. You got that?"

"Sure. And if you let your guard down for even an instant, I'll splinter your neck like a chopstick. You got that?" I think he got it, all right. He didn't say.

I conducted my watchdog to the rear of the building, out to the fire escape. A thick, heavy snow had fallen on and off most of the day—it was back on. The blurred sky cast uninspiring shades of gray across our little corner of the world. Our steps spattered through the clumps of off-white slop as we trudged down the iron steps. We sloshed our way to the side alley and followed that to my car. My uninvited guest told me to get in. I got in. He got in. He set the forty-five's muzzle at rest on the duffle in his lap, pointed straight at me. Your cross-eyed uncle could not miss at that range. Even my Aunt Sylvia could've hit the jackpot.

"So what'll it be? The Cook's tour? I'd like nothing better than to show you Graceland."

"Head downtown."

"And after?"

"Head downtown."

"Anyone ever tell you that you blab too much?"

He sneered. He made it look natural.

I inched the coupe to the end of the alley. Traffic floated down Clark Street slow and steady. I slipped the coupe into the southbound lane. Every now and then Little Scarface snapped his head about with a ducking motion to peer through the tiny rear window. Reminded me of an automated sprinkler. The rest of the time he fixed his cool, mannequin glare on me, out-staring the steely stare of the forty-five.

One panorama slopped into another across the windshield. The wipers slapped left, slapped right, the snow globe view went crystal clear, then just as quickly got all fuzzy through the blobs of melting snow. The cars and cabs and buses and pedestrians looked done up in blurred watercolors. I got tired of squinting. I got tired of watching the wipers dance. I was already fed up with Little Caesar's calling the shots. I clenched the steering wheel until it hurt.

"You're going to tell me what's in the bundle?"

Silence.

"Or where we're really going?"

Nothing.

"Talking to you is like smooching an inner tube."

"No questions, no answers, shamus."

We cut over on Wacker, crawling along with traffic toward the Civic Opera House. Crawling like so many, slop-covered beetles. My host kept checking behind us. The constant surveillance went beyond mere vigilance. The mug expected something, something in the shadows. Something followed him. Or waited for him. It bugged him like a false note, whatever it was. I couldn't get a read on his reactions. I tried, but Wild Bill played it blank as white bread.

An unexpected break, a sudden gap in traffic, and we picked up speed. Until a smothered burst erupted. The coupe jolted. Her left front nosed down, careened into a curving, splashing skid. We skimmed the asphalt like an ice floe, pulling a real Nanook number, spraying white and gray sheets in our wake. We spun all the way around. The rear, passenger side caught on something, pulled and scraped, and we sloshed to a stop at the ramp entrance to Lower Wacker Drive.

"A blow out?" he asked. "How do you pull off a blow-out in this weather?"

"That was no blow-out."

A muffled crack rang out, followed fast by a sharp *ping* at the trunk of the coupe. I slunk down and craned my neck enough to peek around the seat. Clyde swung open his door, slid out and crouched behind it. One hand brought up the roscoe, the other gripped tightly on the bag at his feet. Five car lengths back I spotted him, this yahoo leaning halfway out of a standing Yellow Cab, squeezing off potshots. My pal let fly a couple slugs that burst the taxi's windshield like glass fireworks.

The gunman fired one shot, ducked out of the cab, fired once more, spun himself like a whirling dervish behind and around to the opposite side of the hack. Both shooters exchanged another three rounds, shot for shot.

As the pellets rained against the coupe, surrounding traffic ground to a dead stop. Most of the drivers and passengers flung themselves onto their car seats or floors. A few brazen souls braved the slush, scrambling and crawling their way to the curb. Either they had wills of iron or yellow streaks longer than the lakefront.

A slug shattered the coupe's rear window and showered the front seat with fragments. I thought, *You guys are nuts!* I thought it, but I didn't say it. Two loose canons playing Tombstone, in the middle of Wacker, in broad daylight, and me without my opera glasses.

I crouched and crept my way out of the coupe's driver side. I sneaked a quick glance this way and that—the coupe sat dead center in the street, smack in the middle of Wacker, wide open, a sitting duck as prone as the Hindenburg on the fifty yard line at Soldier Field. I squatted low as I could and scooted around the trunk. I hugged close to the bumper and inched my way behind Dillinger.

I kneeled close up and barked, "This another friend of yours?"

Capone had just reloaded. He checked his grip on the satchel, his finger on the trigger, ready for the next frenzy of slugs. Baby Face popped up and caught one square between the eyes. The impact snapped back his neck, spun his torso like a top, and two things occurred in rapid order. The first thing: as he spun, the rod flew out of his right hand, skipped and slid its way through the street slush in the right lane—I watched it sail. The second's a lulu: as he spun, his left arm wheeled the duffle and clocked me a good one across the face. I took the brunt of the blow on my left cheekbone.

I struggled to maintain my balance, gave it my best shot, realized I was already laid out. The johnny by the cab must have been in the dark because he kept sprinkling pills into the coupe's hood and doors. I blinked through the dizziness and caught sight of Napoleon Jr., a crumpled box of Cracker Jack without the prize. Between the bottom of the door and the street I spied the shooter bobbing back and forth from behind the taxi.

I lunged, strained for the duffle, slid it towards me through the slush, leaned on it, wrangled myself to my knees. The contents felt stone hard with no give. The gunman slammed a couple, timed rounds into the door, getting a read on the situation. I glanced left and right. No kind of cover to be found—the stopped traffic stood too far away. He had me pinned but good. I copped a quick glance behind me at the ramp leading down to the shadowy, green luminance of Lower Wacker. Thanks, Mr. Burnham. Sure.

I flexed my jaw, hitched my shoulders, and dashed for the ramp. The damn duffle dragged like a bucket of plaster and held me back until I worked up some momentum. The shooter must've spotted me. A couple slugs whizzed by awful close as I ran, slid and otherwise skidded down the sloping lane to the underground drive.

Lower Wacker's a cavernous throughway, a subterranean crazy house. For mirrors, chutes and rails, it's filled with limestone, green lamps, echoes. You're never certain about the reverberations you hear in Lower Wacker. Maybe they belong to you, maybe to something unseen up ahead, maybe something after you from behind. Or maybe something on another level. Or maybe it's your pulse beating in your ears like an oil derrick from lugging a satchel filled with pig iron.

At the foot of the ramp I maneuvered across the limestone barricades to the opposite side. I set off along the northbound lane, straining to pull off a fast walk. I never heard of anyone hitchhiking on Lower Wacker—I planned to be the first. I kept checking the emerald shadows in back of me, but no cars in sight. The recessed fixtures didn't throw light, they glowed like neon, casting a dim haze of jade twilight on the silent roadway. Between my huffs and puffs I listened for my assailant.

I pressed along until my lack of wind eclipsed the throbbing pain in my cheek. I fell against a cool wall and felt the perspiration running from beneath my hat. For a moment time stood still or took a backseat or become altogether irrelevant.

Pounding footsteps and the crack of a shot snapped me out of it. I made out his dark figure in the foggy green, half a block back and gaining. I hugged the wall and slid myself along until the slightest bobbing of light made my shadow rise and fall like a teeter-totter. I spun about and caught sight of a vehicle coming up behind the shooter.

I stepped a foot from the wall to give the gunman a big, fat target and draw him out. I dropped the bag, tried to catch my breath. He scampered into the traffic lane to get a clear bead on me. I heaved up the duffle and moved as quickly as I could.

The blaring of a car horn wailed, the sharp shriek of tires tacking a sharp turn, the peculiar mix of both sounds as the echo wound through the Drive. The car came up fast, sped by me. I turned around and spotted the gunman pulling himself up, hopping on one leg.

I hauled the valise up the next exit ramp, fighting the angle and the weight, legs burning, all the way, battling for air and traction on the incline. Lugging the bag against my chest, same as the old man, I shuffled out from the ramp. I'd lost track of time—the sunlight had packed it in, the snowfall relentless, large flakes glittering through the beaming streetlamps like sparklers. I stumbled across the wide, deserted intersection with the elevated train tracks overhead, and came to a railing overlooking the river. I dropped the bag at my feet, leaned over the rail, listened to the sound of my forced, heavy breaths. An El train rolled and roared above me, its shrieking metallic whine shattering the silence. After it passed I heard a solitary tread of uneven steps scraping in the distance behind me.

The shooter hobbled his way to the top of the ramp. He spotted me, limped across the intersection with the jerky gait of a three-legged dog. The rod rose in my direction as he neared. I used whatever strength I had left and hoisted the duffle onto the top of the railing—the gunman paused at the sight, posed in the middle of the street like a broken scarecrow. A lone car skirted its way around the gunman and drove on. He renewed his feeble tread and slowly worked his way closer.

When he reached the curb, I raised the bag and held it out beyond the railing. He got the message, all right, and stopped. He wavered, his frame bent slightly, his weight on the left leg. Only the toe of his right shoe lightly touched the pavement. I'd bought a moment or two. I didn't know how many more moments I could buy. I didn't know how long I could manage a standoff. I didn't know anything because I wasn't thinking. All he had to do was wait me out, let the load in the arms do the work, wait for my muscles to give out, give up.

We ignored the traffic, straggling pedestrians, the snow, the man in the moon. My eyes fixed on the gun barrel and his eyes fastened on the duffle. He cocked the gat and took aim. I feinted a jerk of the arms. We both froze in place as a slight breeze spun the snowflakes around us like a knick-knack globe.

I had the nerve, but not the muscle. I couldn't hold out. The spent bands in my arms went to jelly and quivered. It took merely an instant, the slightest relaxing of the fingers, a lost sense of touch, and the duffle slipped from my grasp.

I lunged forward. The shooter squeezed. A pill bit and burned through me above the left shoulder blade. The impact knocked me forward and I struck my chest against the retaining wall. My head sagged and I spied the bag rolling off the embankment onto the river, propped up momentarily on a thin piece of ice. Then the duffle broke through and sunk below the dark sheen of still water.

The gunman stood next to me, gawking as the last bubbles rose, broke to the surface, and dissolved back into the dark sheen. I began sliding down against the railing, but the shooter braced me up with one hand clenching my overcoat collar. He burrowed the gat into my gut. The hammer sounded a hollow click when he pulled the trigger. I used my good arm to slap his hand away and the roscoe spun out of his grasp. His hands came up fast and wrapped tight around my throat. I grabbed his wrist with one hand, my other arm too numb to lift.

Half my face felt half-dead, I could sense the hole in my shoulder, the wound oozing beneath my clothes like I'd sprung a leak. My legs begged to give out. You could say I was near useless. More than useless. I was done for. His dark face contorted as he bent my upper back beyond the rail. I felt the coolness of the end coming over me, saw the flakes dancing past his narrowed eyes. His breathing became rapid and bellowed thick as fog from his mouth. He shook me like he was shaking the last drops of life out of me—he probably was. Then I detected a high-pitched ring.

It started somewhere off in the distance, faster than a blink of an eye, but my senses played things as a slowed reality. I heard a thin whir, the descending whoosh of a large insect flying by, or more like the high-speed whistle of a rifle shell. He slammed into me, almost threw us over the rail, but we caught up on the wall's top ledge and rocked back. We collapsed to the sidewalk. He hacked out a scarlet mist as we fell, leaning heavy against me all the way. I gasped for air and fell to my knees on the wet pavement.

The quick, even slapping of shoe leather came nearer, nearer. I gazed up at an auto parked with one wheel over the curb, a blurred, running figure, a rifle held across his body. He reached me and peered down. He smirked at the body in front of me, leaned down and almost fingered the clean hole drilled through the back.

"Lucky I didn't get you, too."

"I'm the luckiest man on the face of the earth. Sure. You're wearing white socks."

"The bundle?"

"Taking a bath.

"No matter."

"What's in it?"

"Lead."

"That's it?"

"Lead weights. Just a dodge."

"What did they think it was?"

"Counterfeit plates."

"But the first one. The one who stuck me up. He was an agent."

"Save your breath. There's a bus on the way."

"But his buzzer. I got a good look."

"He's federal, but that wasn't his badge. They were both of them agents."

"A G-Man?"

"Yeah."

"What's his real name?"

"Can't tell you that."

"What's your name?"

"Knox."

"Like where they keep the gold?"

"Just like that. Now stop being stupid and clam up. Just sit quiet and wait for the meat wagon."

"Stupid, that's me. Stupid enough to be suckered by a turncoat government man. Stupid enough to let him get the drop on me. Stupid enough to not give in when it would have been the easiest thing in the world—just leave the satchel. Give it back, even. Instead, I'm just stupid enough to get clobbered in the face and take one in the shoulder and probably contract double pneumonia, all for the sake of a hunk of lead."

"Does sound kind of stupid," Knox smiled.

"Maybe you get that way in Washington, once in awhile, maybe. I play at stupid a lot. Sometimes my line of work calls for it."

Statement No. 10:
Jane Doe

She gave off the impression of being alone, all right. Abandoned child alone. War widow alone. A class all by itself. That grade of alone you only run across in a city of three million strangers. You go for blocks and see nothing but strangers. Miles on end. Strangers far as the eye can see. Strangers with stories all their own and problems all their own. Strangers who look this way, that way, any way at all as long as it's the other way.

Another hunk of human flotsam. A leftover, a scrap. Ignored as a park bench in January. Discarded like that gee waiting for the pellets of Nevada gas to dunk into the acid. That man who can't focus on anything beyond the thick chamber windows. That man with numbered days, with no tomorrow, as good as forgotten. That's alone, and that's how she read.

I've seen some odd ones in my time. That one caught me off guard. Full of atmosphere, that one. Mysterious forebodings. You boys like that? Forebodings? I'll have you going all a'tremble. Sure.

But she must have clued you in already. She must have laid it all out for you. It's her story and she can tell it now. For a while there it was touch and go. I had my doubts. Plenty. You'd of had your doubts, too. Anybody would've.

You're just looking for a little corroboration, isn't that right? You've got to make sure the evidence jives with her story. Coming and going. I'll square it up for you, all right. We'll have it all tied up in pretty pink ribbon. The captain likes pink ribbon, doesn't he? I know I heard that one place or another.

Call it the case that wasn't. This was no case at all. I was minding my business when she popped into my life. Maybe it's more like I butted into her life. I guess that's neither here nor there.

I can't tell you how long it took before I noticed her. I can't even tell you how long she'd been there. Had no idea what she was doing there.

For all I knew she could of been waiting for something. Could be she waited for someone. Could've been as simple as waiting for the bus. But it wasn't.

One bus passed by. Then another. Passengers got on, passengers got off. Miss Lonelyhearts remained on the bench, screwed to it, staring at the hands in her lap. I took note.

Raven hair framed her square face with cropped bangs, the sides curled to points at the jaw. She wore a heavy, grey cardigan wrapped close around. Could've been a guy's sweater, it ran so large. Wide and loose at the shoulders, ending inches below her hips. A plain, white organdy dress, ankle length, flowed from beneath the sweater. From where I watched it appeared stained or soiled down the front. The shoes, simple black flats. She carried no purse, no shoulder bag, no clutch.

I paid my check and caught sight of a third bus. It pulled up across the street and blocked my view of the bench. I could make out the movement of passengers inside the bus as they jostled and shuffled into place. The vehicle lurched into gear, began to glide forward, and rolled its way from the curb and into traffic. I could see the bench again. She read all alone, all right.

I exited the restaurant and lit a cigarette. I stood under the sidewalk awning and smoked and watched her from across the street. She existed in her own world. What world that could have been escaped me.

It got me thinking about another young jane. A woman I never met. A woman who one day just up and disappeared. I can't imagine that one's ever coming back. I recalled her father and the story he handed me. About the way he lost his wife, too. The poor sap seemed lost without his daughter. I guess he'll go on feeling like that for a long time.

As I watched and smoked and studied her, some sorry-looking joe approached the bench. Real down on his luck sorry-looking. His advance startled her back into this world. She clutched harder at the sweater and wrapped it tighter. He spoke at her, yapping and gesturing with outstretched palms. She gazed down at the street and shook her head. The vagabond kept up the patter. He wouldn't blow. He kept at her and he kept at her.

I griped to myself through a puff of smoke. I figured the last thing the lady needed was this tramp. I took a quick pull, flicked the butt into the curb, and crossed Clark Street. I stopped when I hit the far end of the bench. I faced the girl square, hands in my pockets. I looked her straight in the eye. She clutched at the throat of the cardigan and brought her dark eyes my way. A white cloth or handkerchief wrapped around her left hand. The beggar shut his trap at the sight of me.

"Drift," I said.

I only had eyes for her, but the tramp knew who I meant. His mouth dropped open. They both gave me the stare. Yeah, I'd take her gaze over his any day.

"I said drift."

The tramp's mouth closed and popped open again, a couple times, and he turned tail and scurried off. Something about me must've told him I wasn't fooling. That made things all right. The day a gumshoe can't run off a hobo is the day to apply at the civil service.

The girl tilted her head to one side, big eyes taking me in, making a real good study of it. I didn't budge. I figured if she wanted to take a good look, I'd let her take a good look. If I could put up with it in the shaving mirror, she could put up with it, too.

Close up she was real easy on the eyes. Those angled, brown orbs set off by a strong, aquiline nose. Full, almost pouting lips. This one wore no makeup—she didn't need any as I far as I was concerned.

In the midst of this silent scrutiny a doddering, old bird wobbled her way around me and sat between us on the bench. We never stopped gazing at each other. The old bird fussed with her purse until a number fifty-one drew up. I assisted the old thing into the vehicle. The bus pulled away from the curb and left us alone like we were before.

I raised my chin to her. "I'd say you're in trouble, sister."

She brought her hands up to her throat. Her forehead crinkled with concern. "What did I do?"

"That was an observation, not an accusation."

"Oh."

"Strikes me like you could use a hand."

She gaped at her shoes, then brought those big brown eyes to mine, slow.

"I spotted you from that deli. People don't usually park themselves on bus stop benches for general amusement or to pass the time of day."

"They don't?"

"No, not usually they don't. Mostly they'll go in for a picture show at the Oriental. Maybe at the Woods. Maybe catch an exhibit at The Field Museum, or drift through the zoo. Or catch a ball game, maybe. Tourists go for the view from the top of the Prudential. But hardly no one just sits on a bench."

"I don't know who I am." She blurted it out. Frank as that. Like she meant it.

"That's a riddle and a half, sister."

"I guess it is." She raised and lowered her shoulders quickly.

"You mean you don't remember anything."

She raised and lowered her shoulders quickly.

"A lost lamb, are you?"

She crinkled her forehead again.

"Were you planning on staying here all day?"

"I have no plan. No idea."

"Would you like me to get the police?"

"No, don't do that. The idea frightens me."

"It does, does it? All right, lamb."

She kept gazing at me. A deep, full gaze.

I said, "I don't know what you expect to see. I don't have any answers. I barely know the questions."

"I know." She looked away for just a moment. "I don't know."

"You don't leave a fella a whole lot of choices. I guess there's nothing to do but get you some grub. Are you hungry?"

"A little bit. I don't have any—"

The sweater fell open for a moment. She realized what happened, grabbed it quick, wrapped it close.

"Skip it, sister. I can't imagine your appetite would break anybody's bank."

I stepped off the curb and leaned into the street. I turned to look behind me. She hadn't moved.

"Come on, lamb," I said calmly. I started to cross and tilted my head. "Come on."

She rose slow and followed me, hesitating, lagging several steps. I waited for her beneath the awning, holding the door. For what it was worth I led her to a table towards the back. There's no such thing as a quiet booth at the Belden. I placed a business card on the table and slid it over as the waitress showed.

"That's right, Patricia," I said. "I'm back. Bring the lady here some scrambled eggs, white toast, orange juice and coffee."

"No coffee, please."

"I'll have the coffee, Patricia—just a moment." I turned to the lamb. "Show me your left hand, angel. Palm up."

She placed her hand on the table, gently. She rolled it over. A stain of dried blood created a blurred crease across the cloth wrapping.

"You have any bandages, Patricia? Or maybe just a clean handkerchief. Can you do anything about that?"

"We'll fix her up," Patricia winked at me. Pat's smile could warm up a judge at a murder trial. "Come on, honey."

The lamb gave me a hesitant look.

"It's all right, angel. You go ahead."

Patricia turned the grin up a couple degrees. The lamb clasped the cardigan tightly at her throat, slid out of the booth, and followed Patricia to the ladies' room.

Patricia returned in a couple minutes with the coffee and orange juice. "Sweet doll you got there," Patricia sniffed. "Something of a mess, I'd say. That doesn't look like any of your doing."

"That's right, Pat. Just performing my good Samaritan bit."

"You just keep it up, honey."

The lamb got back to the table in time to exchange a hesitant smile with Patricia. She said, "Thank you," with a half-nod.

"Don't mention it, hon." Patricia winked over her shoulder.

"Stand there for just a moment," I instructed. She did as I asked. "Turn it around." She did, craning her neck my way. "Okay, you can sit down now. Those light smears down the front of your dress look like paint. The dark streaks are blood."

She cleared her throat. "The buttons at the top of my dress are missing. I'm not wearing a bra."

"How about panties? You wearing those?"

"Yes."

She showed no shame or embarrassment. No hesitation in her voice.

"Those blood stains on your dress—"

I waited while Patricia dropped off the eggs and toast.

"Go ahead, lamb, dig in."

"What about the blood stains?"

"Un-huh. Your hand sure didn't make those stains on the dress. Too much blood for that."

"I'm not hurt anywhere else." She spoke between bites.

"Do you remember anything at all?"

"Nothing. You're a private investigator?"

"Sometimes more private than others. What's the last thing you recall?"

"Just walking along the street. Clark Street." She glanced towards the front windows and back down at her plate. "That's all. I was walking up Clark Street and felt so awfully tired. I had to sit down think. When I did, there was nothing to think of. That scared me."

"Sure."

"How long have you been a private detective?"

"Feels like a couple of lifetimes."

"Hmm. Curious. Is that a tough sort of life?"

"Whatever you say, kid."

"You rescue a lot of damsels in distress?"

"You're the first missing person I've ever bought lunch for." That effort got a very nice grin out of her. "So you came up Clark."

"Yes. I look around me, and there I am, shuffling along the sidewalk. It's as though I simply showed up, almost out of thin air."

"As though you just woke up? Or came to?"

"Yes...in a way. With all these strangers buzzing past. Taking notice of me, then not. The cars. The traffic signals and signs. I began moving faster, and faster, until I had to sit down. I felt I had to. I tried to think. But empty. You see? I knew I was on a bench. I saw buses and stores. Webster, Clark, Grant, Belden. Only street signs. They didn't mean anything. Does that make any sense?"

"Just like you know how to read. How to talk and walk."

"Yes."

"Nothing signifies nothing. None of it means a thing."

"Yes, that's right. Nothing I saw meant anything to me."

She gave me the emptiest look in the world, this quiet, sweet pan wearing an expression blank as a skillet. A thing like that can spook you, if you let it.

"Anything else?" Patricia asked.

The lamb closed her eyes. She gave her head a slight shake.

I said, "If you don't mind, Patricia, see if there's any kind of label in that sweater."

The lamb crinkled her brow at me while Patricia took a peek inside the collar. "The Thrifty Men's Shoppe," Patricia read. "That's spelled *shopee*. Nothing but the best for our little girl. No store label in the dress."

"Good gal. You got a phone book behind the counter?"

"Sure do. Back in a jiff."

"Might pan out to be a lead. Then again, might not."

"I suppose a maybe is better than a nothing."

"You want a cigarette? Do you smoke?"

"I don't know. I guess not, thank you."

I lit up and pulled off a couple drags before Patricia came back with a Wells Street address. I settled up with Patricia and stood.

"What do you say, kid? Fortified enough for a walk?"

"Sure. Walking I can do. Thanks awfully for the square."

We started out headed south on Clark. We set a leisurely pace. It made sense to give backtracking a shot. She had come to at Webster. Before that, everything blanksville. I tried pointing out this and that and the other thing in the long-shot hope of ringing a bell. All real low pressure, of course. I kept it real casual, low-key. Clark Street could've been the surface of the moon for all she made of it. People, shops, diners, laundries, streetcars. As good as a foreign country to her. Like she's just off the boat. All the while she kept a tight grip on the cardigan with her right hand. Her left played with my business card, flipping it over and over in her fingers.

"Have we passed your office?"

"Not yet. Coming up." I pointed ahead. "About a half-block before Dickens."

We stopped when I thumbed towards the entryway to my building. She gave it a good once over.

"I could've told you. Nothing special."

"Can we take a look inside?"

"You're the subject of this investigation, not me. Keep walking, kid." The fleeting glance she shot me accompanied an appealing curve of the lips.

We kept quiet for the next four blocks. We took a hundred-foot jog on Lincoln, skipped over to Wells, strolled down the east side. We passed an occasional shop on the street level. A single-family house tucked in between here and there. Mostly older residences. Red brick and brownstone two flats. Four flats. Nothing taller than three stories.

"Anything familiar?"

She pressed her lips together and swung her head.

About two blocks down we hit upon the tiniest gallery. I paused to light a smoke and took a peep in the display window. We found a range of contemporary works, most of them city landscapes. A couple abstracts comprised of large sections of bright colors broke up the monotony.

Towards the back of the window I spotted a portrait. The artist had broken the surface of the canvas into flat planes of muted colors. The female subject posed on a straight-back chair. She held one arm slung behind the back of the chair. Her gaze came straight out at us, direct and cool. You felt as though you were the painting and she was staring at you.

"I don't know art..." I turned to the lamb. She looked absolutely absorbed by the portrait. Downright mesmerized, I'd call it. Her right hand floated in front of her, she almost reached out to touch the painting. Her fingers rested lightly against the pane of glass. Her eyes locked on the damn thing, to the point of tearing.

I glanced back at the portrait. Leaned back. That's when I saw it. And I got it. The resemblance in the eyes. The structure of the face. The likeness was a soft one, all right, but it was there. The lamb got it in a flash and it grabbed her, took hold of her. I let her be, without making a move, without a word, without a sound. I watched her close.

Her lips parted, slightly. Slowly, the right hand floated towards her face, one fingertip softly touching her lips. Then the hand opened and began caressing her cheek.

She spun around, swift, facing the road. I followed her gaze and it led me across the street. The opposite corner of Wells and St. Paul. She stepped straight ahead, focused only straight ahead. I tossed down the butt and grabbed her arm to keep her from reaching traffic. She flailed against my hold, strained against me, and slipped off my leash.

I made one wild, empty grab for her, then dashed into the street, waving my arms to the oncoming cars. Northbound traffic stopped easy, but a southbound cab only gave in at the last minute. The hack jammed the brakes, the tires shrieked, and the thing lurched to a stop barely inches from my legs.

"Where's the fire, Mac!" I barked and the jerk laid on his horn.

The lamb kept right on crossing, gliding, smooth as if she had training wheels. Her stare never broke. Nothing averted her eyes. Like a sleepwalker, she was. Like in a trance. The cabbie and me shared a bewildered look as she reached the sidewalk and continued down St. Paul.

I raced up to her side. I was going to stick to this one like glue. She stopped hard when she hit the second door down.

"Two hundred seven West St. Paul," I said. "All right. Mean something to you?" Her breathing ran shallow and fast. "What gives?"

She faced the door square. "Open it." She spoke quietly and firmly.

I tried the knob. "No dice. It's locked. See?" I rattled the thing nice and obvious for her.

"Open it."

"You want me to bust in?"

"Open it."

"That's what I thought you said."

I took out my pick-set, lowered to one knee, and set to work. She stood over me, close, tensed up, breathing rapid.

"You know it's not like I jimmy locks every day, sister."

The lamb never said a word, and she didn't have to. She worked the silent pressure bit pretty good. Eventually I got the tumblers to jump, the cylinder slid nice and easy, I pushed the door open.

"After you, lamb."

She ignored the buzzers, the mailboxes. She sailed through the vestibule, set her sights up the flight of wooden steps. Her right hand skimmed the top of the banister as she began climbing, her eyes fixed on the top stair. I came up right behind her. She didn't pause at the first landing, but kept right on and made for the top floor.

One door stood at the peek of the stairway. Her hand quivered as she twisted the knob. The door gave in to her light push and swung easy.

I stayed on top of her as we entered the expansive loft, mostly left wide open. The space equaled that of a decent two-bedroom apartment. Scarred wood floors and molding. Brick walls in need of a fresh coat of paint. Three skylights ran the length of the place. Roughly two-thirds of the accommodations gave over to the work area containing an easel with two art lamps, workbench, etcetera. A couple drop cloths draped the floor, spread beneath the easel and bench. Plenty of brushes, tubes of paint, old coffee cans, blank canvases. Used up brushes and tubes scattered across the drop cloths. Vertical stacks of paintings leaned to against one of the short walls. Must have been maybe four or five dozen works. On the easel I spied a large canvas with rough charcoal lines of a figure and a few splashes of primary colors.

A little ways beyond the work area there was this pair of long, folding screens that came off the wall to create a hidden alcove. Past that, at the farthest end, you could make out a small kitchen set up. The narrow door next to that probably the john.

I glanced over at the lamb. She surveyed the room with a slowly turning head. Her breath became more and more regular as she took it all in, her eyes narrowed. She pointed across the work area toward the wall beyond the easel. She took in a small gulp of air through her mouth. She swallowed and cleared her throat. She released the words in a voice out of practice, faint and horse.

"That's where he attacked me."

The lamb's right hand rose, the index finger pointed beyond the easel.

"He grabbed me with both hands as I got dressed. There were two detail brushes in his right hand. He smelled like gin and turpentine. More so than usual, stronger. I pushed him back a couple of steps and the brushes dropped to the floor. That enraged him. He came right back at me, moving wildly, trying to seize hold of my arms and wrists. He caught me, the collar of my dress in his grip. He swore at me. I slapped him. He staggered one step, then slapped me back, very hard."

Her voice began to tremble.

"The blow knocked me sideways. I fell away from him, still in his grip. That's when my dress tore. I fell that way, to the floor."

I followed the pointing finger. It moved towards the easel.

"He picked me up and reeled far back with his fist. His swing was so big and so wide that I easily ducked out of the way. But his momentum pitched him forward and he caught his leg on mine. We tumbled over in a tangle. We must have bumped the worktable because brushes and paint spilled over us and onto the floor. I clawed and crawled away as swiftly as I could, and scrambled to my feet. I would have run to the door, but couldn't. There he was, between me and the door, standing there, releasing this hideous rasping noise as he exhaled. Smears of fresh paint streaked his pants. Pink radiated from the jawline and ear where I struck him. I stepped back, he moved towards me.

She continued aiming her finger at the empty spaces. She placed her other hand over her heart. Her chest rose and fell rapidly.

"Directly behind me were the kitchen and the bathroom. The back door was too far away. I turned and I ran. I ran for the bathroom, and I slammed the door behind me and I tried to throw the bolt as he pushed on the door. I leaned against it with all the strength I had and fumbled to catch the bolt. He pushed harder. The door flew open and I flew. It knocked me and I reeled across the sink. I must have fallen against the medicine chest mirror because I remember closing my eyes to the terrible, shattering sound. When I opened my eyes he was right next to me, grabbing at me and touching me and leaning against me and making that rasp, that ugly breathing rasp. His breathing sounded like the vilest excitement and hate, and I couldn't push the sound away. I tried but I couldn't push him off me, but I kept trying and trying and I couldn't. And my hand found that slice of mirror in the sink and I took it and I brought it around as fast as I could and as hard as I could and as deep as I could. And I buried it into his back. I pushed at it and I pushed at it and made it go in as deep as I could.

"He jerked up straight and burst into these hideous shrieks. His body lunged and flinched as he tried to reach the thing stuck between his shoulders. He twisted and wrenched and screamed as he tumbled past me and over the side of the tub. I covered my eyes and heard the low, dull slam, the thud of his skull meeting the tile. I heard quiet after that. And then I realized I was shaking and I tried to stop shaking. I wanted to stop shaking. All I could do was keep my eyes closed."

The lamb's eyes had clamped shut, her hands balled into fists. But now the fingers gently rolled open and relaxed. Her breathing let up. She calmly lowered her arms to rest at her side. Her face came up towards mine and she opened those warm, dark eyes. She looked full at me, but I couldn't tell if she recognized me—it was that kind of gaze.

"I opened my eyes and I was walking down the street. Everything was strange. All the people were strange. I had to sit and rest until it stopped making no sense. Nothing made any sense. Then I saw you." Her stare was penetrating. "You'll find him in there."

"I know, lamb. I'll go check it out. You'll be okay out here?"

She gave me a little nod. I knew what I'd find. I believed her. She remembered, now. The whole ugly mess had come back to her and left her to pick up the pieces. I could help with that.

The door to the can was closed. I gave the knob a twist and shove. I entered careful, groping for a switch or a chain, feeling the crunch of glass and broken mirror under my step. I felt an overhead chain and gave it a yank. The hard glare of the naked bulb didn't pretty things up. The medicine cabinet ajar with collapsed shelves, scattered contents. Fragments of the half-shattered mirror lined the basin and the rim of the sink, sprinkled across the peeling floor. The body parked on its back, short ways across the tub. An awkward, distorted pose. The head and neck wedged up against the backside of the tile wall, the chin tight against the throat. The arms spread wide with tensed, curled fingers. Blood capped the fingertips. Legs flung over the side of the tub, the feet dangling above the floor.

You couldn't miss the real discovery, the real eye-opener: four bullet holes in the chest. Right at the heart. Small caliber and close up. Burn marks mixed in with the shredded cloth and blood. Very close up. Exceptionally close up. The killer could not have been any closer. I found it hard to believe she told it wrong, conscious or unconscious. But that was a possibility. The other possibility meant a surprise guest.

I unholstered my thirty-eight and called out. "Lamb, you there?"

"Yes?"

"You all right?"

"Yes. I am. Are you all right?"

I heard her move. "Stay where you are."

"What is it?"

"Just stay where you are, get me?"

"I got it."

I exited the bathroom nice and easy. I twisted back toward the lamb, held up my palm for her to stay put.

I inched my way down the far wall, down to the rear door. The safety chain held fast. Lofts don't offer a lot in the way of hide-and-seek games, so that left whatever lay behind that partitioned alcove.

I advanced along the wall and came up on the screens. Behind the dividers I found a large bed, blankets and sheets thrown about. I also found a woman on the bed. She lay on her back, like she was resting. Having herself a nice siesta. Peaceful-like, you could say. The hands folded across her stomach with a nickel-plated twenty-two tucked against her waist. I leaned over the muzzle. I couldn't mistake the faint odor of fireworks.

An empty glass stood on the nightstand. Also an empty prescription bottle labeled *chloral hydrate*. I leaned over and put my head to her breast. No sound. No sensation. No rise and fall. At the wrist, no beating beneath the cold skin. I pocketed the roscoe and returned to the lamb.

She hadn't moved. I brought her a chair. She sat down while I told what I found in the bathroom. I told her what I found in the bed. I gave her a couple moments to let it sink in.

"That's probably Delores," she said. "She was like a wife to him."

"I have to call the police, now. Do you understand, lamb?"

"Of course you do."

"Do you mind waiting here? I could take you somewhere else."

"No, that's all right. It is. You go ahead. Make your call. The telephone is by the bed."

"Thanks."

I crossed towards the partition and it came out of her. A quick eruption, almost like a laugh. "I didn't tell you—I remember my name!"

I'll never forget her name. I'm damn good with names. Sometimes my line of work calls for it.

Statement No. 11:
Marcel Dupree

Five whores, an infant child, and a flask of gin. How's that for starters? Just the launch of another unusual case, all right. Or the makings for one helluva party. Or maybe both. Put that down on the record. Sure.

You could bother to chase down my original statement at the Third District Station House, maybe. That *maybe* is the point. That *maybe* is what I'm doing here at the Eighteenth. The South Side's as good as another burg altogether, so far as anyone else cares. That's the truth and you know it. Whether you'll say it out loud's another thing. It's like they're running a private police force down there. On the one hand justice, on the other corruption—that keeps their hands full. What's kept inside that force is as good as buried. And our mayor's office doesn't help any.

The bulls on the South Side look after their own, like anywhere else in the city. Only more so. They have to. They're on their own. That means reports get mislaid or misfiled, sometimes. That means, sometimes, a report never existed in the first place.

So here I am, talking to you. I'm here to finish the job I was hired to do. That means setting it down. I want this on the record. I can't count on the Third District to speak for my client. I won't count on it to speak for those who can no longer speak for themselves. I'm here to make sure this one gets in the books.

A lot of principles balled up in this one, sure. All ways around. I take it personal, being played for the patsy. But I swallowed it, all right. Jamaica played it shrewd, as shrewd as they come. But I can't hold that against her. Not with everything in her world being threatened. Jamaica saw every last thing hanging by a thread. Ready to consider anything, do anything. Ready to try anything, even me. Sure. That leads me back to that crowd in my office.

I found them laying in wait for me. The five of them, plus the kid. They ringed my desk like front-row fight fans at the International

Amphitheatre. Maybe I am laying it on a little thick—that papoose didn't come across as too vindictive.

One dame stood firm as a potbelly stove. She had one fist fastened at the hip, the other hand tipping a sparkling, silver flask to her lips. A couple ladies leaned backsides against the desk, taut arms crisscrossed over their chests. Another cradled this infant in her arms, swaying gentle-like, side to side.

I've saved for last the ensemble's most striking member. Her lean form traced tight circles in front of the others, a tigress on the prowl. Brown, almond eyes peered from beneath angled lines. You'd cast her for Asian if not for that rich complexion. She kept her jetty hair close to the skull in short, closed curls. High cheekbones set off full lips from her thin face. She modeled a close-fitting number, oriental in flavor with high collar, low hem, and a side slit as long as your imagination. You could see the material was cheaper than day old bread, but she sold it like a million. A million bucks on the shoulders of a thirty-year-old diplomat of the streets.

I hung by the doorway and drank them all in—not exactly my kind of mixed drink. I met each gaze, one by one. I've seen coroner's juries with happier pusses.

You don't get a whole lot of *happy* in this racket. That must go for your line, too. You can do right by clients, but that doesn't exactly make them cry for joy. You can mollify them and satisfy them maybe, up to a point. Maybe set their minds at ease. That's at best. At worst, you confirm their darkest suspicions. This group? Some of those dames looked out for blood. I had to wonder whose blood they had in mind.

I parked my hat on the coat stand, closed the door, swung around with my hands in my pockets. The tigress halted in front of the others, one arm wrapped across her breast, the other supporting the hand that caressed her chin. She eyed me up and down, real slow.

"As long as you already helped yourselves in," I said, "you may as well help yourselves to a seat."

The broad in the brightest blue wrap dress you ever saw, the one with the passion for bright flasks, snapped back, "We prefer to stand, thank you!"

"Speak for yourself, honey, if you don't mind." The jane toting the baby sounded downright demure. "I'm eyeing that cushy sofa."

"In that case," I said, "make yourselves at home, by all means."

Three of the dames maneuvered to the couch, led by the one with the kid. The bright blue, thirsty one took a chair in front of my desk. The tigress held her ground and made a study of me.

The flask tipper half-sipped, half-spat, "The sooner we get on with it, the sooner we can bug out of here."

"First things first," I said.

"You want to know," the tigress said in a breathy rasp, "how we got into your office." She held her chin high.

"That would be swell, for starters," I replied. "Of course I could check the lock for scratches, but I'm betting you didn't pick your way in."

"Mm!" The drinker finished a swallow. "We met the sweetest old man while we were dawdling around in your hall. That custodial man."

I nodded. "Sixty or so with a bum leg that trailed him by a step?"

"He's the one I found. And what do you think?"

"I haven't the slightest," I said.

"He's a man what appreciates a taste of the juice himself!" She winked.

"Nathan. Sure. Just for the record, in case I need to do some second story work myself, what kind of hooch did he go for?"

She jiggled the flask, "Gin. A little taste of gin." She smiled.

"And now you'd like to know who we are." The tigress gave me a one-sided smile.

I stepped over to the last chair and held it for her. "Allow me."

She hesitated for a beat, swiveled, and melted into the straight back like a bar of chocolate in the sun. I headed to my side of the desk. I felt her eyes on my back.

"You girls appear a ways from home."

"You telling us to get lost?" Bright blue was itching for a fight.

"That's not what the man said, Agnes." The tigress caressed her chin with the back of a hand.

"Just a simple observation," I said. I put an edge on it. "Nothing more, nothing less. That's my business."

"Agnes is in a bit of a state. But I'm not apologizing for her. We're all a bit fired up. That's why we came."

"All right, she's Agnes. You all got a gander at the stencil on the door before you forced your way in, so you already know who I am. Who are the rest of you?"

"On the couch there," the tigress spoke with a wry smile, "we have Annie and Coco. Ophelia's the one with the child. My name is Jamaica."

"Jamaica what?"

"Smith. Plain old Jamaica Smith."

"There's nothing plain about *Jamaica*. Not in this burg. What's the kid's name?"

"No need to involve the child." Agnes clenched her jaw.

"I was just being polite. Skip it."

Ophelia spoke softly and sweetly, "Her name is Juliet."

"That's a beauty," I nodded.

Ophelia smiled to herself.

"She's crazy," Agnes said. "Juliet."

"All right. Now everybody knows everybody. Annie, Coco, Ophelia, Agnes, Jamaica—what makes you girls worm into my humble office on this lovely spring afternoon?"

Except for Jamaica, my callers lost their nerve. Jamaica poked her tongue in her cheek and rolled her eyes. Her compatriots fidgeted every which way. Annie and Coco exchanged shy glances. Agnes threw back another swig. Ophelia mouthed baby talk with the cherub. Annie considered her nails. Coco smoothed out her skirt.

I lit up a cigarette and waited. Coco finally gave Jamaica the eye and jerked her head twice in my direction. Jamaica returned Coco's prodding with a coquettish smile, then dropped it hard to address me. "I'll take one of those," she said.

I took out my pack of cigarettes, shook one loose, and Jamaica delicately plucked it out of the deck. I struck a match and held it above the blotter. Jamaica leaned the end of the butt into the flame.

"I guess it's up to me," Jamaica exhaled a blue cloud. "I'll lay it on the line. I'll give it to you fast and straight. Then you can see what you make of it. Fair enough?"

I said, "Fair enough." An underlying chuckle peppered my words.

Jamaica cocked her head. "I didn't say anything funny. We didn't come all the way up here to be laughed at."

"You think you can laugh at us, man?" The indignant Agnes straightened in her chair, poised to stand fast.

"Excuse me, kid," I said, "but you know who you sound like?" That caught Jamaica off guard. "You sound like me talking to the cops."

Jamaica covered her mouth, and I detected a faint giggle. That put her on the spot. She had to save face in front of her friends and get real serious.

"We mean business, here. Don't go getting cute with us."

"I don't mean to be cute. Sometimes my line of work calls for it."

"Now ain't that a laugh. We have something in common."

"Being cute?"

"We're working girls, if you hadn't figured it out, and we came to you because we're in a spot."

"I take it you don't mean elementary school teachers."

"All right, Mr. Private Detective. You want me to say it? You're dealing with five girls getting on some stiff time as streetwalkers. Okay? Five of the best from the South Side."

"All five you say? You're practically a union."

"We're in a serious fix."

"Now how serious is that?"

"As serious as it gets."

"In my book that makes it life or death."

Coco chimed in, "Show him the clippings, Smitty."

Jamaica fingered through a leopard-skin clutch, pulled out some scraps of newsprint, handed them across the desk. I stubbed out my smoke, tilted back in the swivel, and ran through the first article, carefully torn out from *The Defender*. It began,

"The body of Rudolph *Pockets* Patterson of South State Street was discovered early yesterday morning in the alley behind Thirty-seventh Street and Princeton Avenue. According to police, Mr. Patterson suffered multiple stab wounds from a long, sword-like weapon. Authorities pronounced him dead upon arrival at St. Bernard Hospital."

I fingered through the other snippets. The second clipping reported the death of William "Chills" Clay. The last article noted the demise of Ontario "Pinky" Trane and Marcus "Middleweight" Monroe. All four men murdered violently. All four done in with some kind of sword, of all things. Or something damn close to it—reports got hazy on it. All on the South Side. All within the last three months.

"You catch those dates, Mr. Detective," Jamaica told me.

"I got it."

"What if I told you they were all hustlers?"

"Any of you turn tricks for these guys?"

"Annie and Ophelia worked for Pockets. Coco worked for Chills. Agnes worked for Monroe—on and off, anyway."

"I was pulling part-time," Agnes tossed in.

"Uh-huh. Go on."

"Okay, now dig. What if I told you that in the last two months six of our sisters have crossed over?"

"Murdered?"

"Murdered."

"Cut up the same way?"

Jamaica took a long drag. Her eyes clamped shut and she nodded.

"Okay, sister, you've got my attention, in more ways than one."

"That's not all."

"There's more?"

"Last week. Mama Rose passed over."

"Mama Rose?"

Annie and Coco repeated in a simultaneous whisper, "Mama Rose."

Agnes managed between swallows, "Mama Rose was everybody's mama. She looked after everyone in The Belt."

Jamaica's eyes narrowed. "That's the gospel. If you needed any kind of help, in any way, shape or form, you needn't bother even asking. You just turn around and find Mama Rose by your side. No matter what. No matter who you were. Even girls like us. It didn't matter to Mama. We were all her children."

Ophelia chimed in soft and low, "I wish I could've said a prayer for her."

"Amen." Agnes threw back a shot.

Through a gray cloud I said, "Murdered, I take it?"

"So violent," Jamaica said in a hush. "How could anyone treat her so bad? That's the mean thing about it. To end someone's life that way. Who in the world could have anything against sweet, old Mama Rose?"

"Allow me to get this straight. In the last three months four pimps, six hookers and Mama Rose, the neighborhood saint, have met their maker, and the mug responsible for it made none too pretty a job of it."

"As wicked a death as there is," Agnes bobbed her head.

"Mama Rose was the end, Mr. Detective." Jamaica's eyes fixed on mine.

"Uh-huh. Okay, give it to me."

"What's there to give? After Mama Rose, we couldn't sit by no longer."

"There's something evil after us," Agnes declared. "No two ways about it."

Ophelia rocked in place. "He's a madman. It's the work of a madman."

I asked, "What's the city's finest doing about it?"

"They doing what they always do. Sitting on their ossified hands." Coco swung her head. "Just sitting on their hands."

"You don't strike me as someone born yesterday," Jamaica said. "You know the bulls don't do any crime solving in The Belt. Half of them are on the take and don't give a damn. The rest are intimidated or have better things to do. As long as it stays in The Belt? No one's to care. That's why we're here. We all figure we have to pay someone to care."

"And you've chosen me."

"Someone should send the SOB to West Hell," Agnes raised her flask.

"We want you to solve the case." Jamaica spoke it slowly and distinctly. "That is your racket, ain't it, Mr. Detective?"

"Uh-huh. That's what it says on the license."

"A waste of time," Agnes muttered.

"Ain't no one," Annie spoke up, "in our neck of the woods who do what you do."

"That's solid, Mr. Detective," Jamaica appealed. "No one in The Belt's going to stick out their neck. You're our best hope."

I'd never been anyone's best hope before. And just for the privilege I'd have the honor of sticking out my scrawny neck. You boys know all about that one.

So we kicked it around a while longer, like pushing bocce balls with a feather. The girls had no more ideas about the killings than I had about changing Juliet's diaper. As for leads? They had about as much of a clue as a republican candidate for mayor. I'd of done better writing to an advice column.

They did offer one contact to look up. When I say *they* I mean Jamaica, of course. She scribbled it down on the backside of my business card. The man I wanted could be found at The Club DeLisa on South State Street, a Mr. Socrates Jones.

It was getting on late afternoon by the time the coterie waltzed out. I decided to take a stab, got on the blower, and got lucky. I caught up with Mr. Jermaine Hawkes, *Defender* reporter, lead man on the pimp slayings.

Hawkes second-guessed my interest at first, so I gave him a cursory rundown of my credentials and investigation. A couple of past cases rang a bell with Hawkes and convinced him of my sincerity. Hawkes turned out to be one of those civic-minded journalist types. He got a righteous thrill when an outsider showed concern for his beat. Hawkes relished being asked what he actually thought for a change. A man like him, he said, could write up the stale who, what, when and where in his sleep. The *why* fascinated him like the apple fascinated Newton.

Hawkes boiled it down convincingly. He couldn't tie it up in pink ribbon, yet, but he leaned toward a cut and dried solution. Each death occurred within a twelve-block radius inside the Grand Boulevard neighborhood—that covered a lot of nightlife, including clubs like The Club DeLisa. The slayings fit the same pattern. Hawkes eye-witnessed the bodies, and he described the stabbings to me in all their colorful and brutal detail.

The butcher made thorough work of it. More than thorough—multiple wounds approaching the sensational, but in a methodical sort of way. The corpse of William Clay, for example, displayed no less than fifteen separate stab wounds. Clean punctures, deep and controlled thrusts. None of the victims, however, exhibited signs of mutilation. That proved the key to Hawkes. One big show, he surmised, a pointed message as lurid and violent and loud as possible.

Hawkes asked about my next move.

"You mean after this conversation?"

"That's right."

"You mean after a bite to eat?"

"Yeah, man, what's it to be?"

"Looking up a gent at the Club DeLisa. I'm supposed to see some egg named Socrates Jones."

"Him you can see all you want, but he'll never see you, square man."

"I've got riddles enough without playing twenty questions, Hawkes."

"I'm just telling you. The man'll never, never ever see you."

"And why is that, Hawkes, because I'm just a square?"

"Socrates Jones won't see you because he's *blind*, baby."

"You're a card, Hawkes. A regular pistol. About as funny as a match in a gas pipe."

"Whatever you say, square man. You just watch yourself in The Belt. If you stray too far from those black and tans you might wind up meeting the wrong kind of barber. You dig?"

I noted that "dig" had more than one connotation. That's the kind of double-talk you get from writers. I thanked Hawkes for his help. He wished me plenty of luck. I promised to give him the story, if I ever got one. Hawkes presumed there'd be a story, all right, no matter what—the catch was whether or not I'd be around to tell it. He really broke himself up.

I drove my coupe straight through the city, cruising Wabash on into the loop. I grabbed a sandwich at the Wonder Bar at the corner of Jackson before heading to the South Side. I followed a beeline down State until I reached Garfield and the site of The Club DeLisa.

I hung a right on Garfield and pulled into a spot half a block down. One storefront over, three kids pitched pennies beneath the cool, fluorescent glow of a pharmacy sign. I got out of the coupe and felt the night air, dry and mild. The boys took notice of me as I stood at the curb, loosening my tie. The squirt of the group, a gangly runt with a face all eyes and yap, sauntered my way.

"You leaving your car there, Mister Charles?"

"That was the general plan. The coppers don't take kindly when I leave it on the sidewalk."

The kid leered over his shoulder, "Tommy, we got ourselves another comedian." He puckered his lips and scrunched his nose. "You think your machine be safe here?"

"What do you think?"

"Mm mm. I don't like the looks of it. You never can tell, no sir."

"Maybe you'll keep an eye on it for me."

"Maybe I'll do just that—you make it worth my while."

"What do you have in mind?"

"Fifteen cents comes to mind."

"Fifteen cents, you say. Sounds kind of steep, kid. The going rate in the Gold Coast is only a nickel. You wouldn't be trying to take advantage, would you?" I worked awful hard to hold back a smile.

"Let me tell you how it is. The first thing is, see, that this here isn't the Gold Coast. The next thing is, there's three of us to take care of. You take that nickel three ways and you've got yourself three times the protection."

"You've got it all worked out."

"I've got it worked out plenty. Deal?"

"Sure. You got yourself a deal, kid."

The youngster held out his hand. I shook it firm. He tightened his mouth and squeezed his mitt as hard as he could, mustering every ounce of pressure he had into his puny grip. While he grappled, I pulled some change out of my pants pocket with my left, turned over his hand, dropped three nickels into his palm.

"Real coin of the realm, kid," I said. I winked and turned on my heels.

"We'll keep that bus safe, mister," he called after me.

The brute hovering outside the doors to The Club DeLisa must've had about six inches on me. I considered asking him if he got his tux from a tentmaker, then nixed the thought. He didn't say boo and let me pass.

The interior of The Club amounted to a gigantic hall, crowded, noisy, smoky, wailing, vibrating. All that on a Thursday night. At the back on the right side a throng of chorus girls, done up in silly Mexican hats and blouses tied above their navels, twirled and kicked a raucous floor show. Each dame wore the same frozen smile plastered across her kisser. Their out-of-sync kicks and turns delighted the audience—those paying attention. I turned my back and inched my way through crammed tables and roving patrons to the long bar on the left. I copped a stool, spun around to face the crowd.

A passing drunk tripped and nearly landed in my lap. He let loose a good-natured, "Whoa!" and stood himself up. He must've been flying higher than Lindbergh. The sight of me caught him by surprise.

"Christmas!" he leaned way back. "But you so fair you could pass—" He stopped himself, bent in close, squinted, threw up his arms. He turned away and ambled off announcing, "I beg your pardon, I beg your pardon."

That's when I spotted a sharpie duded up in a tux at the far end of the counter looking my way. He'd been watching. He sized me up for another half minute before signaling a barman working near my end.

The barkeep leaned over, "What can I do for you, mister?" His eyes never rose above the top of the bar.

"Maybe you can help me out. I was told to look up a man by the name of Socrates Jones."

"I asked what are you drinking?"

"Do you know where I can find Socrates Jones?"

"What are you drinking, mister?"

"Uh-huh. Make it scotch and water."

"Oak," he said, and walked away.

I took in the scene while I waited: the people, the floorshow, the hot brass and loud percussion. The music swung, the crowd enjoyed its energetic self, and only the wait staff out-paced the dancers, bopping across that spacious floor like mad ball bearings in some wild arcade. I heard the clunk of glass on wood at my elbow. I twirled around to catch that tux man, the one who gave the sign, setting down my glass.

"One scotch, mister."

I slapped a fiver on the counter.

"What's that for?"

"That's for the drink and some information."

"We don't sell information here, mister. You're looking for Socrates Jones? You found him." He leaned in a bit. "You see that curtain at the end of the bar? All the way down? Go right through there. You want the door at the end of the hall."

"Where does that lead?"

"That'll take you to Mr. Socrates Jones. Have your drink, keep your money, and don't be hanging around out here."

That was too easy. Way too easy. Maybe the word was out. Or maybe I'd been set up. In any case, I figured a stiff belt would be in order.

With the glass at my lips I asked, "This slug ain't going to kill me, is it?"

"Haven't had no fatalities, lately." The man didn't break the tiniest smile.

I threw back the shot fast and it burned through me like a cigarette burns through a cheap mattress. The tux man saw it in my eyes, snorted once, and began wiping down the bar.

I gave my head a slight shake, nodded to the man, pulled myself up. I got plenty of looks as I snaked my way through the mob. I reached the deep red, velvet curtain, glanced around one time, then pushed my way through. Low-watt bulbs lit the dark, brick corridor in a sickly, pale yellow. I made my way slow. As the music faded behind me, the door at the end came into sight. I gave the wood panel two solid raps.

"Come in, come in," boomed through the door.

On the other side of that door I found a cramped setting, a kind of dressing room and lounge combination. A full-blown dressing table butted against the long wall on one side, its illuminated mirror providing the only light around. The tiny bulbs made me squint as I struggled to make out the rest of the joint. A long white couch lay jammed down the opposite wall. A barrel-shaped man occupied the desk coming off the furthest wall. His face tilted up with eyes squeezed tight, two eyelids wrinkled shut like sealed folds of flesh. On a black, glass rectangle before him his thick digits rolled a reefer with the grace of a cardsharp. A phonograph droned the thick strains of something torpid and classical in the background.

"Mr. Socrates Jones?" I asked.

Jones curled an off-center grin. "They call me Socrates because I make a mean dialogue".

"Uh-huh. And the high-brow chicken scratching?"

"That is Mr. Wagner. You dig music?"

"I never found much time for it. I've caught *Your Hit Parade* on occasion."

"That's truly a pity. No personal favorites at all?"

"Sure." I planted my hands at my hips. "Teddy Wilson's pretty good."

"Mm. Very nice choice. Delectable." The wide face beamed and the head tilted further back. "A very smooth sophisticate. Man, I could listen to good music and talk good music and forget about everything else."

"How do you account for good?"

"Whatever I take great pleasure in is good. Now, while I'm certain a dissection of my habits and comforts could prove quaint if not absorbing discourse, I am willing to suppose you have other things on your mind. Am I right or am I right?"

I approached the desk as I spoke. "I'd say that's about right. I've got the bodies of four men and six women on my mind."

"Yes, yes. Ten neighbors who have prematurely cut out to their final repose." Jones pinched the reefer between his fingers. "We all loved Mama Rose."

"That's right." I stood just opposite Jones, the black glass panel between us. "Four hustlers, five streetwalkers, and Mama Rose. I was told you might have some information for me."

"Yes, yes. Maybe I do and maybe I don't." Jones struck a match and brought the stick to his short, wide lips.

"I didn't come all this way for maybes."

"Of course, of course. And who might of told a daddy-o like you a thing like my having the information you seek?"

"Miss Jamaica Smith."

"Jamaica Smith, where the commonplace meets the exotic."

"So you've heard of her."

"I am familiar with Miss Smith's work. Not personally, you dig. But excuse me." He held out the juju. "Do you imbibe, man?"

"No thanks, it hurts my teeth."

"Yes, yes. It was at Miss Smith's request that I agreed to grant this audience, to look you over, to coin a popular phrase. That must sound immensely haughty to you, but a man like you is ignorant of such things in The Belt. I have earned a fair deal of reverence in my little world, a sort of wise old cat of South State Street. I consider the accolades somewhat exaggerated, but then it would be bad form to turn down such honors. Am I right or am I right?" He fired up the stick.

"Sure."

"Bringing your investigative experience to bear upon these most unhappy and unfortuitous events, applying all of your very own professional wisdom, what do you make of it these sorry circumstances?"

"As a professional I can picture an oodle of possibilities."

"Is that a fact, man?" Another puff sucked in his cheeks like collapsed grapefruits.

"Could be a crusader running around with a few screws loose."

"A misguided deviant attempting to cleanse our evil citizenry?"

"I don't buy the zealot angle, but it's always possible."

"Good. What else?"

"Could be an old working associate with a score to settle. But then the number of scores seems to be running a touch on the high side."

"Better and better. Any further suppositions to suppose?"

"Sure. The most likely set-up goes like this: some ambitious wise guy, probably a recent import to The Belt, sets himself up to spoil the competition. He's thinning out the resistance and sending a message to the rest."

"Ah. Bravo indeed. And how do you explain Mama Rose?"

"Mama Rose saw something she wasn't supposed to see."

"Ah," groaned Jones with a Cheshire cat grin. "Yes, yes." He took a long, slow drag and the vapor floated from his lips like an Indian rope trick.

"Any new blood around you can suggest? Some hotshot who blew in from out of town? Say in the last half-year or so?"

"Yes, yes. That is an astute interpretation of the situation. And I do believe I can think of at least one cat who fits your proposition."

"I'm not so sure how astute it is, but it's plain enough and simple enough. I like simple. Complicated almost never works."

"Yes, yes."

I leaned across the desk. "Has he got a name?"

"The cat goes by the name of Marcel Dupree. But I hasten to add that it's most likely an established alias, you dig?"

"From the South, is he?"

"Monsieur Dupree purportedly hails from New Orleans."

"Which means there's got to be a reason he left The Big Easy in the first place. You know where I can find the mug?"

Jones pulled another drag and placed the reefer in a small ashtray at his elbow. "I hear tell Dupree fancies himself quite the proficient at billiards. The local establishment in which to indulge oneself in such activities would be Whitey's. Shall I write out the address for you?"

I found that an interesting offer coming from a blind guy. "No, just point me in the general direction. If I get lost I'm sure there's plenty of folks down here more than willing to help me on my way."

"A curious turn of phrase."

"I thought you might go for it. You have anything else for me?"

"You will find Whitey's on Garfield, two blocks east of State. I do recommend you take care. Your investigation may require the greatest delicacy and tact. In any case, may you go lightly, slightly and politely."

"I catch the drift, but I don't find anything tactful about being sliced open with some kind of saber."

"Yes, yes. Well, it may be that you know what you're doing more than it appears."

"Then again, maybe not." I gave Jones my back and strolled towards the door. "But that's okay, Mr. Jones. I don't mind working in the dark. Sometimes my line of work calls for it."

I lit up as soon as I hit the street and felt a chill on my neck. Could've been the cool breeze or could've been the old stranger in a strange land routine. Could have been the cool reception I found at The Club. And from Jones. Plenty of character, that one. I had no way of telling if he was on the level or feeding me to the wolves. Either way, he sure put out the minimum.

The State Street I knew in the Loop and on the north side of the city must have been some other State Street. Traffic outside the DeLisa lingered at a casual crawl. Motorists visited with each other, and pedestrians mingled in between lanes. I couldn't help notice that foot traffic on the sidewalk parted before me. Folks stepped out of my way, leaned away. They avoided me like I was some kind of path-crossing black cat.

A young punk with nerve jumped in front of me as I turned the corner at Garfield. "Are you lost, little man?" Junior stood no more than five-two himself. That made me Goliath to his Toulouse-Lautrec.

"No more astray than usual," I said.

"I think you're lost and don't know it." He kept tilting his head from one side to the other. It annoyed the hell out of me.

"Sure."

"What do you think you're doing here?"

"I'm looking for someone."

"Yeah? Who? Who you looking for?"

"Is your name Algernon?"

"That's right. I'm Algernon."

"It so happens I'm not looking for Algernon."

I brushed by the egg without waiting for any witty rejoinder. I wanted to get on with it. His goading calls trailed me, but I carried on to Whitey's, as seedy a pool hall as I've seen in my own neck of the woods. I pushed through the swinging door. A few of the patrons noticed me, their pans displaying the disbelief of the ages. The rest of the folks couldn't have cared less. I sauntered straight for the man behind the counter.

"No open tables," he announced.

"You could at least ask me if I want one, first."

"Nope."

"For instance, you could say, *Can I help you?* Or *What'll it be?* Something like that."

"Nope. No open tables."

"It just so happens I'm not interested in a table."

The door to Whitey's whipped open hard with a slam against the inner wall. Sure enough, the punk from the street couldn't let it rest. He posed in the doorframe like some puny cowboy of a punk, his thumbs tucked in his belt loops.

"Don't be knocking around my door, son," the counterman scolded.

I planned to ignore the kid as best I could. "It so happens I'm looking for someone," I told the counterman.

"We just run a clean hall here and we got no open tables."

"Tell him you're looking for Algernon!" the kid barked in his thin, nasal voice.

The counterman motioned with his head, "He with you, mister?"

"No, sir. Not by a long shot."

"Well, I guess that's one thing in your favor."

"I've got enough problems without that. I'm looking for a man by the name of Dupree."

"If I knew of any man by the name of Dupree, I'd have to tell you I don't know any Dupree."

"That's Marcel Dupree."

"Yeah, that's the Marcel Dupree I never heard of."

The kid sauntered in my direction. The counterman held up his hand with a start.

"You hold on there, son. If you need to do any whooping now, you don't do it in here."

"That's right, kid," I chided. "Take it outside."

"Take it outside?" His twang got more annoying with amplification.

"Forget this man, here," instructed the counterman. "Besides, why let all these good folk see you get your butt thrashed?"

"Okay. Okay, old man. I'll be outside—waiting," and the kid swung his way back out the door.

"If you've never heard of Marcel Dupree, I guess you've never heard of Marcel Dupree."

"I've never heard of him being in tonight. Not since this afternoon."

"Sure."

"Some of us know the score, but we got to look after our own selves. You with me?"

"Uh-huh. But I bet that never stopped Mama Rose.

The counterman sucked in his lips. He looked to his shoes. The door slammed wide again and the kid took two big steps inside.

The counterman nearly screamed, "What I tell you about that door?"

"I said I was waiting for you, mister!"

I turned away from the kid. "Can you tell this punk I'm saving my fight for someone else?"

"I don't think there's telling him anything, mister."

"Kid," as I turned back around, "You're all hopped up on bad westerns."

"I'm through talking, mister."

"Outside!" the counterman roared.

"I'm way beyond that, old man!" the kid roared. His head jerked left and right until he spotted a beer bottle on a nearby table. He grabbed the bottle by the neck and a sneer came over his punk face. The kid gauged the twenty feet that separated us. I guess sticking his tongue out the corner of his mouth helped with that.

Customers in my general vicinity began to fade. The counterman gave me room, too. I snapped up a cue stick from the hand of one of the patrons sidling past me. I held out the stick with both hands, like a dumbbell, and waited.

"Make your move, kid."

Junior jiggled the bottle in his fingers. He slid one foot forward, leaned over as a feint, and froze. With a jerk he wound up and unleashed the bottle with a ferocious fling. The kid's follow-through reminded me of Luke Appling. I raised the cue in front of my face in time to shatter the bottle. Green shards splintered past me. His arm impressed the hell out of me. The crowd hushed. I felt like Stokowski.

"You're out of ammo, kid," I said.

I moved one step forward, the kid shifted back his weight. He spread his legs and bent his knees, held his arms at his sides. His hands flapped like a runner on first base trying to distract the pitcher. I stared straight into his bulging eyes. He gawked at the stick gripped tight in my right hand. I raised the cue to shoulder level, took one step closer, and another. He threatened to lunge with only four feet separating us, but the movement of the stick balled him up. I raised it higher, swung it to my right, then whipped it in a half circle, down and around and it snapped sharp against his left shin.

The kid went down like a cheap marionette, his whining screech filling the hall. I glanced at the counterman. He had nothing to say. I dropped the stick in front of the kid and hit the door. The punk's nasal wail trailed away as I hoofed it up Garfield at a steady clip.

No Dupree, no lead, no soap. Sometimes things pan out, sometimes you've got a bad pan. Figured to be high time I got back to the coupe before I rankled anyone else. The next mug might turn out to be a lot better at pool. It was time to refigure things. Maybe press Jones again. Or look up Smith. With the right lead I figured it couldn't take that long to track down Dupree. Or some stooge or chippy working for him.

Two cars down from my coupe that fifteen-cent kid, my carhop, slammed into me blind. He practically bowled us both over racing out from the wide corridor between two buildings. I righted him by a hand on each shoulder, steadied him with a quick shake. Smears of blood streaked his shirt and windbreaker.

"It's bad," he whispered. He held up red-stained hands. "Bad." His head quivered. His eyes blinked like Morse code.

"Look at me," I said. I repeated it, stern as I could without shouting. He brought his eyes up to mine. "I want you to telephone the police. Can you do that?"

"Yes."

"Do it. Do it now."

"Now," he echoed. He swiveled both ways, then took off like a gangly rocket.

I glanced to the side, swept that corridor between the buildings. A place of shadows. At the corridor's far end, cut off by a windowless building of brick, a small globe shone weakly above a doorway. Shades of gray and black saturated the rest of the passage. Stepping into the walkway felt like a game of high stakes hide-and-seek. I listened hard, peered hard. Something moved near that distant doorway, something a few feet in front of the entry. Something low to the ground. I continued carefully, slowly, eyes adjusting to the underexposed passage. That moving thing, that quivering blur, took shape. My pace quickened. The form turned into a body sprawled on the pavement just to the right of the rear door. I broke into a run as the face and figure became familiar. I reached her and knelt down. Stripes of blood streaked below the jaw line.

"Agnes," I whispered.

Agnes groaned, an ugly kind of grunt, and her eyes fluttered open. She stabbed out her hand and I caught it. Her grip was strong. I told her to hold on. I told her I'd get her help. Her fingers convulsed, my entire arm jerked in response. I'd steadied her arm before I registered the odd sound behind me: stride, scrape, stride, scrape, stride.

Imagine coming that far only to let a gimp get the drop on you. I gently laid Agnes's hands on the pavement and swung around. He shambled in and out of the pockets of darkness, a long, lean figure that bent forward with every lunge of his good leg and straightened out with every drag of his bad leg. He lugged himself along with the aid of a tall cane. As he entered the dim circle of light thrown by the door lamp he pulled up, no more than twelve feet between us. He reared up, showing off a perfectly cut suit of clothes—vest, derby and spats—all in the same remarkably gaudy, bright red.

"You the gumshoe been seeking me? Well, you find me, now. The name is Marcel Dupree." He spread his arms wide to augment the announcement.

"This some of your work, peddler?" I jerked my head towards Agnes. Her eyes had shut. Her breathing went shallow, but even.

"My, now," Dupree scratched his jaw. "So many accidents in this quarter. And the poor lady's throat so badly cut. A shame she can't tell us what happened."

"Never mind the dance, Dupree. We're both wise."

"Maybe so. And that is why I be looking for you, man. This *my* business. *My* people. But you try to make it *your* business."

"You made it my business, but I'm not going to waste my time drawing you a diagram."

"That's a pity, man. A mistake and a pity."

"I make a lot of mistakes. Sometimes my line of work calls for it."

"You talking strange, man. I don't like this kind of talk, and I tire of it." Dupree planted the cane in front of him with his left hand. He rested his right wrist across its knob.

"Sure, peddler."

"My name is Mr. Dupree."

"Dupree, peddler, trash. All the same to me. On my side of the city we throw out the trash."

"Then there is no more to be said, detective *privé*."

Dupree quickly withdrew the end of the cane to reveal a slim blade. Something out of a bad costume spectacle. He flourished the steel to catch an angle of light that glinted straight into my eyes.

I squinted. "How can there be nothing more to say when you haven't said anything yet?"

Dupree waved the blade above his derby. "Are those to be your last words, then, man?"

"No. I'd also like to say go to hell."

"But you already there, man. You have found your eternal damnation. Prepare yourself to die."

"This isn't The Bayou, peddler."

I reached quick between my hip and belt and pulled out my thirty-eight. I drew up the muzzle, aimed easy, and fed one round point blank. The slug speared the center of Dupree's chest, his body recoiled, but the damn derby defied some physical law and stuck tight.

As the echo of the volley faded down the corridor, a gurgling sound escaped Dupree's lips. He coughed softy. Two crimson bubbles formed over his lower lip and then oozed down his chin like Hershey's syrup. The sword fell to the ground with a clang and Dupree dropped to one knee.

"Aw hell, man" Dupree said.

I raised the muzzle one more time and finished off Dupree with a clean shot to the temple. His head spun, his limbs flailed and gave out, and he met the concrete like a wilting flower. The damn derby rolled clear, traveled five feet, and settled down like a manhole cover.

I listened for sirens. I heard the distant sound of traffic back on Garfield, like some muted breeze. I bent down to Agnes. Agnes was dead. I kept her company another forty minutes before the cops showed up.

I felt worn, beat. They'd pulled me in every direction and sucked me dry. The cops from the Third District interrogated me for hours. Two pairs of plain clothes ran me through the ringer until I barely knew my own story. Sure. The boys in blue didn't want me around, but they made a good show of it. They'd handled the likes of me before. None of it really mattered a damn to the cops in The Belt, anyway. They knew it. I knew it.

Jamaica propped up a no parking sign in the cool dawn light. I spotted her as I exited the station. A floor-length evening dress flowed out from the thick sweater wrapped about her shoulders. She hugged her arms around tight to keep out the chill. She made for an elegant vision parked outside the precinct house, a touch of class misfit. I recognized something defiant in her stance. Maybe she was just tired. Maybe she was just cold. Maybe she was a lot of things. I could have slapped her around.

I walked up to her close. The time was quiet. Dead quiet. She plucked two cigarettes from the pack in my pocket. She placed one between my fingers.

I said, "You take chances, lady."

She said, "That's everyday life in my world."

"If I wasn't so beat I'd throw you across my knee."

"Maybe another time, Mr. Detective." She almost smiled, but the expression died like the setting sun. "I'll miss Agnes."

"I didn't like Agnes one bit. But no one deserves to go out like that. None of them."

"That's the truth, Mr. Detective."

"You set me up, lady."

"I didn't see any other way to do it. I wonder if you can understand that."

"I understand it, all right. You figured you'd get to Dupree through me. You made sure of it. You told everyone and their brother. You figured if I actually solved the case I'd find a way to make it stick. If Dupree found me first and took care of me, then maybe someone up at City Hall would pay attention. Didn't it go something like that?"

"Something like that."

"I guess we all got a raw deal."

"What the hell else was I going to do?"

I gave her a stare warm as frostbite. "You know how I made out tonight. How'd you make out?"

"Don't go trying to turn me into some kind of cliche. All the little girls in The Belt— Her eyes teared up. She raised her chin. "All those little girls. Ain't none of them dream of this. Ain't none of us dream of this, Mr. North Side Detective. We don't wake up one morning and say, *Momma, you know what I wanna be when I grow up?*" She dropped her head.

I pulled out a match. I struck it. I lit the end of my smoke and took a pull, long and deep. I blew out the gray vapor and let the match drop. The flame died before it hit the pavement.

"Find yourself another match," I said. I walked away, wondering how the hell I was going to get back to my coupe.

ABOUT THE AUTHOR

Ben Solomon grew up with Picasso, Cagney and Beethoven. Classical arts training, comic books and Hollywood's golden age rounded out an education fit for a renaissance-hack, and provided inspiration for a lifetime. He's worked across disciplines, attempting to capture music upon canvas, translate oils and silver nitrate into words.

Movies, painters and comic books infused Solomon's Chicago childhood with a dazzling kaleidoscope of nonstop sights and sounds. Keaton and Krupa, Nijinsky and Chaplin, Marvel and Mozart—in Solomon's boyhood mind, influences existed side by side, alive and kicking all at the same time, artistic contemporaries in a never-ending universe. Warner Brothers provided Solomon with knights in shining armor played by Bogie, Raft and Robinson; Chandler and Hammett provided the dragons. Chicago sports proved that winning wasn't everything, and Ellington taught him, "It don't mean a thing if it ain't got that swing."

Solomon studied at some of Chicago's best institutions, including the Stone-Camryn School of Ballet, the Art Institute, St. Nicholas Theatre and Second City. Among his early claims to fame, Solomon hoofed as an extra with the Bolshoi and Joffrey, worked tech behind William H. Macy and John Malkovich, and performed in David Mamet's only children's play.

Solomon's passion for the tough guy world of early gangster and PI flicks led to his creation of his short story series, "The Hard-Boiled Detective." He premiered the adventures online in February 2013, offering three yarns a month to subscribers. His hard-boiled and other fiction have appeared in e-zines across the web as well as the 2014 anthology "The Shamus Sampler II." Another adventure is scheduled for the "Drag Noir" anthology from Fox Spirit in October 2014. Samples and more information about Solomon's old-school crime series can be found here: http://thehardboileddetective.com/

Solomon appreciates your taking a flyer on "The Hard-Boiled Detective." He hopes you enjoyed reading these yarns as much as he enjoyed writing them, and that'll you'll consider posting a review online.

Praise for Ben Solomon and *The Hard-Boiled Detective*

Solomon strikes a perfect chord in his voice reminiscent of Bogey, and most certainly a mix of the classic tales of Damon Runyon, Raymond Chandler, and other great practitioners of the dark and brooding noir story.

–Robert W. Walker, author of *Killer Instinct* and *The Edge of Instinct*

If you're looking for fast-paced stories in the pulp style with a hard-boiled narrator, snappy patter, solid mysteries, and a period setting all filtered through a modern sensibility, "The Hard-Boiled Detective" fills the bill. Check it out.

–Bill Crider, author of the Sheriff Dan Rhodes mystery series

Pure pulp for now people. A delicious and unapologetic throwback to another, simpler era, an era of cheap thrills printed on cheaper paper, full of broad-shouldered he-men and soft-shouldered broads, where fedoras and trench coats are the order of the day and the roscoes spit ka-chow ka-chow all night long. This ain't no Chandler, this ain't no Hammett, but the ghosts of Daly and Bellem and a million other forgotten word slingers are ready to kick up a little dust. Sure.

–Kevin Burton Smith, The Thrilling Detective website

Ben Solomon writes terrific stories that catch you by the throat and won't let you breathe until the last words of his yarns end. Dames, booze, guns, betrayal, a world where nothing is what it seems. What's not to like? His dialogue is crisp and snappy and laced with gallows humor. The stories hit you like hard slaps across the kisser, forcing you to pay attention. And I'm thankful I did. This is Noir with a capital N. But be warned: read Mr. Solomon's stories only when you don't have anywhere pressing to go, and for damn sure don't read them in bed if you expect to get to sleep anytime soon. Oh, did I tell you I loved these stories? Keep 'em coming, Mr. Solomon.

–Nathan Gottlieb, author of the Frank Boff mystery series

As timeless as he is nameless, Ben Solomon's "The Hard-Boiled Detective" embodies everything that is cool in a PI.

–Jochem Vandersteen, author of the Noah Milano mystery series

www.ingramcontent.com/pod-product-compliance
Lightning Source LLC
Chambersburg PA
CBHW020114180626
46812CB00006B/2598